T0146481

Everything's bigger in Texas . . . including love.

A deputy sheriff in Houston, Avery Humphrey is ready for some hometown comfort when she heads back to Kasota Springs, but one kiss from Brody VanZant is enough to make her trade "soothing" for "sizzling." When it turns out hot, hard-headed Brody is another Bonita County deputy, sizzling gets complicated, especially after Avery is made the interim sheriff. Brody knows romancing the boss isn't on the duty roster, but to him it's a state of emergency to prove to Avery that he's the partner she needs—in her life and in her bed—and he's ready to give her as many kisses as there are stars in the Texas sky to convince her.

Visit us at www.kensingtonbooks.com

Books by Phyliss Miranda

The Tycoon and the Texan
The Troubled Texan
Out of a Texas Night
(with Jodi Thomas, Linda Broday, and DeWanna Pace)
Give Me a Texan
Give Me a Cowboy
Give Me a Texas Ranger
Give Me a Texas Outlaw
A Texas Christmas
Be My Texas Valentine

Published by Kensington Publishing Corporation

Out of A Texas Night

A Kasota Springs Romance

Phyliss Miranda

LYRICAL PRESS
Kensington Publishing Corp.
www.kensingtonbooks.com

First Electronic Edition: May 2018
eISBN-13: 978-1-60183-382-2
eISBN-10: 1-60183-382-2

First Print Edition: May 2018
ISBN-13: 1978-1-60183-383-9
ISBN-10: -60183-383-0

Printed in the United States of America

Out of a Texas Night is dedicated to my sisters, Clara "Pumpkin" and Martha Ann, along with my cousins Vicky Johnson and Mike Johnson. I love and miss you all. May you rest in peace for now and forever.

Chapter 1

Kasota Springs, Texas
Spring Festival 2015

Avery Danielle Humphrey shaded her eyes from the stark white sunlight with her lace-trimmed, large-brimmed bonnet. She watched thirty or so Texas longhorns, with horns as wide as the length of her bed, strut down North Main Street flanked by cowboys from the surrounding ranches.

She took a step to the side. Forgetting to pick up her big hoop skirt, she nearly tripped. She couldn't help but wonder how in the world Southern belles wore such garb without falling head over teakettle. No wonder they walked slow, didn't look down and had such a measured, Southern drawl from holding their breath. They were praying they didn't fall.

As previous parades crossed her mind, heartwarming memories flooded her thoughts. She figured many of the steers were so old they were likely in the first Kasota Springs Rodeo and Reunion she had attended twenty-seven years before.

She smiled, thinking about sitting on her father's shoulders so she'd have a bird's-eye view of the majestic, once nearly extinct, cattle drives that were only one of the traditions associated with the century-old spring festival and rodeo.

The pleasant memories faded as quickly as they appeared.

If only she had returned to her hometown under better circumstances.

If only life hadn't dealt her a blow she wasn't sure she could recover from.

If only she were an innocent four-year-old sitting on her father's shoulders, mesmerized by the customs of the historic town where her family was one of the founders.

Avery had been hoping and praying she wouldn't give her mama and daddy a heart attack by surprising them and showing up for the festival. However, that concern had faded when she got to the gathering place for the parade.

By staying out at her friend's ranch, and the workers being sworn to secrecy, she had been able to keep the knowledge of being in town from her parents. As far as they knew, she worked twenty-four seven in Houston and didn't have any extra time on her hands.

Since her folks had always led the processional in their classic Corvette convertible, she had planned to stun them by showing up at the parade. The problem was that when Avery arrived, she was told her parents had been called out of town unexpectedly. Although sadness set in because her scheme to bushwhack her parents had blown up in her face, happiness filled her heart when she saw Sheriff Deuce Cowan and his wife leading the parade riding two of Mesa LeDoux's show horses.

The thought of missing Avery's parents again weighed on her like a concrete cowboy hat. She surveyed the crowd that tripled the size of the one-horse town, as she affectingly called Kasota Springs. Fortunately, the small community was within driving distance of several larger towns that had plenty of hotel accommodations. She figured this was the only town in the world that had four streets named Main, and they were built around a square that now served as a park. Of course, she hadn't forgotten that at the pulse of the town still stood the first little white, wooden church built in Kasota Springs. It had a beautiful bell tower that housed the original bell created in 1889 by her father's great-grandfather, who was also the town's first blacksmith.

At the other end of the park was wrought iron fencing that kept watch over five graves, each with the name of one of Tempest LeDoux's husbands and engraved with the words *The Beloved Husband of Tempest LeDoux*. Avery quickly searched the crowd for her best friend Mesa LeDoux, descendent of another founding family of the quaint community in the Texas Panhandle and beloved feisty great-granddaughter of Tempest.

Kasota Springs was definitely a town where more death certificates were filed with the county than birth records issued.

While the high school marching band passed on the other side of the square, ahead of the longhorns, Avery took out her phone and glanced at the time. In less than an hour the booths for the festival would open, and she had volunteered—rather, been volunteered by Mesa—to work. A shiver ran up her spine at the thoughts of what else she'd been volunteered for. She suspected her friend thought beginning at the kissing booth would be therapy for Avery.

Except for a couple of new additions, everything seemed exactly as she remembered from the last spring festival she had attended several years ago. Of course, Lola Ruth Hicks had made her famous peach-apricot fried pies. The sign above the booth priced them at a dollar each with the funds being donated to the American Cancer Society.

Since Avery had been staying out at Mesa's family's ranch, the Jacks Bluff, where Lola Ruth was the glue that held the big ol' ranch house together, making it run as smooth as silk on glass, Avery had had the opportunity to enjoy more than her share of Lola Ruth's larrupin' good handmade goodies. Somewhere deep inside, she figured Lola Ruth had lied for years about not using lard for the pies. Somehow, Avery couldn't see the lovable woman turning to shortening or vegetable oil, much less coconut or avocado oil, after all of this time. Avery's ideas of being a vegetarian fought against her repulsion at using animal fat in any food, but her taste buds kept telling her she was oh so wrong.

Slowly, keeping her typical trained eye on everything and everybody around her, she walked toward the kissing booth, hoping to catch up with Mesa.

Off to the left, a tall, strikingly handsome man, with charisma dripping off him and dressed like a pirate, stood talking to a group of people. Mostly women. Avery didn't recognize him, but with the increasing crowds and her years of being away, he could be anybody. Somewhere within her inner-core, she realized there was something special about him. The way he stood proud like a man in the military, except for his shaggy hair and beard. He held his head high and from a distance seemed to be totally engaged in the conversation taking place. No doubt he was likely a force to be reckoned with. She even caught herself being a little jealous of the women who seemed to hold his undivided attention. A jealousy she had no right to delve into.

Avery recognized the deliberate footsteps of her friend, Mesa, closing in from behind. The women had worn the same Lucchese boots since either could remember, making them both about three inches taller than many of the guys around.

When she was young, Avery kinda enjoyed the boys having to look up at her and, to tell the truth, she still liked the fact that most men still did. It had served as an advantage many times.

Avery glanced over her shoulder. The man had disappeared, but the women had their heads together like a gaggle of geese preparing for flight. "Hi, Dannie. I've been lookin' for you." In Mesa's typical sassy Texas drawl, she called out to her friend with the nickname only Avery's parents and the LeDoux family used.

"I was watching the parade. Glad you caught up with me. Do you know what's going on with Mama and Daddy?" Dannie adjusted the cap sleeves of the antique *Gone with the Wind* Southern belle dress she wore as part of the festival's traditions.

"Kinda." Mesa fiddled with her turquoise squash bloom necklace that went beautifully with her antique blouse, jeans, and boots. She tipped her head back and looked skyward. "I've never known them to miss the festival. All I know is that they notified the event chair that they had to go to Dallas and wouldn't be back for the parade." She pulled her braid from the middle of her back to over her shoulder. "I know you're disappointed, but we've got a full afternoon and evening of activities that'll take your mind off things." Mesa made small circles in the ground with the toe of her boots.

"I think this is the first time a Humphrey or a LeDoux hasn't led the parade in years," Dannie said, feeling a lot of nostalgia. She'd known Mesa since they were little girls and saw through her. There was something Mesa wasn't telling her.

"Well, semi-technically a LeDoux did lead off the parade because Rainey and Deuce rode two of our prized show horses."

Their shared laughter drifted through the air.

"Let's get over to our booth and make sure everything is set up properly," Mesa said.

Dannie frowned and glanced at her friend. "How much setup is needed for a kissing booth? The last I recall the only requirement is lips."

"And a cash box. Let's go." With her long strides from years of riding horses and training rough stock, Mesa headed toward their booth. "We're donating to the Wounded Warrior Project this year."

"Got a check in my pocket already made out."

"Great. I'm sorry I couldn't watch the parade with you, but I was needed to help bring over some of the rough stock for tonight's rodeo."

"No problem. It was the same as always, just different members of the high school marching band." Dannie held tight to the flamboyant headgear she and Mesa had purchased at the local antique shop owned by Rainey Cowan. It matched the dress but looked like a lost bird had settled in her hair. The two friends chatted as they took a shortcut across the park to the vendor area.

"Slow down," Mesa said. "You're obviously still into martial arts and working out to the extreme. To keep in shape, I'm only riding horses and bucking broncs, hauling hay plus just about anything our ranch hands don't have time for or I get to first."

"Intense exercise is part of me. Releases the tension and stress in my life, especially since I don't have a horse in Houston to ride. But I am doing a lot of running, considering my apartment building has a full gym." Dannie laughed then turned to Mesa. "Okay, I'll race you to the booth."

They both took a runner's stance with hands on knees, although Dannie had to hike up her dress to give her long legs room to move. On a joint count of three they made a mad dash across the perfectly manicured grass, reaching their destination in a photo finish.

Winded, Mesa said, "By the way, Sylvie Dewey and her friend Raylynn are due in for the first hour. I see them coming with Sylvie having her phone glued on the side of her face. I swear she should get that dern cellphone pierced to her earlobe."

"Or at least get an earplug."

"Guess we'd better get in gear; it won't be long before you and I will be up," said Mesa.

"Two women kissers at a time?" Dannie raised an eyebrow.

"Yep, it's the biggest money-making booth of all, after Granny and Lola Ruth's fried pies." Mesa handed Dannie a fancy, feathery party mask that covered only the top half of her face. "And don't forget we have to wear these. We don't want the guys to know who they're kissing."

"Maybe next year when they'll have a booth the men will do the coordinating and wear masks and the ladies have to donate." Dannie chuckled softly, thinking that might not be such a bad idea. Plus, at the moment, she weighed her options: stay in her hometown or go back to the big-city life. Regardless, she planned to be in town for the next festival.

She leaned against a post holding up the tent in their work area, and the tall, rugged, bearded man once again caught her attention. "Hey, do you know that guy standing across from us with his back to the old Kasota Hotel?"

"The one with the long dark hair tied in the back with what looks like a leather strip? Sounds well prepared and kinky to me, but oh well. I think he probably has more facial hair than about anybody around. Love the white pirate-style shirt, fluffy sleeves and that silk red sash around his waist. Even with the vest, I can see his pecs and oh what pecs—"

"Yeah. That's the guy. Dressed like a pirate, tall with taut muscles across his shoulders to die for. I bet he has a tat or two, but I didn't notice as much about him as you apparently did. So do you know him or not?" "Nope, but then I can't see him as well as you obviously can." Mesa laughed then rolled up the canvas tarp to get ready for the first customers. "If you pass on the pirate, let me know." A trace of a smile tipped the corners of Mesa's mouth. "The parade has ended, so I guess we'd better be prepared for business before Sylvie and Raylynn get here. You remember Raylynn, don't you?"

"O'Dell?" Dannie asked. "I just now realized who you were talking about earlier,"

Mesa nodded. "She's a little older than we are, but I figure if you remember Sylvie, you'd remember Raylynn."

"Both are unusual in more ways than their names." Dannie smiled, knowing Mesa wouldn't think she was making fun of them but would admit the eccentricity of the two women.

Two boys about ten or eleven ran up to the booth. The shorter of the two said, "Hey, how much for a kiss?"

Mesa and Dannie exchanged puzzled looks, then Dannie said, "Dudes, come back in about ten years and they might be free."

The youngsters ran off. Youthful glee floated through the air.

"That's the reason the festival committee added a fun house for the kids at the high school gym beginning at four o'clock. That way the adults can enjoy themselves and know at the same time their ankle biters are safe and out of their hair for the evening," Mesa said.

"Good idea." Dannie handed over a check for a generous donation to their cause. "Is there a minimum donation?"

"Nope, but if asked, get as much as possible. We want to win again."

Sylvie and Raylynn reached the booth just before the first lines of men formed. Although everyone was dressed in costume, Sylvie had made little changes in her daily look of being Miss Circa 1955, with her can-can petticoats and a felt poodle skirt, a fashion sense she'd worn since high school, which was about twelve years prior. Her hair looked as if she'd just stepped off the cover of a 1950s *Seventeen* magazine, although it was now several years after the turn of the millennium.

After exchanging greetings and a short catching-up, Sylvie and Raylynn donned their masks and cleaned not only their hands but their lips with liquid out of over a half a dozen bottles of hand sanitizer sitting on the counter.

While Sylvie dickered for a price with one man, she noticeably kept an eye on her phone and even excused herself once to respond to a text.

Raylynn leaned into Mesa and whispered loud enough for Dannie to hear. "I think she has a boyfriend, but she wouldn't tell me anything about him. I'm glad, as he seems to make her very happy."

"We're glad, too," Mesa answered for both of them.

To Dannie's surprise, the two women brought in a whopping six hundred dollars for their hour of kissing mostly the older men, who gave them either a watery kiss on the cheek or obviously tried to slip them a little tongue, which wasn't allowed. But Sylvie and Raylynn, who appeared past their kissing booth appeal, made the rules known loud and clear.

At the end of their shift, Sylvie pulled off her mask and laid it on the counter. In her soft Texas drawl, she said, "That was more fun than trying to pluck a dozen chickens in a tub of water without drowning them."

Dannie laughed with the others and adjusted her mask, trying her best to not look for the man who had intrigued her earlier. Her eyebrows knitted together as she watched a long line of men form.

"Okay." Mesa took Dannie by the arm and pulled her away from the window. "Quit frowning. Our only rule, other than not letting the guys manhandle us, is not to haul off and hit any of the slimy ones. Just please remember, although legally you are still a resident here because you own land and it's your primary residency, you don't have any jurisdiction. This isn't Harris County, so don't go thinkin' you can go wake the judge for a restraining order and have a kisser's ass hauled off to the hoosegow. They are buying a kiss, not a night in the hammock."

"Well—"

"I know you could get a judge in a heartbeat, since he's your uncle." Mesa shook her head.

While Mesa laughed in a deep, jovial way, Dannie stared at the line waiting for the bells on the tower to chime the hour, so they could begin their shift.

Dannie gritted her teeth and made a choice...suck it up and set a goal. By damn, they'd make more money for their charity than Sylvie and Raylynn. "I don't know how in the living hell you got me mixed up in this anyway. I don't recall volunteering."

"Poor, pitiful Avery Danielle Humphrey. Don't you remember when we swore we'd always have one another's back?"

Dannie remembered the life-changing decisions they made years before. They'd been friends forever and they'd always been there for one another. They'd proven it more times than she wanted to remember. Biting her lower lip, she closed her eyes and reminded herself this was going to be a fun day and she had to let the bad thoughts evaporate like too little water on a flower bed in August.

"I need space, Mesa. You of all people know it." She finally mustered up more of an explanation. "As much as I love you, I'm afraid this is one time our pinky swear won't pull me up out of the ashes I've found myself wallowing in."

"You've wallowed enough. Now you need tough love, and I think you know better than anyone that any LeDoux has plenty of that to dish out." Mesa twisted her head a tad. "Remember, *God grant me the serenity to accept the things I cannot change, the courage to change the things I can, and the wisdom to know the difference.*"

"One of Granny Johnson's sayings."

"Remember, for years we thought she stole it from a famous author then learned, as both of us know oh too well, it's AA's Serenity Prayer. One we'll never forget."

Dannie chuckled but deep down felt a calm the prayer always brought her. "Your grandmother is one of a kind. Gotta love her. Okay, let's get our shift over and done with. I want to get to the Buckin' Bull and have the biggest Coke they have. I think after we kiss all the men lining up, we'll need to cool off."

"Well, I want to eat first. Then we'll clean up from the last shift and can go have some fun … not that kissin' isn't fun." Mesa adjusted one of her turquoise-and-silver earrings, then looked out at the two lines of men forming.

After the first dozen customers, Dannie shifted, already tired of negotiating for a kiss, not to mention standing like Angelina Jolie with her lips stuck out for some stranger to end up pecking her on the cheek.

Dannie placed the twenty she'd just received in the cash box, while Mesa negotiated with the next man in line. Her friend could have been a soiled dove from the Wild West, as shameless as Mesa was in making the next kisser pay more than twice what the guy in front of him had contributed.

In her typical fashion, Dannie surveyed the crowd while she touched her hat to make sure the feather was still attached. Suddenly, the man she had been watching from afar appeared in her line of sight. Reaching to the ground, he picked up the purse of an elderly woman who had just dropped it. In the process, the pirate vest he wore pulled up, exposing what no doubt was the outline of a weapon in his back waistband beneath the red sash, likely in a suede and saddle leather holster. She knew the outline only too well.

After tenderly making sure the woman was safely on her way, he got back in place. A half a dozen men stood in front of him and then it'd be his turn to begin negotiations. Perspiration dampened Dannie's hands while her heart beat like someone who entered a murder scene not knowing what to expect. Did Dannie want to make sure Mesa was the one to give out her affection or did Dannie wish to be the lucky woman?

The Howard twins, who probably were in the first graduating class in Kasota Springs, stood before Dannie and Mesa. Harold said to his brother, "I know I put those two bucks in here somewhere, but I can't find them." He continued to dig in first one Levi jean pocket then another. "Maybe I gave it to you."

"No, no you didn't. Let me see." Jarald began removing items from his jacket, while he asked over his shoulder, "Are we holding you nice ladies up?"

"Take your time, Mr. Howard. We'll wait for you." Mesa smiled at both men.

Dannie stepped back, tugging Mesa with her, to give the two elderly citizens some room as the men unloaded their pant pockets and placed the contents on the narrow counter separating the men from the ladies.

Lowering her voice, Dannie said, "See the man you don't know who is seventh in line—"

"He's the one you've been ogling all afternoon, isn't he?"

"I wasn't ogling him, just observing. Notice the necklace he has on?"

"I see it. It looks like one your grandfather had," Mesa said then continued quickly, "something to do with his Texas Ranger badge, wasn't it?"

"Exactly. Carved out of a Mexican five-peso silver dollar; perfect for a man's neck."

"I don't understand. Anybody could buy one nowadays." Mesa kept watch, as the twins continued sorting the contents they'd laid on the counter.

"No. Well, yes, there's a lot of fakes out there, but I think his is authentic. I'll bet the ranch that he comes from a line of lawmen and might well be in law enforcement himself. No doubt in my mind. A handsome, gentlemanly lawman who is definitely not a Ranger, so he's likely working undercover the way he's dressed."

"But, remember most everyone is wearing costumes, so that might be his," Mesa suggested.

"No. He screams undercover. There's no place in this part of the country where he could get by being a cop of any type wearing hair like that and a pierced ear. No way. He's undercover for some agency."

After the twins put their possessions back where they belonged, Harold said, "Miss Mesa, we didn't find that money, but we've got ten dollars apiece if that'll work."

"Yes, sir, that'll work."

Before the ladies stepped forward, Mesa leaned into Dannie and said, "So you think he's undercover and from here? Remember nothing newsworthy has happened here since Sylvie's brother cut his hand by accident and died when we were in the sixth grade."

Chapter 2

Brody VanZant stepped away from the kissing booth to check on a man who had lingered too long around the girl's portable potty for Brody's liking. In short order, a young girl of about four or five came out screaming, "Daddy, I did it. Right down the hole. I watched it until it was all gone." She giggled, while her father squirted liquid sanitizer from one of the bottles on the post outside the bathrooms. She took her dad's hand, and as they walked away, she said, "Now I want to get my face painted."

Brody mumbled to himself, "Okay, she's safe." Being a lawman, he couldn't help but stay alert and observant to everyone and everything around him. But this time, it cost him his place in line to get a better look at the elusive woman who had caught his attention. Maybe it was the headpiece that sported a gigantic feather from some unfortunate bird. The lady with the mahogany-colored hair piled beneath the hat was striking. But something about her made him feel uneasy. One thing for sure, he planned to get back in line before she had a chance to escape.

He passed the gazebo where quite a few senior citizens were playing bingo and headed to the area where booths were set up.

"Hey, man, you gonna ignore me?" Deuce Cowan called from behind.

Brody turned and shook hands with the sheriff of Bonita County.

"Nope. I was trying to find you." Brody skirted the truth.

"I'm glad you were, because if I hadn't seen you in one of our undercover stings, I wouldn't have recognized you. Frankly, you could easily fit into a homeless shelter for druggards and drunkards."

"Thanks. That's what I'm supposed to look like." They took a few steps and Brody said, "You and your beautiful wife gave the festival a great kickoff."

"Thanks. Mesa's horses made me look good, but nothing could make Rainey any more beautiful."

"She is as pleasant as she is pretty. How is her law practice going, considering her responsibilities as owner of the antique store?" Brody asked.

"Really good. She's gotten a number of regional clients once they learned her background as an L.A. assistant district attorney. She's turned most of the antique store over to Sylvie Dewey, who is doing a great job."

As they neared the area crowded with people playing Texas Hold'em, Deuce stopped and said loud enough for everyone to hear, "Now, if I see so much as a penny at any table, you know I'll have to arrest you on charges of illegal gambling. Stay with the Monopoly money; it's worth more than bail." He laughed and was quickly joined by the majority of the players.

"Yes, sir, Sheriff," one petite woman dressed like Annie Oakley responded, then threw out a hundred-dollar Monopoly bill and turned back to the table. "Call."

After Brody and the sheriff got out of earshot, Deuce lowered his voice. "Thanks again, man, for coming over from Amarillo to help me out, especially being the first day you've come off undercover duty. We're really short on deputies right now, with you being on loan to the joint task force, so I owe you."

"No problem. With everyone in costume, I just blend in like any other pirate looking for a night of fun."

"I mean it. Your ass will always be covered as long as I'm around." Deuce slapped him on the back. "But don't forget if you ever want to permanently leave the JTF and work out of here as a detective just let me know. I can make it happen."

"Yeah, but I really enjoy putting my life on the line every time I stop someone for speeding on I-40." Brody double-checked the kissing booth to make certain the pretty lady was still on duty. To his surprise, she raised her head and their gazes met, but he continued talking to the sheriff. "Two nights ago we busted a ring at a house we'd been surveilling for a while. Got a search warrant and came up with over two hundred pounds of marijuana worth nearly a hundred thousand dollars on the street. When convicted, that'll extrapolate to about a ten-thousand-dollar fine each and twenty years in the pen. They had nearly seventy-five thousand dollars hidden in the floor. They didn't even have enough sense to put a rug over the part of the flooring they removed to hide the money. Just a coffee table." Brody glanced back at the kissing booth. Miss Southern Belle was still there. "Of course, local dealers are small potatoes considering who we're really looking for."

"Just remember if it wasn't for the work you guys on the JTF do and the money you all find in the drug busts that's shared with all the counties on the team once they are through with it as evidence, I wouldn't have a decent pickup to drive," Deuce countered.

"Yeah, when the trial is over," Brody said. "I'm sure the dealers would cry their eyes out if they knew how and where we destroy the drugs. I'll take cruising around this town waiting on something to happen. Oh yes, and I almost forgot we serve papers all over Bonita County. I love the look on the face of men who have no idea their wife has filed for divorce until they see us drive up with papers in hand. Generally, some woman is trying to dress as quickly as possible in the background." He laughed richly. "Now that I came out from UC, I'll be free to return to you all, if you still need me. I've always wanted to drive a forfeited Mercedes, but if we don't impound one, promise I'll get one of those new Impala PPVs once I'm back here full time."

"You got any kind of police pursuit vehicle you want."

"I'll remind you of this conversation when you try to pawn off one of those antique units on me." Brody looked up and wanted to laugh out loud when he saw the Turtle Race booth. "What the hell, Deuce? I can't believe we're prejudiced against snapping turtles." He pointed to the sign above the event sponsored by the Bonita County Sheriff's Department that read, "No Snapping Turtles Allowed."

"I can't put that much liability on the county, in case somebody gets hurt." Deuce laughed.

Brody said, "What's the phone number for the people who handle discrimination against turtles?" He shook his head. "I guess I could call 911." He rubbed his jaw then said, "Maybe it's my civic duty to hire a lawyer for the turtles." He chuckled aloud. "Maybe your wife would handle my case."

The lawmen guffawed as they meandered toward the area where exhibits were set up.

"Hunka hunka studman." Deuce slapped his thigh in amusement.

"I haven't thought about that song in a while. It was the beginning to one of our many frat songs. As I recall back then neither of our mothers could remember the words the same way," Brody said.

"Yep, I thought at one parent-athlete event, they were about to hit one another. But then 'YMCA' came on and it stopped their bickering," Deuce said. "Well, until the next time they heard one of our made-up songs."

The two lawmen let out hearty laughs. As they got out of the less-populated part of the square, they sung together, *"Hunka, hunka superstud. Whatta what a man."*

"Hey, who's the lady over there at the kissing booth with Mesa LeDoux?" Brody asked.

"Don't recognize her. I only know it's Mesa with her but have never laid eyes on that Southern belle."

"And you didn't recognize those long legs that make her nearly as tall as either of us—and we aren't midgets. I know you're taken, but I didn't know you were so far gone that you can't look at an attractive woman," Brody teased.

"Rainey keeps me in shackles most of the time. I'm taken and happy about it. My world sure is different since we got married. She's a wonderful woman, as you know. Mama just loves her." Deuce lowered his head a little and said, "Certainly more than me, but that's okay. I know Mama loves me whether she recognizes it or not." Deuce looked down at the ground, obviously uncomfortable thinking about his Alzheimer-ridden mother. He took a deep breath. "As far as that long-legged cowgirl is concerned, I just haven't been around this part of Texas long enough to get to know everybody. Lots of folks come into town just for the festival and rodeo. That gal is probably one of Mesa's rodeo buddies. Likely a barrel racer, if I had to guess." Deuce raised an eyebrow. "Got a suggestion. Get in line and find out who she is for yourself. I've got to go find Rainey." Deuce adjusted his tan Stetson. "Could always use some help with the cleanup. Seems everyone disappears when it comes to the end of the festivities. Then we could go over to the Buckin' Bull for a cold one. You available?"

"Yep, I'll be there. Then I'll head out to my ranch and catch a few winks, so I'll be fresh for tomorrow. Plus I've got to get an appointment to get this hair cut, since this undercover job is over. Don't trust myself to even shave much less cut this shaggy hair I've had to grow out."

"Being on the joint task force can be pure hell, but it looks like you all are closing in on the scumbags involved in at least one of your cases," Deuce said.

"Closer than anybody knows. See you later," Brody said as they went their separate ways.

The sheriff had no idea just how close to home the bust might be, but there was still a lot of work to be done.

Brody passed up the pie-throwing contest, since he really didn't want to run into his sister at the moment. Plus, he hated to see two grown women who had feuded for years waste good ol' fashioned whipping cream on paper plates by having it thrown at them.

In true Texas style, Brody's sister, Winnie, and Clara, owner of Pumpkin's Café, had come together for the benefit of the Kasota Springs Museum. They actually looked like they were having fun. He shook his head and in a moment or two found himself in line at the kissing booth. A big mistake, likely, but he had to know more about the pretty lady with the crazy hat. The smell of Winnie and Stanley Mitchell's barbecue lunch hung in the air like honey butter on hot biscuits. Brody had skirted the area of the catering truck. He was happy that his sister had finally settled down with a man she'd loved for so many years. From the times they'd visited, the couple seemed as happy as any married folks Brody knew. The only rub he saw was Stanley's baby brother, fresh out of the detention center, had come to live with them. Obviously, a bright kid because he avoided Brody like a scared prairie dog facing a coyote. Although staying on alert with Tommy, the lawman was willing to give the kid the benefit of the doubt until he proved Brody wrong.

Brody scrubbed his hand against his cheek. Working undercover for months had left him unable to visit his only sister. That was certainly the downside of his job. While he waited in line, another thought came to him.

If I spend more time in the sheriff's department here, I could move back to my ranch and be part of the only family I have left.

That was certainly food for thought.

It'd been a good ten minutes since Brody had gotten back in line. He stood on one foot then the other, patiently waiting his turn to kiss the lovely woman he'd seen watching him off and on throughout the day. He looked up at the sign above the booth. He was taken back that the only reference to prices read, *Price Negotiable. Donations Welcome!*

As he kept an eye on the crowd, time flew by, and before he realized it, he was the next man in line.

"May I help you, Mr. Blackbeard?" asked a voice soft and sexy enough to melt away a Rocky Mountain ski slope.

It'd been a long time since so few words disturbed him in the way this green-eyed vixen did. He looked her squarely in the eyes. "Evening, Miss..."

"Miss O'Hara, but you can call me Scarlett. Now, sir what can I do for you?" A sensual little smile crossed her lips She obviously was more uncomfortable playing a role of a Southern belle than he was in his garb.

Brody would have loved to have seen more of her face, but half of it was covered with a decorative mask.

He glanced over to Mesa, who was busy negotiating with a strapping young cowboy. "Twenty," she said. The cowpoke slid the money across the counter and puckered up like he'd never kissed a woman before. It wasn't a good time to say hello.

Brody looked back at Miss Scarlett. "How much is your beginning price?"

"A donation, but I'd give you one for thirty." She hesitated for a second before adding, "It's for a good charity."

"Since it's for charity, forty."

"Deal." She flashed a smile of thanks. "No tongue and no touching besides the lips."

Although a counter not much wider than a cafeteria tray separated them, Brody leaned into her and found himself checking to see if she wore a wedding band or any evidence of one.

Nothing.

His gaze moved upward to the creamy expanse of her neck. He looked up and their gazes met once again. Something intense flared through his body as he kissed her lightly on the lips then said softly, "Do you have a special for a discounted second kiss without having to go to the back of the line?"

The smoldering flame he saw in her eyes, from behind her decorative party mask, startled him as she whispered, "Twice the money, twice the kiss."

He gently lifted her chin with his thumb and ran his index finger across her soft lips. "Deal." Brody pressed his lips against hers and gently covered her mouth. A kiss as electrifying as he believed he'd ever experienced followed. It was all he could do not to jump over the counter and take her into his arms, although he knew there was a time and place for everything. This was neither the time nor the place.

Raising his head, Brody silently cussed a blue streak because the kiss hadn't gone far enough. From the expression on Scarlett's face, he believed she'd enjoyed the kiss as much as he had, although he'd never had the desire to analyze a women's affection until now.

Brody took out a hundred-dollar bill and slid it into her open palm. "Worth every penny, Miss Scarlett."

One of the prettiest, most sexually attractive women Brody had met in years slowly tucked the money in the valley of the bosom of her dress, leaned into him, and softly whispered, "Thanks. But a piece of advice? If you don't want the world to know you're a lawman, you'd better take off the Texas Ranger badge around your neck."

Damn, he'd been made by some Southern belle in the Texas Panhandle. Brody's heart beat out of control. "And you know this how?"

"My grandfather was a Ranger, and he had a badge just like that. You're no Ranger, Mr. Blackbeard, but you are a cop. Probably working undercover."

"When you're finished here, why not meet me at the Buckin' Bull and we can talk about the Texas Rangers in our families? It's a family heirloom, that's all the necklace means. I'm anything but a cop."

"Sure you are. And I'm Scarlett O'Hara."

Chapter 3

Once their shift was over Dannie and Mesa walked around and visited other booths, until it was time to close up the kissing booth. When the crowd began to clear out Mesa put up the closed sign. She sorted the cash and placed the bills in a bank bag.

Dannie began cleaning up the trash around the booth that had accumulated during the day.

"I didn't count the money, but it looks like we did really good. I don't remember getting a hundred-dollar bill, so it must have been you." Mesa quirked her head toward her friend. "So what's the story?"

"You remember that tall, dark, delicious pirate?"

"Of course. Not many women could forget him. So tell me....Tell me." Mesa shook Dannie's shoulder to solicit a response. "Well, tell me, girlfriend!"

"You said to get as much money as possible, so when he asked for a second kiss—and oh man, was it the best I've ever had in my life...."

"So, Brody VanZant paid you a hundred dollars for a kiss?" Mesa's excitement rang through the night.

"Yeah, he did, but it was actually two. So you knew the pirate after all. You creep." Dannie grinned mischievously.

"Well, more or less. After I got a closer look, I realized who he was. It's his eyes that gave him away. It's like he looks right through you and digs deep inside to draw out your most intimate secrets. Who could forget those baby blues? Before you ask, he is in law enforcement; actually, with the Bonita County Sheriff's Department. He's a detective, and if my sources are right he works with a special crimes unit made up of several Texas Panhandle counties. Not sure what they do or what they are handling. I know he does undercover work a lot. I think he splits his time between living in Amarillo and his ranch. He purchased the WBarT Ranch a few years back."

"So he owns our old family ranch." Although Dannie felt a little surprised, she continued, "I'm betting he's coming out from UC or he wouldn't have shown up here dressed the way he was."

"I think you're right, but I don't know it for a fact. Sheriff Cowan keeps the county horses over at VanZant's ranch, but sometimes, if a horse needs medical attention, a deputy will bring it over to our ranch for treatment since we have a vet on staff. That's the least I can do for the county. I've seen Mr. Blue Eyes there," Mesa said.

Dannie placed the last bottle of hand sanitizer in the supply tub on the counter and looked up as a yellow cab crossed onto North Main. "I'd already pegged him for a lawman, even without seeing his baby blues, as you called them."

"It takes one to know one." Mesa picked up the money bag and her shoulder purse embossed with a big Texas star on the side, then continued, "I know he has a sister here. Her name is Winnie and her husband is Stanley. They have the barbecue café and bakery on the east side of the square. Pumpkin's is on one end of the block and their place is on the other. They're doing the catering. Evidentially they're estranged, because when Brody does come over here, which is rarely, he never sees her to my knowledge. Some kind of a family feud with Stanley's younger brother moving in with them. I heard from Lola Ruth that Brody wasn't too happy about it, but that's all I know. Anyway, let's get over to the Buckin' Bull before they holler *last call*."

"Yep, it's Saturday night so they have to shut down by one in the morning." Dannie tossed her half-mask in the tub on top of the cashbox. "Some things never change, regardless of the county you work for."

Dannie watched as the yellow cab drove off after obviously picking up its passenger. "What in the heck is that?" She pointed across the park to North Main Street.

"That's simple. A yellow cab. Don't they have them in Houston?" Mesa laughed. "That's how Granny and Lola Ruth get back to the ranch after dark."

"You're kidding me. Your granny has a brand-new pickup and a beautiful Caddy in the garage," Dannie said. "Not to mention that antique F-110 she loves to drive all over you all's ranch."

"Her good automobiles are for special events like weddings and funerals. The truth, I think neither of them can see as well as they once could, so instead of depending on our foreman or someone to drive them around at night they get a cab."

"I guess I should know by now not to be surprised at anything your grandmother does. If she could talk Lola Ruth into being her sidekick in the dunking tank and both wear scuba gear at today's festival after they sold out of pies, I shouldn't be shocked at anything those two come up with. Life really begins at eighty, doesn't it?"

Mesa looked at Dannie with such a funny, surprised expression that both women opened up into a full belly laugh, something Dannie needed desperately.

After a short stop by Mesa's F-150 pickup truck, marked clearly with the Jacks Bluff brand and the Ford Built Tough logo, where she secured the money bag in the glove compartment and locked it and Dannie put the tub of supplies in the back seat, they continued their leisurely walk to the honky-tonk around the square.

As they passed the only dress shop in town, Mesa pointed to a light blue spring dress.

"I really like that. I might come back and get it next week," Dannie said.

"You are feeling better, aren't you?"

"Yes. I feel bad hiding out at the Jacks Bluff for ten days, but I just wasn't ready to answer all the questions that I know Mama and Daddy have for me. Thanks for taking me in like I'm one of your rescue horses."

"No problem. You know they'll want answers because they are concerned and love you, don't you?"

Dannie hesitated but didn't have to give thought to the question. "As Mama used to say—'To the moon and back.' She still ends most of her notes and cards with those words."

"*Guess How Much I Love You?* The storybook my mama and Granny read to me every night before bedtime. That was after I had my midnight snack of one cookie and milk." Mesa's smile shone brighter than moonlight.

"We're very lucky to have families who care so much for us. I truly feel bad that I couldn't go straight home, but I needed time to think things through, and with Granny and Lola Ruth staying so busy with the festival preparations, plus you off to pick up a trailer of rescue horses, I had time to sit out in the shade of those big old cottonwoods and think. Not to mention run three or four times a day and ride horses until my butt hurt. I bet I covered two, maybe three hundred miles, but I do feel better."

Dannie thought back over the last ten days. "You know Lola Ruth tried to feed me to death, all along telling me how dangerous a vegetarian diet could be for me. I finally gave up. Don't believe I ever took a 'death do us part' oath to vegetables."

Like two schoolgirls having fun, giggles filtered through the evening air. "Back to Brody VanZant. Dannie, no matter how luscious the man appears, stay clear of him. You don't need to get involved with any man right now, particularly a lawman. He has baggage and you don't need that. You can use more time to come to grips with your own situation."

The statement made shockwaves run through Dannie. She was hiding from herself, much like when she put on the festive mask and became Scarlett O'Hara.

"That's been going through my mind. After losing my best friend and partner who I depended on for my life, all at my doing, the last thing I need is to get involved with any man, much less a cop." Dannie pretended she was pulling a medieval mask over her face. "See, my protective armor is in place. But I am considering resigning and not returning to Houston or law enforcement in any type or form. I'm not sure I can shuck the memories that haunt me while trying to do a job the citizens deserve."

"That might be a good idea," said Mesa, as they took the two steps up to the front door of the Buckin' Bull Saloon.

Laughter blended with ol' time honky-tonk music settled over cigarette smoke and the smell of beer reached Dannie's nostrils as they entered.

"This place hasn't changed at all except probably more pictures of Bulls of the Year, bull riders, and wrecks. I'm sure each one is signed, as always. I guess Woody and Bunny have personally known every bull rider for the last fifty years." Dannie looked at the wall but it was too dim to see much. It didn't matter because Dannie knew every picture by heart. Photos depicted bovines and cowboys in about every position a bull could get into, not to mention a half a dozen famous wrecks between bull and rider. As her eyes adjusted to the dimness, her gaze settled on a bigger-than-life framed photo of Mesa's grandmother and grandfather. "I guess that one is the favorite of all." She smiled with the fond memories. "I know it's my favorite."

"Of course, because she's the town sweetheart and our family was rough stock, particularly bull contractors, for so many years. She might be a Johnson by name, but LeDoux blood runs through her. She's not about to forget that her family was instrumental in founding Kasota Springs." Mesa gave one last long look at the wall and said, "Let's find a table, if she isn't here yet."

"You never told me who we are meeting." Dannie followed Mesa trying to avoid the much beer spattered wooden floor. They stepped out of the way of two cowboys who obviously had had their share of beer. "Oh, it's Rainey Cowan. She's married to Deuce and came to town about two years ago. I don't know much about her background except she went to school with Sheriff Cowan, and I'm fairly sure Mr. Blue Eyes played ball with Deuce at UT. For reasons unknown to me, Rainey chose to come here and open an antique shop at the ol' train depot, where we got your costume."

Almost before Mesa could finish, Dannie asked, "Then she's married to Deuce Cowan, All-American from the University of Texas and quarterback for the Steelers?"

"*Ex*-quarterback and *ex*-specialty coach. I figured your parents had told you about him being our sheriff. Got injured playing, as we all see over and over on replays, and decided to go into law enforcement. He already had his degree in criminal justice, so he was hired with little if any debate. I heard that Rainey didn't know he was even the sheriff when she moved here. Kind of a heartwarming Texas story about lost but not forgotten love. They are inseparable. You'll like her a lot. What I've found so far is that she's genuine and honest, like most Texas gals. I've grown fond of her. She gave Sylvie Dewey a job when she really needed it." Mesa changed the subject. "Maybe the guys will come by for a drink, after the cleanup of the grounds is finished."

About that time a woman a little over five feet tall with short auburn hair motioned from the bar.

"There's Rainey. Now if we can only get through the crowd." Mesa raised her voice even more to be heard above the music.

"She's really attractive, but we're both at least a foot taller than she is." Dannie waved her hand in front of her face to chase away some of the smoke. She wasn't even sure how Mesa recognized Rainey with the dirty haze hanging in the air.

"Haven't you heard that big things come in little packages? She's very sharp and likeable to boot. Rainey opened a law practice here."

Mesa had barely finished her introductions when she reached into her pocket and pulled out her phone. Apparently, she had felt the vibration, as she punched in her security code, put up her index finger signaling she wouldn't be long, and walked toward the bathroom.

"Mesa tells me that you own an antique shop where I got my costume." Dannie tried not to delve into Rainey's personal life and figured talking business was the best way to begin getting to know her. "I've always loved antiques."

"I have, too. When I was in high school, I worked at an antique shop owned by Deuce's mother, and she taught me so much. In those days, we'd have lots of books for research, but now it's so much easier with the internet. But there is still nothing like holding a piece of antique glass in your hands and looking for proof of authenticity yourself." Rainey took a sip of her drink at the same time the bartender appeared.

"What can I get for you this evening?" He wiped the counter off and put out napkins with a huge bucking bull embossed on the front. "We've got Bud Light and Miller on draft, but about everything you could want in the can or the bottle."

"How about two Cokes with light ice and a lemon, please." Avery ordered for both Mesa and herself.

Rainey and Dannie continued to get to know one another while they waited on Mesa and their drinks. Mesa returned and took her seat just as the bartender showed up with their order.

"I see you two got acquainted." Mesa accepted the cold drink murmuring a thank-you. "That was strange. Our foreman called to say he caught a guy in the horse barn pilfering around. The kid wasn't messing with the horses. Teg was afraid he was trying to steal saddles, but he wasn't even in the tack room, plus it's locked up tighter than a chastity belt. Caught him in the veterinarian's barn. So many of my rescue horses need medical treatment, so we keep meds, particularly stuff to sedate a horse, antibiotics and the like stored out there." Mesa took a sip of her Coke. "Of course under lock and key, too."

"Have you ever had it happen before?" Rainey asked.

"No. It's just weird. Teg called the sheriff's office and reported it. He couldn't get a good look at the intruder because the kid ran for his life when he saw Teg. It's just strange."

Rainey frowned. "That's probably the reason Deuce called right before you all got here and said he had something come up and couldn't make it tonight but would see me at home. He's taking who I presume to be one of his deputies with him, but I couldn't hear who it was because of the noise. I did get that he said to please send his apologies to both of you." Rainey smiled, as if she and she alone knew a secret. "He suggested that we have a cookout very soon."

Dannie answered, "That sounds like fun."

Mesa nodded as if she hadn't heard a word, obviously thinking about something else. She finally looked up. "They probably had to go out to the ranch. But, I've learned years ago to trust our foreman and not get involved unless he needs me. His family has been here as long as mine, and Granny is on her way home. The rescue horses are my project and the rough stock is Granny's. I'm sorry if the problem out there ruined your evening." Mesa touched Rainey's hand and looked up at Dannie. "Really sorry."

"That's part of being married to a lawman." Rainey turned to Dannie and asked, "What kind of job do you have in Houston?"

Before Dannie could answer and without warning, a bigger-than-life boom rattled the building, shaking the antique chandeliers.

A second and third boom shook the wooden door, and nearly knocked the ladies off their barstools.

Dannie's heart jumped into her throat. The sudden noise sounded like the backfire of an old engine combined with the recoil of a shotgun. Chills ran down her spine, and her hands began to shake like they had only one other time in her life. She closed her eyes, but all she saw was red. Blood gushing like it was coming from an open fire hydrant. She jerked to her feet, mumbled that she had to go to the restroom, and headed in that direction, praying she'd make it before she passed out or vomited. Luck was with her, as nobody occupied the only stall. She rushed to the toilet and threw up. Sliding to her knees, she hugged the toilet seat without the thought of germs or anything else; she needed it to keep from falling to the floor.

All she could envision was blood flowing freely, rushing to the door. Every time she lifted her head, another round of rancid liquid hit her mouth.

Shaking her head didn't dislodge the sound of an exchange of gunfire. Memories flooded back like a dam overflowing.

One. She turned slightly toward the first shot.

Two. Her partner Lee stepped in front of her, but she tried to move him out of her way so she could get a better aim.

Three. Lee grabbed the side of his face as he tumbled to the ground. Dannie got off numerous shots at the shadow before her, but the man returned fire, hitting her right forearm. Her Glock service pistol flew from her hand and slid across the floor.

Four more shots from the perpetrator before she could slither toward her weapon and retrieve it, leaving a trail of blood from her arm. Rolling over to her back she saw the figure, although he obviously couldn't see her, and she unloaded the remainder of the magazine. Unable to reload without being seen, she laid her head on the floor tainted with her own blood mixed with Lee's and prayed.

While pushing away the memories, she choked as though a python clutched her neck.

Vaguely she heard Mesa call from the door. Dannie couldn't respond and put her hands over her ears, not wanting to hear anything. All she wanted was for the visions before her to go away, far away, and never return. But she knew that wasn't going to happen.

"Dannie, let me in. I know what you're going through. Let me in," Mesa called loud enough to be heard over the music of "Big Balls in Cowtown."

"You don't know." Another round of nausea slapped Dannie in the gut.

"No, you're right. I don't know, but I do know that you need someone right now. I'm your oldest friend, so please, Dannie, let me help you. Please!"

Dannie laid her forehead on the toilet seat, while the camera in her mind began the recurring nightmares she had dealt with for months. Through a veil of blood, Dannie heard sirens in the distance. Louder and louder. Even louder, until she put her hands over her ears again to drown out the shrill noise. The flashing yellow, blue, and red lights blinded her.

"Tell them to turn their lights off. Go black! We don't need them. I don't need anybody. Everyone, please go away. I must help Lee." She had felt a dozen arms trying to pull her to her feet.

"Dannie, I'm not going away." Mesa pounded on the door. "Open it or I'll tear it down with my own hands."

Dannie tried desperately to chase away all the memories and breathe at a normal rate. She tried again and again until finally she moved to the door and unlocked it, sliding down the wall behind the entryway and barely brushing her hair by the paper towel dispenser.

Mesa squeezed inside.

Dannie heard the click of the lock and knew she was safe. She fell into the arms of her best friend.

"I shouldn't have said that I know, because I don't, but you're safe with me, Dannie. You'll always be safe." Mesa smoothed her friend's hair.

Time slid by like watching a bull rider being trampled by a Brahma bull in a death-defying wreck.

"I'm sure Rainey has crossed me off her list of people she might like to get to know." Dannie pulled up straight and looked in Mesa's eyes.

"Nope. She got another call about the same time. I told her that I was I going to follow you because I figured you'd eaten too much BBQ. Rainey said she hoped you got to feeling better and she'd see you later."

"I'm still sorry that I ruined your evening." Dannie deliberately changed the subject, trying to gather her wits about her. "The rodeo last night must have been a lot of fun. I love the wild cow milking. Do you know how it got started as a rodeo event?" Dannie asked, although she knew Mesa was a walking encyclopedia on the rodeo.

When she didn't answer, Dannie continued, "They had to haul the mamas out with their calves for calf roping and then decided to justify hauling them out for nursing purposes only, so they made up the event." Dannie made an attempt to get her wits about her. "It's always been one of my favorites, except of course bull riding and barrel racing—"

"You're not getting off by changing the subject," Mesa interrupted. "And don't you dare try to convince me this is the first one of these episodes you've had." She took a hard stance against her friend. "What has your psychiatrist said about these incidents?" She unwrapped and handed Dannie a mint.

"Not a whole bunch. I've been cleared to go back to work on desk duty, not in the field. But sometimes when there's an unexpected loud noise like a gunshot, I go into one of these...whatever you want to call them. Episode is as good as any word."

"Eventually, they'll end. Right?"

"Whenever my mind is healthy. My last psych eval showed I'm nearly there, but I know otherwise, when something unexpected like tonight happens. I've been working at the shooting range on a regular basis with no problems. My aim is as good as it's ever been. I'm cleared there. And, I've been on the street with more experienced officers and detectives." Dannie let out a heavy sigh. "Please, please don't tell anyone about this. Especially my folks, please. It'd ruin my chances of returning to Houston or any law enforcement agency." Her breath caught in her lungs, but she continued, "I'm not certain what I want to do in the future but don't want to shut any doors in case I want to go back into law enforcement. So, it's really important to me that you keep this just between us."

"You know I won't tell. I never told anybody about you going swimming nude out on the ranch, and that's been twenty-something years ago." Mesa hugged Dannie tight. "And I never have spoken of what occurred in college either and never will."

"Mesa, sometimes I see what happened in Houston flash before my eyes so vividly it's like I'm there all over again.

"Standing there with my weapon drawn and my flashlight, backup for Lee, and suddenly out of nowhere the first shot came. Later I found out it wasn't the kill shot. More shots came and grazed my left hand, making me lose my grip on my flashlight. The second one hit higher up on my right arm, and I dropped my weapon. Lee stepped between me and the shooter.

"Casings flew around like Fourth of July rockets. I finally reached my Glock and emptied it, but it didn't make any difference. I never had a clear shot, it all happened so fast. At least that's what I tell myself. But could I have gotten a kill shot off sooner? The statistics say no, I couldn't." Dannie wiped tears from her eyes with a piece of toilet paper. "Nothing makes sense, except seeing blood rushing from Lee, and no amount of pressure I put on his chest helped—"

Mesa broke in. "Precious friend, you don't have to do this right now."

Lost in the moment of reliving the nightmare, Dannie barely heard her friend. "I had blood all over my uniform. It was taken as evidence, but I could have never worn it again anyway. Lee's blood was all over me. My face and up to my elbows. Even my boots were covered with blood. Yet, there was nothing I could do. The smell of blood still haunts me—"

"You never get accustomed to the smell of blood whether it's human or animal.... You know that," Mesa reminded Dannie.

"You're right. I remember the sirens from the units we'd called for backup. And the worst part, the son-of-a-bitch got away, although I emptied my service pistol.

"Lee lost his life because I didn't provide cover like a good partner should. I didn't have his back like he would have had mine.... Like he did." Dannie wiped her eyes again. "Other than my father, Lee was the only man I could count on. I relied on him for my life and he depended on me, but I let him down."

Mesa pulled her friend tighter to her. "Please, please, remember it wasn't your fault." She lifted Dannie's chin and gave her the stern look Dannie was familiar with. "I know one thing, missy—beginning tomorrow we're going to target practice at the ranch every day, so you can keep in practice. Even more rounds than the miles you ran. We can get that sound out of your head, but you must get the other memories and visions out of your system yourself. I can't tell you how, but I can get you help. And, if nothing else, I know a lawman or two here who will help out."

Softly and slowly, Dannie said, "I truly want to get back to one hundred percent because I don't really want to be tied to a desk all day, while other officers are out there putting their lives on the line for the people when I should be there right beside them. I'd rather work at a Dairy Queen." She stopped and took a deep breath. "Let's get out of here."

"Now there isn't anything wrong with a Dairy Queen. I happen to love their Blizzards."

Far enough away from the Buckin' Bull where no music or laughter clocked them, Dannie felt the stillness settle around her. Fresh air and Texas. The scent of cattle, oil rigs, and the red delineators of wind turbines that lit the sky to the northeast. She missed her hometown, but something was wrong. Very wrong.

An extra sense that comes with being a lawman lingered heavy in the air and filled Dannie with hope that she might be able to overcome the trials and tribulations of Houston.

Yes, she was on the right track by returning to Kasota Springs.

Dannie made an honest attempt to get the thoughts of Lee and Houston out of her mind. She now realized they were slowly being replaced with those of one strapping and handsome pirate. She kept going back to the kisses that seemed stuck to her lips like a wonderful, light, and favorable mouthful of cotton candy.

As they journeyed back to Mesa's truck, she said, "Oh, by the way, while you were washing your face and I went out to pay our tab, I found out that the shots came from an ol' coot who was drunk and shooting into the night air celebrating. He's now in the hoosegow and he'll see tomorrow how much trouble he's in."

They continued to walk.

"Well, I know of several charges I'd be jottin' down if I was the investigating officer, beginning with shooting a firearm off in the city limits, disturbing the peace, disorderly conduct, and let's not forget public intoxication for starters."

Mesa shot Dannie a raised eyebrow. "And you don't think you want to stay in law enforcement?"

The night air filled with the women's laughter.

"I'm gonna walk to my folks' house. It isn't all that far. They should be back by now."

"Are you certain you're ready to surprise them and then spend the rest of the night answering questions?" Mesa clicked the button on her key to unlock her pickup. "You've had a pretty traumatic time this evening, plus your car is out at the ranch."

"I have access to several vehicles at the house."

Again, Mesa asked, "Are you absolutely sure you don't want to spend one more night at our ranch?"

"Positive." Dannie gazed into the starry spring night.

As Mesa drove away, Dannie waved and thought to herself, *I'm as positive about this as I've ever been with anything in my life.*

Chapter 4

Brody VanZant slid his phone back into his pocket. He sighed loud enough to wake the LeDoux men buried in the park on West Main. Someday he planned to ask about the history behind them, but that'd have to wait.

He couldn't believe the first night he'd come out from undercover, and gotten a lot of the park cleaned up after the Spring Festival, Deuce had ordered him to come to the sheriff's office. He'd said it wouldn't take long, but Brody was pretty sure there wasn't a *Welcome Back* cake waiting for him.

To his surprise, when he parked in front of the town hall, there were four Bonita County Sheriff's vehicles outside. Add his vehicle, and that accounted for the full Kasota Springs Sheriff's Department.

"Something is seriously up," Brody said under his breath. "Very serious."

When he walked through the door to the Bonita County Sheriff's Department, Chief Deputy Scott met him.

"I wasn't sure if you'd ever return to us, but glad you did." They shook hands. "*You* might not be as glad once you find out why Deuce called you in." He turned to Jessup, another deputy, who had just hung up the phone. "Where did they put the suspect?" Scott asked.

"In the SODDIT room." As if Brody didn't know the acronym, Jessup continued, "Some-other-dude-did-it-room."

"Thanks for the reminder. That's interview room one, and two is the pucker-power-room—"

Before Brody finished, Deuce appeared and said, "Yep, only if we need to scare them shitless. I think this dude needs to go there."

"Who is it?" Brody asked the sheriff.

"That's why I called you. Let's sit down for a bit and let me take a second breath. We need to talk."

Brody knew that Deuce was loose with names and speculations within the walls of the sheriff's department and rarely wanted to sit and chat. Brody took a chair across from Deuce. "What's going on?"

"You remember the call I got about an incident out at the Jacks Bluff?" Brody nodded.

"Scott caught the perp and brought him in." Deuce hesitated and clasped his hands loosely behind his back. "It's your sister's brother-in-law, Tommy Mitchell."

"Are you sure?" Brody cussed a blue streak beneath his breath and clenched his fists while staring at the certificates on the wall behind Deuce's desk, not seeing one, just focused on the anger hitting his stomach like a cresting dam on a rainy day.

"He won't give us his name. Just a lot of street-talkin' smut, but of course we knew exactly who he is."

Anger rose even stronger inside Brody. "So he was the one in the ranch's tack room? What'd he steal?" Brody addressed his question to Scott.

"Nothing, as far as inventory was concerned. So far, if Mrs. Johnson or Mesa want to file charges, I think it'd be for trespassing. But their foreman said he couldn't identify the intruder."

Brody slammed his fist into his open palm. "Sonofabitch. Did the little numb nut ask for a lawyer?"

"No." Chief Deputy Scott stopped and handed papers to Deuce. "Here's my report. I'm off again to make sure the partiers get home safely." He turned to Brody. "Truly glad to see you back with us; only wish it was under better circumstances."

"Thanks, but I'd like to be locked up three minutes in a cell with the little bastard." Brody gritted his teeth.

Deuce placed a hand on Brody's shoulder. "Anger won't get us anywhere, Brody. Even a minor offense of trespassing could send Tommy to the slammer for probation violation. That's why I called you in, as a friend. I don't think he needs to go to prison unless there is no other way. Since nobody wants charges filed, do you want me to scare the living hell out of him or let you take him home? Having to face his brother and your sister might be worse than anything I can say."

Brody weighed the options. "That won't do any good. I've talked until I'm blue in the face about what a second offense could do to him. He swears he was set up on the dope sting."

"What do you think?"

"I'm really drawn on it. The professional side says he did it, while the personal side of me thinks he didn't. He has money but doesn't work except at the café. But then I haven't seen him high. His worse trait is being stubborn, having a filthy mouth and bad temper, which can be attributed to being young and stupid." Brody formed his hands in a steeple, giving him time to think through what the sheriff had said. "I've even talked to my brother-in-law about Tommy hanging out with the wrong crowd and I've gotten nowhere with either of them. Stanley defends Tommy and is adamant that the kid just needs a break. The little filthy-mouthed bastard needs a break okay, but it needs to be at the elbow or knee." He took off his pirate skullcap and threw it across the room. "Deuce, right now I'm too mad to think clearly, so do whatever you think is best."

"Let's move him over to the pucker power interview room," Deuce said to Brody but gave an undisputed order to Deputy Jessup.

After more bad language than you'd get down at Huntsville State Prison and the rattling of chairs stopped, Deputy Jessup reappeared with two canned Cokes. "He wasn't too happy about being moved, but I got the job done." The deputy handed the cans to the sheriff.

"Thanks, Jessup. How about getting out on the square for a while and making sure there's no problems with the partiers. One arrest for causing a disturbance for shooting a gun in the air is one too many." Deuce turned to Brody. "I know how badly you want to be involved in the interview, but you can't, so just sit tight behind the one-way glass window and observe. If there's anything I need to know and there isn't anyone else around just tap on the door and step away so Tommy doesn't see you, and I'll come out."

The sheriff stood and so did Brody, coming eye to eye. Deuce continued, "I don't care what you hear or how mad you get, just don't come in through that door or I'll put you in the cell right next to Tommy. Do I make myself clear? You want a 'pray for the devil to intervene' talk and that's what I plan to give him before I turn him over to you to take home."

As much furor as Brody felt throughout his body, he knew Deuce was right, but he couldn't acknowledge it. Sometimes not saying anything was all an officer needed to know that he had the green light to make his point.

Brody watched Deuce enter the interview room. It really didn't make any difference which room Tommy occupied; it was nothing but a tactic. Both rooms were identical. Very sparse, with a table and a chair on each side and nothing else but a one-way, break-resistant window where observers could see in but nobody could see out. Cameras were positioned in all corners to catch several views of every person in the room, while microphones were mounted in the corner of the conference table near the investigator.

Since it was standard procedure, Brody had no doubt that Tommy had been given his Miranda rights plus been advised that everything he said was being recorded.

Brody settled into his chair, cleared his mind, and reminded himself that he was there not as Tommy's family member but as a cop. It didn't take long for the kid to begin running off at the mouth.

Deuce took the chair directly across from Tommy. He just kept an eye on Tommy, watching and listening to his obnoxious, hostile behavior.

"So they called in the *big* pig...oink, oink." Tommy slumped in his chair and folded his arms across his chest. "Do they think you'll get more out of me than junior pig did?" Tommy tapped his toes on the floor and pulled his hoodie down, shading his face.

Deuce slid further into the table, putting his legs between Tommy's knees as a way of invading his personal space mentally.

"Want some Coke?" Deuce asked, as he sat the two unopened cans of soda on the table.

Tommy leaned further back in a relaxed position and dropped his arms to his sides. After trying to move his legs but failing, Tommy let fear cross his face, which only added to his glazed-over eyes. "Not from a pig, I don't." He slumped further in the chair.

"Not what I've heard. It's my understanding that you'll take coke, meth, ecstasy, angel dust, even a little dust blunt—whatever is available from anybody offering it. Well, I'm gonna drink mine." Deuce snapped one of the cans open, took a long drink, and slammed it on the table.

Tommy Mitchell jumped at the sound.

"Gonna tell me your name or try to be a hard-ass like you thought you were to my deputies?"

"I don't have to give you a mother fu—"

"Don't go there with me, dude." He sat up straight, and although he didn't have a gun in his holster, he touched his jacket as if he did, as a reminder that the sheriff still had the upper hand on the kid.

"Talk about losers. You oughta know. A washed-up football player that couldn't even hack it as a coach, so he had to take on being a cop. I guess you know more about roids than any other drugs," Tommy snarled.

Deuce stood so quickly that he knocked his chair over. Putting both hands on the table, he spoke within four or five inches of Tommy's face. "Let me tell you something, you little punk face, if you continue to screw up you're going to be in the big house in no time. The scum inside don't much like second-timers because they have enough sense to know that you're getting another chance and they only wish they had one. You'll be somebody's bitch or in the hospital halfway beaten to death before the sun comes up on day two." He set his chair on its legs with purpose but never took his eyes off Tommy.

Tommy continued mouthing off at the sheriff, while Brody looked on, wanting to toss the biggest thing he could get his hands on through the window, knowing it would do no good but make a big dangerous mess and piss off the chief. Brody swayed between being so angry at the total disrespect Tommy showed and wondering how in the heck the sheriff kept his cool. He knew the answer. The difference between being professional and making it personal.

"We've been at this for nearly two hours. I know who you are and you know who I am. That's about all we've got accomplished. The county doesn't pay me by the hour, so I can sit here until doomsday. One question, do you prefer charges of trespassing and going to the big house for probation violation? It's all your choice, Tommy Mitchell."

"I want my lawyer." Belligerency filled the room. "You didn't even give me my rights." Tommy tightened his arms across his chest.

"Oh, but I did. So I guess that means you want a charge filed against you. Nothing was said about that but it can be arranged. I simply asked you a question. Since I'm finished with my drink, guess I'll go outside and give you time to think." Deuce stood and took a step toward the door. "And when I come back, you better not have that hoodie covering your face."

"So, if I'm not being charged with anything, I can go home?" Tommy slowly removed the hood from his head and let it hang down his back.

"I don't think so. You asked for your lawyer, so apparently you have *something* you don't want me to know." Deuce knocked on the door. "I'll tell you when a lawyer gets here, but remember I can hold you for forty-eight hours without filing charges."

"I don't need time to think." Tommy put his hands on the table and stood. "I don't need a lawyer. Just let me go and I'll stay out of your hair."

Deuce turned back to him. "How about a please!"

Reluctantly, Tommy replied, "Please."

"I'm giving you one and only one warning. If anyone in the sheriff's department catches you with as much as an eighth of a leaf of marijuana or a grain of any drug that you're not supposed to have in your possession while you're on probation or you are thirty seconds late for a meeting with your probation officer, I can promise that I'll personally see to it that you're back in the slammer for violating probation. I'll have every eye in the department squarely on you and if you ever call me or one of my deputies a pig again, it might be met with a fist. You got it, dude?"

"I've got it, all right." Tommy glared at Deuce. If looks could kill Deuce would be on his way to the morgue. "And if *damn* isn't a word that sends me to jail," he sneered, "I damn sure don't want the cop who is Winnie's brother to come get me. I'll walk before I'll let that jackass take me home."

The sheriff slammed a file about five inches thick on the table and planted his hands on either side of it. "You're pressing your luck. If you want your worst nightmare to come true, just keep it up."

The two deputies had returned, and Jessup stood with his elbow on Brody's shoulder. Time crawled by, but when Jessup saw the chief's signal the deputy went to the interrogation room, opened the door, and stepped inside.

Deuce addressed Jessup. "Release this asshole before I find a charge to keep him for a while." He picked up the fake file and stomped out.

As Sheriff Cowan exited, he turned to Tommy. "I think I'll go out to see Mesa and Mrs. Johnson and make sure they don't want trespassing charges filed. I bet I can get them to reconsider." He slammed the door behind him.

Both Jessup and Scott remained in the jail area.

After returning to the outside observation area, Deuce threw both cans in the trash. That pretty much told Brody everything he needed to know.

"I'm sorry, Deuce," Brody said, feeling responsible for Tommy, yet knowing he wasn't.

"Hey, it's not your fault. But watch the little bastard. He's up to no good. I don't know what, but I'm gonna take a look between the Jacks Bluff's barn and where he was picked up. He was on foot when Scott found him, so he could have taken about anything and stashed it."

Brody rubbed his forehead. "It'd have to be a small item, and Jessup reported Scott didn't find anything on Tommy. The ranch foreman said he didn't see anything gone."

"That's why I'm taking a drive back to the scene. His car was found about a mile from where he was arrested and it's still out there. Scott couldn't find anything on cursory check. Since Mrs. Johnson doesn't want charges filed, and because we didn't find anything on him, we don't have any reason to keep his car. I'll just sleep better if I get a little fresh air. A walk would do me some good."

Brody picked up the pirate skullcap he'd thrown across the room earlier and put it on. "I'm going with you then."

"No, you're not. If I do find something I don't want the investigation compromised. I probably shouldn't have let you even watch the interview, but since no charges were going to come about, I didn't see any harm. If

I do find something, that's altogether another deal. If I take anyone, it'll be Deputy Scott."

"Okay." Brody looked at the clock on the wall. "The Buckin' Bull has been closed for a couple of hours, so I guess I'll drive out to my ranch." He sighed. "I've been thinking. If I work out of Kasota Springs, I might just close up the family home in Amarillo permanently. Maybe even put it up for sale, if Winnie agrees, and move out to my ranch. It's closer to Kasota Springs and all I need is the cupboard stocked with food and some Lone Star beer in the fridge for my days off."

"And your gym."

"Of course. But I think tonight, you're the one who needs to work off your frustration." Brody had known Deuce for years and had rarely seen the sheriff out of control like he was in the last couple of hours.

"That's why the walk is gonna help. Also, if you haven't heard, I've got approval to hire someone new for the task force."

"Hadn't heard. How'd you manage this in such short order?" Brody rolled his eyes when Deuce didn't answer. "I know, chatting with the city commissioners while you were roaming around, huh?"

Deuce shrugged his shoulders.

"So, I guess you knew my answer about coming back on regular duty before I did. Who is my replacement?"

"Remember Rocky Robertson? And, before you say anything else he is *not* your replacement unless you've changed your mind about staying on the task force full time."

"Gotcha. So, we're talking about Marion Frances Robertson?" Brody laughed. "Sure. I know a lot about him. From the California Central Coast area. Expert on human trafficking and a DRE, as I recall." Brody pushed some of his long hair away from his face. "He's the one who helped you out with Rainey's ordeal last year, wasn't he?"

"Yep, he did, and yes, he's one of only a few thousand drug recognition experts in the US. He wants to get away from the human trafficking and focus on narcs, so I've hired him."

"Auh, that was the purpose of your trip last month out to California for a..." Brody used air quotes, then continued, "A training session."

"Yep, sure was. He won't be here for a while, but I'm positive he'll be an asset. I'm thinkin' you and he can alternate working with the Joint Task Force plus help us out on day-to-day ops. Kasota Springs is growing by leaps and bounds, and it'd be dereliction of duties not to hire someone like Robertson when we have the chance."

"I totally support your decision. Old M.F. will bring a lot of skill and talent with him." Brody couldn't help but believe the timing was perfect. "Are you bringing him in as a detective?"

"First, you can't get into the habit of calling him by his initials, thus the nickname of Rocky."

"Which fits him to a tee, as I recall. He's tall and fills out every inch of a big lawman's uniform. Also, works with a trained K-9," Brody said.

"You've got his number. He loves his dog, Bruiser, who is a dual-purpose narcotics and tracking K-9. He's trying to buy him now. Of course, likely they won't sell him to his handler. But, in answer to your question, right now, I'm thinkin' Rocky will be more useful keeping his scrubby looks and working as a regular deputy. That leaves a lot of opportunities open."

"Smart thinkin'," Brody stated. "If he and Bruiser need a place to throw out a cot, he's always welcome out at my place or the house in Amarillo. Of course, I'm presuming his dang dog takes to me."

From somewhere in the back of the sheriff's office, Tommy Mitchell bellowed, "I ain't going with him. A pig is a pig. You got the wrong dude, but you all have blinders on when it comes to an ex-con...whether they are guilty or not."

Chapter 5

Dannie watched Mesa turn off Arrington Street in the historical district of Kasota Springs, headed for the Jacks Bluff. She set her purse on the wooden porch beside the swing. Time flew by like lighting bugs, as she took in a breath of the clean, fresh air she so vividly remembered. As tired as she was, sleep avoided her. She watched as the sheriff's unit passed and presumed he was finally on his way home. Dannie continued to sit in the swing on the porch and reflected on not only the great day at the festival and looked back over the ten days she'd been in town. But for some reason the handsome pirate kept creeping into her mind, which particularly lingered on the two kisses like she imagined the hero did in her first romance novel.

In the distance, the chime from the belfry at the original Kasota Springs Methodist Church a couple of blocks away caught her attention. She smiled, thinking about the story of how her great-great-grandparents had met on a snowy Christmas at the turn of the century. As the town's blacksmith, he had built the belfry for the new town's bell that her ancestors brought to the community. Being related to two founding families made her feel responsible for the town.

Guesstimating at the amount of time she'd spent on the porch, she figured it was probably three in the morning. She took out her phone and checked. She wasn't off much. Although she should be tired enough to sleep, she knew it was senseless to try. In her line of work, it wasn't uncommon for her to stay up forty-eight hours straight, particularly, if she was in the middle of a case.

Her conversation with Mesa about why her parents had to leave town suddenly weighed heavily on her mind. It wasn't what she said but what she didn't say that bothered Dannie. That, mixed with the stunning pirate, might keep her awake for weeks.

She found her door key and took a cursory look at the Texas Historical Commission medallion securely installed to the right of the front door. As usual, the entrance was illuminated. Next to the table lamp, Dannie noticed an envelope addressed to her. Chills ran down her spine as she stared at her mother's handwriting. The thoughts of what her mother might have written tore at her insides.

Tucking the embossed linen envelope in her purse, she climbed the stairs to her old bedroom, which reminded her of where Sleeping Beauty might have lived. She dropped her purse on the embroidered white bedspread with yards and yards of material making up the skirt, smiled at the black silhouette pictures and sat at the antique secretary desk. Carefully she opened the letter. Tears filled her eyes.

My dearest darling Dannie,

I'm so sorry that I'm not there, but I was called out of town on personal business. Your father accompanied me.

Darling, Dannie, I haven't intruded since your return because I know you must have space and my excessive mothering isn't needed right now. I pray you know as long as the good Lord allows me to walk on this Earth I will always be here for you no matter the circumstances. I realize there are things that have happened in your career that only personal closure will take care of, but I know you'll come to me when the time is right.

I can't say that I know how you feel because I don't and never will. Losing a partner in the line of duty must be a very difficult situation. When we talk on the phone, or even in your emails, I can feel the hurt you are experiencing.

We will be home on Tuesday morning, and hope you've had enough rest where you feel like seeing us. Your daddy and I love you and have been hurting also.

Love you to the moon and back, Mama

P.S. Wednesday night, we're having your favorite vegetarian dinner, if you come by. I'll get Winnie or Pumpkin to make a tofu dessert. I know I'm being too motherly at the moment!

Swallowing the sobs that rose in her throat, Dannie whispered, "And I love you more." She put the note back in the envelope and placed it in the Bible her mother still kept in the secretary.

Dannie walked around the room and stopped to stare out into the crystal-clear night. Confusion made her desire to sleep float away like delicate bubbles on a windy day. Similar to Mesa's comment about Dannie's parents being out of town, her mother's letter left even more questions. There was something going on that they thought she was too fragile to handle...and maybe they were right.

She sat on the bed and picked up a small music box with a white rose on an embossed pink circle and twisted the tiny tuner. Tears came to her eyes as she listened to the *Blue Danube*. But they were tears of wonderful memories and joy. She opened the matching pink oval trinket box, and sure enough it had a single Hershey's Kiss in it, just like when she was a little girl. Some things never changed, and her parents' love certainly fell under that category.

Glad to get out of her Southern belle dress and hat, she changed into a pair of Levi's and a shirt, along with boots. She zipped the outfit in the plastic bag it came in.

Fresh air was what she needed. She ran down the stairs and stepped out on the front porch. The toll of the church bells called out in the near distance. She began walking toward the sound, thinking back over the letter, and found herself sitting on a park bench across from Town Hall. For some odd reason, being close to the sheriff's department made her feel comfortable, but then the whole town was like a warm winter coat wrapped around the town's people.

The double doors leading into the sheriff's department area of the courthouse sprang open, reminding her of swinging doors in a saloon. The lawman pirate, still dressed in the costume he had worn at the festival, stomped to a white SUV with the county's logo on the side and kicked the back tire twice. Suddenly, he slammed his fist into the side hard enough that it should have broken his knuckles, then leaned against the Ford with his arms crossed.

Avery wasn't sure what to do. If she tried to slip out of sight he'd likely see her and think she was stalking him. If he looked her direction, with the park lighting no doubt he'd notice her. If she stayed still, he'd know for a fact she was watching for him, which she wasn't.... Or was she?

He paced behind what she presumed was his service vehicle for several minutes before Sheriff Cowan and a robust deputy she had heard someone call Deputy Scott came out. The sheriff gave the pirate a soft slug to his shoulder, as if to say *I understand*, shook his hand, and drove off in a county vehicle headed toward I-40. Shortly thereafter, Deputy Scott's county vehicle left the parking lot heading in the same direction

Avery caught movement behind the building and the parked vehicles but with the lighting could only make out what looked like a young bearded man with pants hanging low on his hips. Could he be another undercover cop? Her professional instinct told her he wasn't. There was no confidence in his stride, although he walked with purpose in the same direction as the sheriff had gone. She'd been around enough to know there was always an answer to anyone sticking around any law enforcement agency, although likely only a few knew the real reasons behind a visit.

The whole scenario of the young man walking behind and away from the sheriff's department bothered her...a lot. She knew Mr. Blackbeard was simply letting off steam. She'd done it herself many times in her career and knew it helped but didn't alleviate the problems. They lingered like unwanted dinner guests.

Suddenly, she became aware of him walking her way.

He'd caught sight of her, and she couldn't think of an excuse for being in the town square this hour of the morning, except for the truth. But, she wasn't about to share the real reason with him.

"Why, Miss Scarlett, would you be sitting in the park at this time of the morning?" He spoke in a deep, slightly authoritative voice.

She'd been in the business too many years to give away her cover this late in the game, so she chose to deflect his question. "Mr. Blackbeard, I could ask you the same. Apparently, from what I observed, you're none too happy at the moment."

His tall, black-clad figure stiffened. The muscles in his jaw tightened. "You've already pegged me as a cop, so you must know that things don't go as well as we like plenty of the time. We have to face adversity. Let's just say I was a little frustrated." He looked squarely into her eyes then continued, "But then I think you know all about being a cop. You're either married to one, divorced from one, or in love with one...but you know lawmen."

"Okay, let's just say I know lawmen." She changed the subject as quickly as possible. "I can't keep calling you Blackbeard and I'm pretty sure you know I'm not Scarlett O'Hara, so I'll begin. My name is..." She paused, not ready to give him her last name. "My name is Avery, and yours is?" she asked, as if she didn't already know.

"VanZant. Brody VanZant." He eased his tall, athletic physique next to her on the park bench, making her very aware of his manliness.

"So what type of business are you in?"

Avery looked up into the sky scattered with glittery stars and hoped her nose didn't grow for telling a lie, but then it wasn't a total lie. She just embellished the truth. "I work for law enforcement in Houston. Right now, I sit at a desk and shuffle paperwork for the detectives. Filing mostly. I'm kinda like a secretary, but with the pay of a file clerk."

"They have a civilian filling that job?" He glanced over at her, making it abundantly clear he didn't totally believe her.

"I have a security clearance." She deliberately diverted his attention back to her earlier question. "Wanna tell me what got under your skin so badly that you kicked the tires on your unit? Only, of course, if it's something you wish to share or can share."

"I was checking to see if the tires needed air." He tapped his fingers on his thigh. "But I think I have a score to settle with you." He shot her a dazzling, devilish smile, and he rested his arm across the back of the bench, so close to her that she could feel the heat from his arm. "As I recall, when we negotiated a kiss it was forty dollars, then you gave me a second one for the same price, which made it eighty. Right?"

"At this point you've proven to me that you can count and have an extremely good memory, so what score do you have to settle with me?" She turned toward him and raised an eyebrow.

"Since I gave you a hundred dollar bill, you owe me another kiss—"

"Technically, a half of one. Since the price was forty dollars each, you'd have a credit of only twenty dollars or half a smooch." Avery couldn't help but smile at the way she challenged the cop.

"How about I donate the extra twenty and I get a, hum, let's see…"

His smile totally took her off guard, and suddenly she felt like she was rolling around in a field of spring wildflowers with Brody holding her hand. "You get a kiss, anyway."

"That's a good idea, but with interest." His arm circled her shoulders and he pulled her to him. Slowly, he explored her lips, leaving her mouth burning with desire. His lips seared a path down her neck and shoulders then worked their way back up. His tongue traced the soft fullness of her mouth before he pressed his lips to hers, caressing her more than kissing.

After a lingering, unforgettable kiss, Brody pulled back and released her from his hold.

The experience made her thoughts spin and her emotions whirl and skid, while being transported on a soft wispy cloud. She turned his head and drew his face to hers in a renewed embrace. She crushed her mouth against his in a slow show of passion.

Leaving her body burning with fire, she pulled away. After taking a second or two to come back to reality and let her heart settle, she said, "The interest must have been one hundred and fifty percent, like a payday loan."

"If that's the case, I still owe you." He took her hands and held them together between his big ones, then said, "Just clear polish and no watch? I thought all women around here had to have their nails painted bright red and can't do without a watch."

"Who needs a watch now days with clocks everywhere you go and with an iPhone?"

Without warning, doors to the sheriff's department opened wide and fast, just as they had when Brody had exited, and two uniformed deputies literally ran to their county units.

One officer spied Brody and yelled across the street. "VanZant, we need your help. Something has happened to the chief. FM208 north of I-40." The officer got into his unit and sped away like the other.

Brody lightly kissed Avery on the forehead. "Sounds serious." In one swift motion, he took her hand and helped her to her feet. "Can I drop you off somewhere?"

She shook her head. "No. It's only a couple of blocks and there's plenty of streetlights along the way." She smiled at him. "Plus, this is the most peaceful community in the USA."

Avery watched him take off toward his vehicle. When he reached his unit, he unlocked the back. With haste, he removed his pirate shirt and vest, exposing his gun and holster in his back belt, just as she had expected. She had no doubt he had a second personal weapon within easy reach. In a matter of seconds, he'd added a polo shirt topped by his bullet-resistant vest.

She observed his every movement until he headed out with full lights flashing in the direction of the other units.

It was then she thought to herself, *That's the road that separates Mesa's family ranch from the Slippery Elm. There must be something seriously wrong when they all head out running hot.*

She sank to the bench feeling empty inside and watched his county unit head in the direction of the others, all racing towards FM 208.

And there was nothing she could do to help. She had no county jurisdiction and had lied about her job, so Brody wouldn't put two and two together and find out not only her real position with the Harris County Sheriff's Department but the fact she came from one of the town's founding families. It would be easy for him to check on her and find out she had been involved in a departmental shooting, but she'd been very careful not to give him her last name.

Helplessness cloaked her. She realized that there was nothing, absolutely nothing, she could do to help them with the emergency involving Sheriff Cowan. She felt totally helpless, and it was not a good sensation. Oh, how she'd change things, if she could go back in time.... If only!

Chapter 6

Before Brody got into his county unit, he looked over his shoulder and saw the woman who claimed her name was Avery standing beside the bench looking up into the sky as if praying. A woman he had kissed several times, yet he didn't even know her last name, where she lived, or if she even resided in Texas. He'd never seen her before, but then he spent most of his time in Amarillo sleeping during the day and running sting operations at night.

But that was about to change.

He'd already told Deuce that he'd make an effort to do less work with the Joint Task Unit and spend more time with the Bonita County Sheriff's Department as its only detective. But now, the way he and Deuce left their last conversation, the sheriff had made the decision for Brody to return full time—especially in view of Tommy's crappy attitude.

Miss Avery had distracted him, yet the minute he drove away his full attention went to the possibilities of what lay ahead. Could the sheriff have been hit while he was walking along the highway, looking for evidence Tommy threw out of the car? Fallen down a ravine? A thousand *what ifs* ran through Brody's mind. Regardless of what Brody thought, Chief Deputy Scott would not have called out all units, including Brody, unless there was some type of search and rescue. Nothing fit together.

The one thing Brody didn't like in the least was that if something had happened to the sheriff, the last person to have made a threat against him was Tommy Mitchell. Worry kept getting in the way of logic as Brody raced to catch up with the other deputies.

By the time he got to the site, there were a dozen or more vehicles on both sides of the road, some with their lights flashing, others probably owned by the Bonita County Deputy Reserves. An ambulance pulled up behind the county's fire truck.

Long before daylight, Chief Deputy Scott had everybody squatting in a circle with flashlights illuminating a county map. He'd already sectioned off the coordinates around FM208, which ran through three ranch properties.

"What happened?" Brody hesitated even asking because he was scared of the answer, but he had to put on his law enforcement persona and forget anything personal. His number one responsibility was to protect the citizens of Bonita County.

"The dispatcher, Raylynn, had just come on duty when she got a call from the sheriff, who said he'd located something out on FM208 involving the trespassing on the Jacks Bluff. He didn't say what it was, just asked that a unit be dispatched immediately to help him process the scene." Scott squared his shoulders. "It didn't take long after I got here to discover help was needed."

Brody's worst fears seemed to be coming closer to reality than he wanted. "Raylynn didn't say what Deuce found?"

"No. His phone went dead, so I headed out here." A worried expression spread across Scott's face. "When I got here, I found the sheriff's unit with his phone smashed on the ground by the driver's side, along with some traces of blood. Not a lot, but enough to be concerned about. That's when I sent out an all-units-available request, including the reserves."

Brody's heart felt as if it were being hoisted out of his body much like a mechanic would pull an engine out of a pickup.

Could Tommy have made it back to the area and hurt the sheriff? After all, the kid had threatened Deuce. Impossible.... No way had Tommy had enough time.

Chief Deputy Scott interrupted Brody's thoughts. "Work in pairs and be thorough." He addressed the whole group, including quite a few reserve deputies who they'd managed to get in touch with. "From the footprints near his unit, it looks like he might have been dragged, so we've got to search around and under every mesquite bush plus every inch of prairie grass. Anything that blood could cling to. Pay particular attention to any stands of cottonwoods. Any place an unconscious man could be hidden. There are plenty of extra batteries for your flashlights, so be sure to take a good supply with you." He paused for a moment and then said, "Remember light is power." Scott looked up at the whole group. "Let's get going. Time is essential. Report back to dispatch every thirty minutes."

It wasn't what Chief Deputy Scott said but what he didn't that disturbed Brody. Scott no doubt kept his private thoughts to himself, just as Brody did.

After the group dispersed, Brody said to Scott, "If we don't find him right away, I can have the DPS chopper with the infrared cameras in the air within five to ten minutes and here shortly thereafter. Just give me the nod, Scott. All I have to do is give the APD Sgt. Clark a call."

They exchanged looks that Brody thought said the chief deputy agreed, but what he said was different. A very firm "No!" came from his lips before he continued, "Let's wait. I'll team with you, VanZant." After making sure everyone else was out of hearing range, Scott said low and emphatically, "Tommy Mitchell's car was nowhere to be found. It was definitely right up the road when I brought him in." Scott tensed his jaw, showing his frustration. "It wouldn't have been all that long of a walk for him to have left our offices and hoofed it back to the car. Damn it to hell, I wish I'd had his car impounded but didn't have any reason."

Brody nodded, not wanting to say anything, afraid Scott might hear the reservation in his voice. "Let's head back to where you last saw Mitchell's car and see if we can find anything. Obviously, the chief did." He ground the words between his teeth. "I hope the rain that crossed over here didn't wipe away any evidence. Scott, can I see the map before you fold it up and head back to the car?"

Chief Deputy Scott hesitated before unfolding the map and spreading it out on the hood of his vehicle. "Sure."

Brody took a long, careful look at the coordinates on the map. "Why isn't this area being searched?" Body pointed to a spot between two pump jacks little more than a half of a mile at best north of a ravine.

No doubt questioning Scott was a mistake, as he jerked up the map and said, "Oh, I checked it out already. Just forgot to mark it and with so much help, I can't remember who I assigned to recheck it. Hey, VanZant, I'm sorry I barked a little, but I'm really concerned about the sheriff, particularly in view of what happened back at the office...." Not waiting for a reply, he folded the map. "Let's get moving before someone messes with any evidence that might be around."

Methodically, the two lawmen divided up and carefully searched the area to where Scott had seen Tommy's car last.

Finding fresh tire tracks, Brody motioned to Scott to come to the other side of the road.

"Fresh muddy tire tracks on both sides of the asphalt, so this happened after it rained out here, but I don't think we even had a sprinkle in town. Looks like he turned around and went back to his place," Scott commented. "Shit-fire-alive, there looks like a second car stopped on the asphalt. See the muddy track?" He pointed to the ground. "But there's no way to identify the tire tracks if someone brought him out here to pick up his vehicle. He could have walked home like he said, but then who took his car home?" The chief deputy removed his hat, ran his fingers through his hair, and put his hat back on. "Everyone has reported in twice and dispatch has called me. Nothing found by foot search, so there's little left to do but suspend the search until we can round up more help."

"We could get the county horses out. It'd be faster than on foot," Brody suggested.

"No!" Concern swept across Scott's face, yet his answer was harsh and emphatic. "Not until it's daylight. It's too dangerous."

Brody knew he frowned at Scott's tone, but he couldn't let Scott's instructions slide without making a rebuttal. "We could have them ready for daybreak, which isn't but an hour or so away."

"No!" The tone of Scott's words left no doubt in Brody's mind that the chief deputy was exhausted either with worry or with Brody.

Chief Deputy Scott turned and walked away.

"I can still call in favors," Brody called loudly.

Without waiting for Scott to snuff out his suggestion, Brody took out his phone and made a call to the tactical flight officer in charge of the helicopter. He got an immediate response and was told he could have the chopper in the air and flying over the coordinates Brody gave him before daybreak.

Brody reported back to the chief deputy, but instead of being grateful for the help, he directed Brody to check on the folks at the Jacks Bluff, while Scott said he'd go over to the Slippery Elm, Deuce and Rainey's ranch.

They agreed that the time wasn't right to tell Rainey about Deuce, because there could be nothing wrong. It would serve no purpose to upset her needlessly. Scott had already done an outside surveillance to make sure everything was okay.

Doing exactly as he was told, Brody drove to the Jacks Bluff. When his vehicle rolled over the cattle crossing guard toward the main house, which had probably been there since the ranch was founded in the mid-1800s, he turned off his headlights and got out.

The house was dark. He stayed away from the outside lights, each illuminating a large area. Everything seemed in order.

The reflection of the tall, stately oil derrick that watched over the ranch headquarters made him almost laugh inside. He was too young to have seen Granny Johnson standing out on the porch-wrapped house, which looked like it'd come straight from a Southern plantation, with a Winchester rifle across one arm and the other on her hip, telling the oil field supervisor that they could pump all the oil they wanted out but they *would not* take down the derrick. It served as a reminder from where she came from to where she was at that time.

Brody returned to his vehicle, made a U-turn, and went straight to town, as fast as he could and stay within the law. Hell, he could be charged with trespassing, too; however, he worked for the county and most of the Jacks Bluff was in Bonita County.

No doubt Scott didn't have his sights on Tommy as a possible suspect or he would have never allowed Brody to be involved in any part of the investigation, even the search. Or did he and didn't want Brody to know? Was it possible the chief deputy had a hidden vendetta against him for being an undercover cop?

As Brody turned onto his sister's street, he switched off his headlights. The only car at the house was Tommy's, which meant he was home, although there had been a lapse of several hours since he'd left the sheriff's department. A dim light came from the living room.

Winnie and Stanley would already be at work. Since adding on a full-fledged barbecue café to their bakery a year ago, it took both of them to keep the business running. Their day began at four or five in the morning and didn't end until sometimes six or seven in the evening.

Parking several houses away, Brody walked back to the Mitchell house, in the shadows of ancient cottonwoods and Siberian elms that nature had planted decades before.

He pulled out two evidence bags, his knife, and a piece of paper wide enough to get some imprints of the tire. Squatting on the dark side of Tommy's car, he'd retrieved a sample of the dirt in the tire treads. To his skilled eye it didn't appear to match that on the side of the highway where Deuce had disappeared. He'd have plenty of time to compare the two, as he'd taken a sample from where the tire tracks were found, without Scott's knowledge. He also took the print of the tire, as best he could, plus pictures with his iPhone.

The car being there didn't serve as proof Tommy was.

A dim lit room certainly didn't mean anything.

Brody knew he'd feel better if he saw the sorry, no-good jerk in the flesh, but daybreak was sprinting across the eastern skies.

Time wasn't on Brody's side.

With all the evidence securely stowed away, he walked to the side of his sister's house. He was just tall enough to get a good view inside the living room.

Tommy Mitchell lay stretched out on the sofa with one shoeless foot touching the carpet. His mouth was open, and he jerked a little as if snoring.

Brody took notice that Tommy didn't have on the same shirt he had worn at the sheriff's department but now sported an old, wrinkled, dirty T-shirt. His eyes were half-closed, but he was breathing, at first in shallow bursts but then more deeply. A scenario Brody had seen too many times. If there were any signs of a drug overdose, Brody would have called for medical help. But it didn't take a physician to see the kid was sleeping very heavily.

For all it might be worth, Brody took a couple of pictures. They could never be used as evidence in court, but he wanted them to remind Tommy what drugs do to a person, if he in fact was stoned. However, without physically examining Tommy's mouth, eyes, and coordination, there was no way for Brody to know if he was stoned or sleeping soundly.

Hopefully, he was sleeping soundly, because all-in-all, the kid was anything but stupid except when it came to his associates and drugs. Credit where credit was due, he was a hard worker and did attend college, but the drugs tore a wide patch of destruction within him.

It was a short trip back to the square and Winnie's café, the Ol' Hickory Inn. Knowing the front door would be locked, Brody parked in the rear next to the huge barnlike structure. Before he entered the back door, he hollered out to his sister and her husband, making sure they were aware he was coming in the back way.

He needed some answers...answers without asking questions.

Likely it wouldn't be what he learned but what he wasn't told that could make a break in the case. The Dr. Jekyll and Mr. Hyde in him wanted to put the little jerk back in the big house, while he hoped to clear him, if he was innocent. There was no doubt in Brody's mind that any DA in America would conclude Tommy had threatened the sheriff.

That was undisputed and would automatically revoke Tommy's probation, if it got before a judge.

But now the sheriff was missing!

Brody tapped on the screen and walked on in. "Is there still some coffee for your raggedy ol' brother?" Brody enjoyed seeing the smile on his sister's face when she pulled her hands out of the soapy water and hugged him. The liquid didn't bother him in the least. Any time he could get a hug from his only sibling, he'd take it.

"Of course." She reached up and pulled his special mug from the top shelf over the sink. "There's always coffee for my big brother." She handed him the coffee cup, which bore his name. She had bought it for him as a gift years ago. "I saw you at the festival yesterday, but we were all so busy, I couldn't even break away long enough to find you."

Brody filled his cup to the brim. "I know the way you're looking at me that you don't care much for my pirate look."

"I'm just happy to see you in the flesh regardless of how you look!" She shook her head and went back to washing a big cook pan. "But, if it weren't for his size and good looks, I probably wouldn't have recognized you." She looked up at her big brother and gave him a quirky little sisterly smile.

Brody leaned against the cabinet and eyed the freshly baked cinnamon rolls, but unfortunately, pastries weren't what he'd come for. "So how have things been going with your new family lately?"

Her smile was replaced with frown lines. "Okay. It could be better...." She dried her hands and glance toward to entry way to the dining room before she added, "But that's how it is when you're running an eatery. Get up early and stay late. Lots more dishes to wash than we had when I had just the bakery, but bills have to be paid."

Winnie looked over Brody's left shoulder, confirming his suspicions that her husband was listening to every word.

Quickly changing the subject, Brody said, "I know you all put out fantastic barbecue, especially the ribs. That's what I hear everywhere I go." He took a big sip of coffee and tried another approach at finding out what he wanted to know. "It smelled really good yesterday. I'm sure it meant a lot to have Tommy helping you guys."

Her brows knitted into a frown. "We were certainly tired when we finished up. Weren't we, Stanley?"

Brody played along and made a slight turn toward Winnie's husband. "Hi, Stan, didn't know you were behind me. Figured you were out putting on some briskets or some of those great ribs in the smoker."

"Winnie, if you don't get your ass in gear, we won't have rolls by lunch." Stanley guided Brody to the dining area.

Before they could even sit, Stanley began. "What in the fu—"

Brody cut him off. "Why so hostile? I just came by for a cup of coffee and to visit you guys."

"Then I'll say it this way—what in the hell, if that doesn't harm your delicate cop ears, do you want? Trying to catch Tommy doing some little minor thing so you can be the one to let the world know that you put away a kid who was caught with only a tiny bit of marijuana? So you can be the big man...the big *law*man?"

Stanley put his cup in the dirty dish tub behind the counter. "Tommy hasn't done anything but stay out of trouble and help us, so let him be." The tone of Stanley's voice was unmistakably harsh and accusatory.

"It's apparent you think I can't even come by and have a cup of coffee with you and my sister without an underlying purpose." Rage roared in Brody's ears. "I'm not accusing anybody of anything, but since you brought it up, where was your little brother last night? I didn't see him at your BBQ truck or at any of the evening festivities." Brody stayed clear of saying he hadn't seen him at all...especially at the sheriff's department. He took a sip of lukewarm coffee.

Safe is better and better is safe went through his mind again and again.

"If you just *have* to know, he was home sick. Still in his bed when we left. Has a cold and took something I got him at the GreenMart. Something for allergies, if you need to know that, too." His words were cold as an ice storm in the Arctic. "Guess you want a receipt, too." He didn't wait, just barreled on. "Now that you got all of your answers, I'll let you out the front door. I'll tell Winnie that something came up and you had to leave without saying goodbye. We've got work to do, so we can stay in business." Stanley unlocked the door and walked him out. "And if there's anything in *my* family you need to know, rest assured I'll send word to you."

"Thanks for the coffee and company." Brody put on his lawman's face and handed his cup to Stanley. "I almost forgot to leave this. Be careful, it's very special to me."

When Brody turned the corner toward his pickup, he heard the crash as his mug hit the concrete.

Chapter 7

Brody slammed the door shut on his vehicle. It took all of his restraint not to peel out and let gravel fly everywhere, particularly along the side of the steel barn he'd parked near.

No words Brody could think of fit how much fury ran through him. And, he'd heard more than his share of profanity in his career. He hammered his hands on the steering wheel and hoped the pickup would outlive his anger. Not that he gave a rusty rat's ass, since it was paid for by shared forfeited money seized as evidence in drug cases from the Joint Task Force.

Now he had a bigger problem on his hands than he had first thought. From seeing Tommy at the sheriff's office, then lying on the couch only a few hours later, there was no doubt of the kid's involvement with the disappearance of the sheriff.

No matter how hard he tried, deep inside he couldn't figure out the time frame and put all the pieces of the puzzle together. Nothing fit like it should. Could the lawman side of his brain be conflicting with his love for family and mixing up his emotions?

One thing for sure, Tommy had been snooping around in the Jacks Bluff barn. But what in the hell had Tommy stolen or planned to steal? There was always the possibility of drugs, but they were locked up tighter than a drum in the tack room. Conflict again churned in Brody's stomach. Tommy had to have had a reason to be out there on Mesa's families' ranch.

At least once Deuce was located and back in the saddle again, Brody could lift the huge burden off his chest. The sheriff would retrace Tommy's steps, ask questions in his capacity as chief lawman, and pick up the little bastard. But first they had to find Deuce.

While Brody trusted Scott to cover his back in the field because he'd want Brody to cover his, Brody trusted the chief deputy about as far as he could throw a couple of hundred pound bags of grain when it came to competition within the department.

He drove to the courthouse and came in the rear entrance. Locking himself in the back conference room, he took out a legal pad and began to jot down notes, as any good investigator would. He folded the pages, with the intention of giving them to Deuce when he was located. Brody locked the notes in his gun safe before returning to the parking lot and driving away.

Just on the other side of the Dairy Queen, he saw Lola Ruth Hicks, the longtime housekeeper at the Jacks Bluff, driving his way. As they passed, he raised his hand to say hello. She waved back, not in her regular acknowledgement way, but a "pull over to the side" gesture.

The last thing he needed was to answer questions, and, with the helicopter flying overhead, he was certain she had plenty.

Before he could get on down the road, she made a U-turn.

Well, now he had no choice but to stop.

Pulling to the side of the highway, he put on his emergency lights as a precautionary measure, got out and walked back to Lola Ruth's car.

"Good to see you, Miss Hicks. I was so busy yesterday at the festival helping out Deuce that I didn't even get over to your and Miss Johnson's booth and get a fried pie."

"Well, you know you're always welcome to drop by. And, if I know you're comin', I'll make sure you have a couple of fresh ones waitin'." She grinned up at him. "Glad to see you. I know you don't spend much time here since you moved to Amarillo, but I'm sure happy to see you found time to come and help at the festival." She continued to clutch the steering wheel and look up at the baby blue Panhandle sky with a light scattering of wispy clouds.

"I'm back working in Kasota Springs full time." Brody tipped up his Stetson with his thumb to see her expression better. One thing for sure, he didn't dare mentioned that he did UC work or was on the joint task force unless he wanted everyone in the county to know about it. Miss Hicks was a wonderful and pleasant person, but some things in police work had to be kept undercover as much as the UC himself.

"That's great." She smiled . "Are you gonna stay in Amarillo? Are you gonna drive back and forth? You know how high gas is, but I heard it's goin' down. You'd save money if you stayed at your ranch. What does your sister think about all this change? I'm sure Stanley had plenty of advice to give. And, of course, you need to take the winter weather, when it comes around, into consideration. And, tornadoes—"

"Yes, ma'am." Lordy, Lordy that woman zipped questions like bullets she thought he could catch on the fly.

Brody's desire to muffle his ears with his hands overwhelmed him. He tried to be kind to the older woman, while becoming more impatient to get back to the scene where the search was taking place. He'd also forgotten that he didn't have anything but his personal phone with him and definitely needed to check in with Scott. The jackass would bitch if Brody was gone longer than necessary.

"I'm so excited you'll be here all of the time to protect us. You know I've always liked you and never thought you should have gone to work for the Amarillo police."

Brody smiled to keep from shaking his head.

"By the way," she continued, "do you have any idea what's goin' on over at FM208? I've been hearin' a helicopter above us for quite a while." She looked up at him with eyes that screamed, *And you better not lie to me, young man!*

"Sorry, Miss Hicks. I was just on my way back there myself. The last I heard there was someone who ran off the road and got lost. There's a lot of land out there to try to find them in the dark, so now they have some light to help out. I did a drive-through around your headquarters before daybreak to make sure everything looked normal."

She pressed the palm of her hand on her chest and said, "Thanks. You guys always look out for us." A worried expression crossed her face. "I hope whoever is lost knows how to handle a rushin' bull or a coyote with a mouth full of goat head stickers. Now, don't forget to come and have a pie or two with me. It's Farmer's Market day on the square. Not many vegetables coming off yet, so gotta get there early if I want anything." She said good-bye, rolled up her window, and pulled away.

Brody watched her make a U-turn and head toward town before he returned to his unit.

The closer he got to the search site, the tighter his stomach clenched. Luck had been with him when he ran into Lola Ruth Hicks. Generally, if anyone started a conversation with her it was like wringing the neck of a rooster, swinging it around and around, until either his neck snapped or everyone gave up and headed home, not planning on having chicken for supper.

Now, Brody had a reason to be gone so long, if Scott were to ask. The more time he had, the better he could decide how to handle the information he'd picked up while he was in town.

Hopefully, Deuce was okay and they'd have an opportunity to come up with a strategy tomorrow. Whether Brody should have been at his sister's house investigating on his own or not was open for legal interpretation, but he didn't want to compromise the case—if there was one against Tommy Mitchell.

As he neared the search site and saw the ambulance, fire truck, and most of the volunteers gone, the worry that had followed him since last night seemed to have dissipated somewhat. For the first time he felt like he could breathe. However, his years as a lawman told him that things were never as they first appeared.

By the time Brody got out of his pickup, Scott had rushed up. "I'm sorry, man, I forgot that you don't carry a department phone and since I had to call in the relief dispatcher and she didn't have your private number, Thelma didn't know to keep you updated."

Brody stopped him with a raise of his hand. "I don't care about that. I presume you found Deuce. How is he?"

As if the floodgates of emotion had just been breached, the look on Scott's face changed to anger mixed with fear. "Damn it, Brody. You were the last person I wanted to have to tell this to." He swallowed hard. "He was airlifted to Northwest Texas Hospital in Amarillo by Lifestar, once the DPS chopper located him." Scott shut his eyes and curled his right hand into a fist. "He must have slipped into a pretty steep ravine."

"Damn it to hell, tell me how he is." Brody planted his legs wide apart and crossed his arms over his chest.

"Not good. With the fall he took he's probably paralyzed from a spinal injury. He's in a coma and of course can't talk. The paramedics on board Lifestar said the trauma team is waiting at the hospital. Did you talk to anyone at the Jacks Bluff?"

"Lola Ruth knows why the DPS chopper was here, but I only told her *someone* was lost and you all were looking for them."

"She's a talker for sure. She probably had you corralled for an hour just yakking. But that's one woman I want to keep on my side. She can tell me more without me even asking questions than anybody I know," Scott said.

"Has anyone told Rainey?"

"Yes. I went up to the main house and I got her. I assigned a deputy to her and got her here in time to ride in Lifestar to Amarillo. I received a report that they should be landing at the hospital any moment."

Scott paused, probably trying to figure out how many more ways he could use the word I, then continued, "I thought you might go tell Sylvie. What about his mother? I know she's afflicted with Alzheimer's and is in no condition to understand what has happened. Why don't I just leave the tellin' to you, while I continue working the case?" Scott shook his head. "I've got a lot ahead of me. Since Deuce probably won't be coming back any time soon...maybe never, I'll have to take over, since I'm next in line. Of course, that'll only be until the Commissioners Court names me sheriff permanently, in the worst scenario. Gonna go by the office and check on things. I'm not the only one who needs sleep."

"You're exhausted and I'm sure your wife wants to see you. I'll be okay to watch over things. We'll rotate people, so everyone can catch a few winks. This will give me some time to think things through." Brody felt totally drained and knew the full magnitude of the situation hadn't hit him yet.

"Get a few hours' sleep, Scott. You deserve it."

Brody's legs shook as he got back in his vehicle. Silence grew tight with tension and apprehension all around him. His chest was about to burst open because his heart was beating so fast.

In his career he'd witnessed bodies lying in fields for days, even months, and child abuse that would make the best lawman in the world get light in the head and want to vomit.

There were some things in life that once they've been seen they cannot be unseen—or unsmelled—but the knowledge that someone had tried to kill his best friend and a fellow lawman made him sicker than anything he'd experienced in his career.

Deuce was too smart, not to mention familiar with the area around the ravine, to have accidentally fallen down the side. The two friends had hunted too many times on the land for the sheriff not to have realized the flow of the ravine, with or without daylight. Plus, he would have never left on foot without his flashlight.

Anxiety made Brody's stomach churn, and he lifted his shoulders to relieve some of the tension. But the idea that Deuce could be laid up a while and Brody would have to work under Chief Deputy Scott was truly more undesirable than putting his life on the line every waking hour. He could tolerate Scott but didn't always appreciate the way he went about doing things, and sometimes, actually most of the time, Scott's ego was way too big for his britches

But still, there was something in the way Scott handled the investigation that bothered Brody big time. But he would not throw out accusations of another lawman until he had facts. There was no way in hell Scott, although he was a total a-hole, would harm the sheriff. If and when the time came that he was convinced Scott had something to do with Deuce's injuries, he'd be the first one to step forward and lay out all the facts like any other case.

Brody needed to go by the office, so he headed that direction with thoughts of Deuce heavy on his mind. Brody had already committed to the sheriff that he'd move over to Kasota Springs, so he wouldn't renege on the deal.

You don't do that type of thing to your friends.

And friends they were. Actually, more brothers than friends.

He'd first met Deuce on the University of Texas football field. The first day of workouts in their freshman year. They enjoyed a great relationship on and off the field. He recalled how happy he was for his friend when the Steelers drafted Deuce and just as sad when they released him because of a broken femur. Together they rode the bubble of happiness until one day it burst. By that time, Brody had already gone into law enforcement and encouraged his friend to do the same.

Whether Deuce was incapacitated one day or the rest of his life, as Scott seemed to think, Brody owed it to Deuce to stay with Bonita County.

That's what friends do. The thoughts continued to repeat as though there were a parrot in his head mocking him.

Driving back into town, the first thing he did was go by the antique store to talk to Sylvie. A note on the door read "Closed for the Day." That told him she had already gotten the news about Deuce and had likely gone to the hospital to be with Rainey, who had no family in town.

Quickly stopping by the sheriff's department, Brody had little explanation to do since the majority of the deputies had had enough of Danny Scott and had found reasons to get out of the office. The relief dispatcher, a woman he only knew as Thelma, told him Chief Deputy Scott had sent the regular deputy, Jessup, home for some rest, since as a volunteer, she could work a few more hours. She told Brody that she had everyone's phone number to call in case they were needed. Thelma apologized for not having Brody's personal phone, but she added it to the list and recited the phone number back to him.

Whether the relief dispatcher knew of Deuce's and Brody's agreement for him to work permanently out of Bonita County, he didn't know. After a brief thought of mentioning it crossed his flooded mind, he immediately considered coming up with an excuse to leave but he had some work he needed to do first. Staying might open the door to more questions than he was willing to answer right now. Leaving well enough alone was good.

A wave and an *If you need me, call*, didn't seem adequate, but Brody wasn't up to any more discussions, except to ask Thelma for two envelopes.

Back in his office, he located a legal pad and wrote a *To Whom It May Concern* letter. Of course, to make a copy he had to face Thelma, who sipped on a cup of coffee but didn't try to engage him into conversation. Returning to his privacy, Brody placed the letters in the envelopes and addressed them, then pulled a worn-out stamp from his billfold and stuck it on one. He slid the envelope in his shirt pocket beneath his jacket.

He strolled to Scott's desk and placed the second envelope in the middle drawer where it couldn't be missed.

On his way out of the back entrance, he stopped by the small lunchroom and grabbed an individual package of cookies and a bottle of energy drink that Thelma used her coupon hobby to keep the department stocked with.

No one except Deuce and Brody knew he had agreed to work out of Bonita County permanently, thus giving up most of his undercover stings. He had no reason to believe his rank would change, so he'd continue being lieutenant detective assigned to special crimes. Same rank. Same offices, but working on different cases.

Realization hit him that he hadn't slept in two days. Nor had he eaten much of anything except the cookies and energy drink. He wasn't sure he could keep his vehicle on the road long enough to get all the way to Amarillo, so after stopping by the post office's outside drop box and dropping in the envelope, he headed toward his ranch, just west of Deuce's ranch.

Brody didn't have any Lone Star beer at the WBarT, but knew of at least one fifth of Black Jack in the cupboard.

Within minutes, he unlocked the door to the rustic ranch house and reset the alarm. Quickly, he secured his service firearm and put his personal weapon in the drawer of the end table. After opening and slamming shut three cabinet doors, he found his favorite glass and poured in four fingers of Jack Daniel's. Planting his feet wide apart, he took two swigs of the whiskey then refilled it.

In the living room, Brody switched on the television and plopped down on the sofa. He swore the dust he stirred up was similar to the Dust Bowl days of the 1930s. Maybe even worse. But then what could he expect from a six-foot, four-inch man who weighed over two hundred pounds flopping down on the cushions like a wrecking ball causing an old building to implode.

He finished off the whiskey and refilled his glass with another two fingers then placed it on the dusty end table. He guessed if he planned to stay on the ranch much, he needed to hire a housekeeper. Or, at least, someone to organize everything where he could find it. He'd given his sister and brother-in-law permission to come out to the WBarT any time they wished. Apparently, they either had never taken him up on his offer or didn't give a hoot about cleaning, which meant Winnie, the queen of clean, had not been there.

Brody looked up when Chief Deputy Scott's voice coming over the television airwaves penetrated his thoughts. Scott was in the midst of an interview with an Amarillo TV anchor, telling the world about Deuce being in critical condition after an apparent attack. And, Chief Deputy Scott was hot on the trail of the person responsible for the sheriff's near-fatal injuries, as if he was the only deputy working the case. Scott rambled on in an authoritative way, promising *he* wouldn't stop until the perpetrator was brought to justice.

The last thing Brody heard before he clicked off the TV was how Scott would protect the citizens of Bonita County as chief deputy. There were more *I's* than *We's*, as expected.

Brody wouldn't allow himself to lose control, although he was tempted to throw his glass and the bottle of Tennessee whiskey across the room. Instead, he let Scott's comments roll off his back as if he'd thrown a bucket of water on Brody.

He directed his attention across the room to his football memorabilia in cabinets with sliding glass doors on either side and beneath the windows. He wanted to go over and examine each individual piece. He needed security, comfort, and his signed footballs, pictures and helms had always done the job. He could remember almost every birthday one of the items his mother and daddy had given him. Even an old girlfriend or two. Most were given to him by Deuce during his football days.

But as much as he wanted to spend time with his special assortment of souvenirs, his legs didn't feel like they could make it across the room.

After he took another swig of whiskey, he balanced his thoughts between sleeping on the sofa, dust and all, and going to his bedroom. He was sure there were no sheets on the huge four-poster antique bed, plus the couch was closer.

It had been one hell of a day and the days to come were certain to be equally as bad, if not worse.

As exhausted, both mentally and physically, as he felt, Brody chose to go to the basement, where he had a full gym. After putting on hand wraps and boxing gloves, he took out his frustration on his punching bag. Although he did a relatively mild workout for him, he walked back upstairs guaranteed to sleep.

Tomorrow, he'd go to Amarillo and check on Deuce for himself. He needed to talk with Rainey and see if he could help handle Sylvie with the antique shop in the ol' Rock Island Railroad Depot. And if he could lend a hand with Deuce's mother at the nursing home.

Just as he closed his eyes, the face of a beautiful woman appeared. A sexy as hell lady, who he felt certain would relieve some of his frustration and heartache. Avery Scarlett O'Hara.

Brody was so exhausted he wasn't sure his mind hadn't played tricks on him and there was not even a woman at the festival dressed as Scarlett O'Hara. Maybe she was nothing more than a character in a dream. She was too perfect to be a living, breathing woman.

As the memories of the kisses returned one by one, there was no doubt in his mind that a Miss Avery with no last name existed and he could sure use her smile and a tender kiss right now.

Like a building collapsing, the realization of the day's activities tumbled down around him. Tears were close to surfacing. There was only one other time he'd cried as a lawman. The day they buried Deuce's father in Denton, a sheriff killed in the line of duty. No way could this happen to two people in the same family, but in reality he knew of more cases than he wished to talk about. He sent up a silent prayer for Deuce and those killed in the line of duty. He'd held back the emotions as long as he could.

He needed to go back downstairs and work out again. Harder than before, to release his anger and frustration, but instead hot tears welled in his eyes. He clinched his fist, and the urge to throw the glass returned.

Brody took another drink.

From the back of the sofa he drew the quilt his grandmother had made for him when he was in college. He shook off most of the dust, wrapped the old muslin around his body, and settled into the cushions of the sofa. The tighter he pulled the quilt around him, the tighter he held back the emotions. Like a pot of boiling water overflowing, hot tears rolled down his cheeks and landed on his arm.

His whole world had been turned upside-down.

Way in the back of his mind, memories lolled around, reminding him of his days in the police academy. The lectures about a lawman being just another human with emotions, but they weren't allowed to show them except in private. And, privacy he had for the first time in months, along with a deep stabbing hurt in his heart.

If only he could go back. Even one day. Maybe he could have changed the world around him, especially for his best friend.

Brody did as he always found himself doing when he'd observed a murder victim or some unsavory bastard who beat his wife or shot up a house full of people. He wept aloud, pulling the quilt tighter and tighter, wishing he could go back and do yesterday all over again.

Sleep overtook him, but the nightmares remained.

What is seen can never be unseen....

Chapter 8

Avery Danielle Humphrey sat in the kitchen impatiently waiting for her cup of tea to brew. Weak arms propped on the table held up her head, but that was the only way she could stop her nagging headache. She'd taken niacin and aspirin, but so far there was no real relief.

Knowing a good run and fresh air would help, she went upstairs and showered. Hot, steamy water helped a lot to clear her head but did little to stop the thoughts of the sounds she'd heard during her restless night.

Although she'd not lived in Kasota Springs for many years, she recognized something serious, very serious, had gone on during the night. Not just the cop in her that felt the urgency, but the sirens, the DPS helicopter, and Lifestar. Each helicopter had a distinctive sound, plus she recognized the infrared beams, which meant a search of some type. Coupled with the other things she had seen when she was sitting in the square with Brody, trouble saturated the morning air.

And there was nothing she could do about it, not even assist in the hunt. With her expertise, she'd be a great resource, yet she'd have to tell Brody the truth, the reality about her job in Houston.

That would have definitely caused an unnecessary distraction, plus open a gate to allow one lie after another to escape. She couldn't afford to tell the story that ate at her daily to a stranger...not yet.

This complication left the door unfastened for Avery to make another decision weighing heavy on her heart. And it wasn't about Brody VanZant, either, especially since he worked with multi-units and she had no idea what agency or county he was employed by. Possibly Bonita County, possibly another one.

When Deuce got back in the office on Monday morning, she might, just might, approach him for a job. That was, if she decided to stick around. From what she'd learned about the sheriff, he was fair to a fault, honest to the core, and had scruples of a five-star general.

Since Deuce and Brody were best friends, she'd think he'd have those same qualities. Again, she had to remind herself the thoughts concerning staying in town had to do with her parents, not Brody.

At the moment, it was her feeling, depending on the advice of her parents, that she'd return to Kasota Springs and leave the big city behind. But there was a lot of thought that needed to be put into the issue.

After dressing in running clothes, she came downstairs and fixed another cup of tea. Realizing the water was hot, she got up, tossed the K-Cup in the trash, and took her drink back to the table. Thoughts scrambling inside her head only increased her headache. Oh, how she wanted to go to where the sounds of emergency vehicles seemingly had come from. Since Mesa had said she'd be working all morning with the ranch hands taking care of the rough stock from the rodeo, Dannie didn't want to bother her. She'd see her later in the day and would find out.

Of course, she knew Brody, as well as Sheriff Cowan, was probably still at the accident scene. All depending on what the scenario had been. Probably an automobile accident, but then why call out all units unless it was a multi-vehicle scene?

And that still didn't answer why the DPS helicopter was out using infrared imagery.

She blew on the hot liquid and ran her hand across her forehead. The other question that had kept her awake was the deal with the young man she had seen leaving from the back of the sheriff's department offices who had walked off into the dark directly where the noise of emergency vehicles had come from.

Possibly the real reason she hadn't been able to sleep were the thoughts of Brody VanZant and his kisses. Those feelings eventually ended up with her wondering how he was going to take the secret that she'd kept from him. Had he ever been in the same position? Many lawmen and women had been. All cops had been trained for her situation; however, most people in law enforcement had never experienced it for real. She wasn't the only detective who had missed a shot, not taken one, or had their partner protect them by stepping between them and the shooter.

The thoughts caused too much ache in her heart. Avery turned her attention back to her tea and drained the cup. She needed to go over to the antique shop and return her costume from the festival. Mesa had said they'd be open Sunday as a convenience. Avery also needed to apologize to Rainey for messing up their evening.

Those thoughts quickly moved on down the line, as Dannie returned to reflecting on the turbulence she felt around her. The unrest that came with working in the judicial system hung around her shoulders like a concrete jacket with a PVC collar.

Topping her list was her worry over the note from her mother, which Dannie had read a half a dozen times before she fell asleep. She saw nothing but a perfect storm racing toward her. She knew her mother well enough to know that if she had to see a doctor or there were any family problems, she would share whatever was going on with Dannie's father and then usually Dannie. She had a feeling this was one of those times that her mother had chosen to not tell her daughter everything, thinking she was protecting her.

It was a Humphrey-Sullivan family trait, protecting each other.

The front door opened, and familiar voices came down the short hallway into the kitchen. She smiled, listening to her father fuss at her mother for trying to bring in too much luggage. If there was one man that could be called a true Texas gentleman, it would be her father. She was sure he got it from his father and grandfather, both Texas Rangers.

Avery stopped at the threshold to the entryway. Her mother, Kathleen Claire Sullivan Humphrey, stood there, surrounded by luggage, looking like Cinderella waiting for directions to her carriage. She turned in the direction of Dannie's father and said, "Ira Lambert, *darlin'*, please be careful and not fall over our luggage."

Kathleen stepped toward her daughter. Gently her mother set her handbag, which cost more than Dannie's two-way airline ticket from Houston to Amarillo, on the antique parlor table. She opened her arms, and Dannie flew into her embrace.

"I'm so glad to see you, darlin' Dannie." Her mother kissed her on the forehead and wrapped her arms around her, pulling her daughter tightly against her.

Avery felt certain her mother had no idea how much she had missed being called Dannie.

Her father obviously had a crisis going on, the way he waved and blew a kiss to Dannie without missing a word of his conversation on his cell phone. As a lawyer, the town's mayor, and chairman of more state and regional committees than she could count, he always had an emergency to be dealt with. This one seemed more serious than usual.

Typically, her father, who had a voice to match his height, could be eight feet tall if she used that as a comparison to how he sounded. His breathing was deep and each breath seemed closer together.

Dannie had gotten her height from her father but was sure happy the Good Lord had seen fit to give Dannie her mother's figure. One thing for sure, they owned the sturdiest furniture in town. Much of it had belonged to her grandfather Humphrey, who was just as large as the life he lived.

"What kind of emergency is going on, Mother?"

"I thought you of all people would know, since it happened last night—actually early this morning." Kathleen kept an eye on her husband, who went into the parlor still talking nearly loud enough for his wife and daughter to hear clearly.

Dannie's leg muscles tightened, as if she were about to buckle over. At least her headache had lightened up a bit. Her premonition must be true.

"Oh God, Mother, tell me. Please don't say that someone from the sheriff's department got injured. Please, Mother, please." Dannie's hands turned clammy. By the look on her mother's face, Dannie knew she was right.

"Darlin', I thought you would have already heard about it, but Sheriff Cowan is in critical condition in the hospital in Amarillo. Or they may have airlifted him to Lubbock—"

"Oh God…I just knew it was the sheriff or one of the deputies. I just knew it." She shook her head in disbelief and clutched her throat. "What happened?"

"I don't know exactly, but it seems there was an altercation near the Jacks Bluff last night and they had to send out a search party before daylight this morning and it took a while to locate him." Kathleen stood unwavering as she walked to the kitchen. "I need some coffee, and your father will tell us what he knows as soon as he gets the final report. Right now he's having a conference call with the commissioners to see what course of action they should follow."

"What they need to do? He's that bad?" Dannie closed her eyes and let the perspiration run between her breasts as she awaited the answer.

"When Lifestar arrived and the trauma team saw him, he was unresponsive. He has a head injury of some sort, but I don't know how serious, and had been out in the elements for a few hours." Kathleen tucked a couple of tresses of hair back into her bun. "Things have taken a turn for the worse and they can't get him to move—and although the doctors said he hadn't been shot, it looks like his spinal column has been damaged. Nobody knows how right now, but there was blood, not a lot but a significant amount. One good thing: although he's in a medically induced coma, it appears there's nothing wrong with his brain. He just can't respond verbally. They said his recovery after surgery might take a while." She lowered her head. "*If* he recovers."

Dannie measured coffee for a regular pot, although her hands shook. Nobody really needed caffeine, but it was such a family ritual that she didn't give it a thought until after she had it on. She'd fix herself some tea.

"I thought from your letter that you all wouldn't be home until Tuesday." Dannie wiped her hands on a tea towel.

"I wasn't sure how long we'd be, when I wrote the note. We'll talk about it later."

Kathleen sat in her favorite spot where she watched the bird feeder right outside the bay window. Being spring, she no doubt could see several little beaks bobbing up and down in the bird's nest. She folded her hands as if praying and looked over Dannie's shoulder. Dannie knew exactly what her mother was thinking, because they'd talked about it hundreds of times over the years.

Out of the blue, her mother said, "You know, darlin', you shouldn't wear a sleeveless top and shorts at the table."

Before Dannie could respond, her father entered, still on his conference call.

Dannie took the chair next to her mother, waiting on the coffee, and listened to her father.

Beginning to feel like an eavesdropper when she didn't even have a bull in the chute, Dannie got up, rinsed out her cup, and started a new cup of tea. Then she filled two more with coffee. After giving a mug of coffee to her father and putting her mother's in a cup with a saucer, Dannie returned to her seat. At least she had showered, washed her hair, and dressed before her parents got home. You'd think her mother would know Dannie had prepared to go running, but Dannie had thought for years that her mother surely carried the genes of Emily Post.

Her father's conversation caught her attention when she heard him endorse Danny as a replacement for Sheriff Cowan if he wasn't able to return fairly soon. A hot, shrinking feeling hit her stomach and she thought for sure she was going to throw up. Daddy had only used his first name, but Danny Scott was the only Danny in the department and to her knowledge was the highest-ranking officer.

She heard him go on to say, "According to Rainey, the doctors said it could be months or more before Deuce will be able to return, and that's after he comes out of the medically induced coma and goes through rehab." He stopped to listen then said, "Whatever you do, don't let the name get out yet. All hell might break lose. Just remember that we can appoint any qualified person we want to be interim sheriff and we're less than six months away from the mid-term elections, and then the citizens can make their own choice." He took a sip of his coffee, sat the mug on the table, and looked over at Dannie. "No, kept it to yourself, I'll talk to the candidate myself, and since we have a consensus all we'll need is to call an executive session, take a formal vote to go into the minutes."

Her father lowered himself into his chair. "Charlie, you aren't out in the open talking to us are you?" He bit his lip listening. "Sylvie Dewey! She'll have it spread all over town before we can talk to the candidate or any of the deputies. We might as well hold a press conference in ten minutes." He rubbed the back of his neck. "That's probably why she keeps her iPhone within easy reach at all times.

"Okay, let's all take time, cool off, and test the waters. Remember everything depends on Deuce. I know you guys are with me and my family in praying that our sheriff comes out of his coma and there's little damage. I want him back as sheriff." He took another sip of coffee. "Yes, I agree, keep it as low-key as possible. As far as I know, it could have been an accident. He could have fallen out there in those old cottonwoods. And if it wasn't an accident, they said we don't even have a suspect." He waited, obviously listening to one of the county commissioners. "I don't know about the crushed phone. It does look suspicious, but he could have dropped it and stepped on it." He stopped to listen again. "I agree. We may never know what happened if Deuce doesn't wake up."

Dannie lowered her head and covered her eyes with crossed hands. The situation for Rainey had to be earthshaking. Mesa had told Dannie about Deuce's mother, who was suffering in the later stages of Alzheimer's. Dannie didn't know much, but she knew Mrs. Cowan lived in the local nursing home and rehab center.

"Mother, who's going to take care of Deuce's mother?" she said in a soft voice. Feeling sorry for Deuce and Rainey didn't even seem adequate.

"Darlin', she's really bad. But in her own way is doing well where she is. She's obsessed with Deuce's football years and doesn't even know him when he visits. She thinks he's someone else. It breaks my heart. Sylvie can't go out there because it upsets Mrs. Cowan too much. She loves Rainey." Dannie's mother clutched the pearls hanging from her neck, twisting them so hard Dannie was certain they would break. "I can go once or twice a week, and we'll get a group of the ladies from the church and various social organizations to help out and see who fits in with her. Of course, we'll talk to Rainey first and hopefully, it won't be long until Deuce will be in the same facility because it sounds like he'll need a lot of rehab.... That is, once he comes out of the coma." Dannie's mother accidentally knocked her coffee over, leaving a dark stain on the white lace tablecloth.

Dannie jumped up, grabbed a handful of paper towels, and dabbed away the liquid. "I'll put the tablecloth in the washer right after I've treated it with spot remover."

"Thank you, darlin'. Generally it could wait until Jennie comes, but I do love that tablecloth and would hate to have ruined it. I need to unpack and make up a grocery list."

Dannie tossed the paper towels in the trash, got fresh napkins from the linen drawer, and sat back down.

Although it was bad timing, she felt like she needed to talk to her parents. She hated to do it with everything happening, but then there probably wasn't going to be a better opportunity any time soon.

"Daddy, I need to talk to you and Mama. It won't take long."

"I need to talk to you, too, sweetheart. Mine won't take very long, either."

The hardcore detective in Dannie made her determined to say her piece first. "Just give me a minute. Mine's a yes or no with little if any discussion at the moment." She went on without waiting for an answer.

"First off, I really have two questions." She turned toward her mother, but kept her gaze on her father to see his reaction. "Is something wrong with you, Mother? Something medically? I've never known you to miss the Spring Festival unless it's an emergency."

"No, darlin', there isn't. My doctor in Amarillo didn't like what he saw on my annual mammogram and wanted a specialist in Dallas to check me out—"

Her father interrupted, "I'm the real culprit. I know her doctor was right, but I wanted her to be seen in Dallas by a specialist."

"Yes, darlin', he's right. Things are fine. I'll have to take some treatments over in Amarillo, but you know me, I've never let anything get me down." She patted Dannie's hand. "I'm sorry if I frightened you. To be honest, I was a little scared myself, but with everything you've been going through, you didn't need to be worried unnecessarily. I'm so sorry, sweetheart."

"Okay, I'll believe you." Dannie smiled at her father, who had taken on a look of *liar, liar, pants on fire.*

Her father had just made the decision for her.

"Daddy, I'm going to catch a flight today or tomorrow to Houston to check on my apartment—"

"Aren't you planning on staying around here a while?" Her mother looked at her with sad eyes.

"Before I do anything, I have to talk to my boss. Then turn in my official resignation. Since I've been on paid mandatory leave I don't think I'll have to go through the normal channels of giving them notice." Dannie folded her arms across her chest. "My apartment is leased for another six months, so I won't have to be in a hurry getting my things organized and making any type of decisions. That'll give me an opportunity to find a job...."

Before she could gather her thoughts to continue, her father blurted out, "Sweetheart, I can find you one while you're gone."

"Thanks, Dad. I don't care if it's working for Pumpkin at her café or the Dairy Queen. Even helping you out at your office. Just as long as I have some money coming in. I've got plenty saved for a rainy day, but one never knows when it will rain."

Her father stood there drumming his fingers on his thigh with a slight glimmer to his eyes. "That's what I wanted to talk to you about...."

Chapter 9

Brody slowly opened his eyes to early morning sunlight filtering through the old cottonwoods.

He blinked several times, sat up, and rubbed his forehead. If anything he might well be more tired now than when he had crashed the night before. It reminded him of frat parties when he was at UT. In those years, he and Deuce thought they were invincible.

As a man matured and saw himself in the victim's place, it grew harder to shake off.

Most of the night he had tossed and turned, wondering what the future held for Deuce. For Brody, too. Damn it, the whole sheriff's department, for that matter.

Any decision he made about his future with Bonita County was now dependent on what happened to Deuce in the long term. On the other side of the coin, he'd already made a commitment to Deuce before he got injured.

Hell, injured! In Brody's heart, he knew it wasn't just a simple injury but an assault. He felt certain of that so did Chief Deputy Danny Scott, but he wouldn't put money on it. The longer Brody waited to act on the investigative work he had done the night before, the harder it would be to solve the mystery...a mystery to all but Deuce.

Before Brody went to the hospital to see his friend, he needed to check in with the department. Afterward, he wanted to have a talk with his sister and, for that matter, Stanley. One of the first things he had learned doing undercover work—hell being in law enforcement period—was the worn out cliché: *Keep you friends close and your enemies closer.*

This was definitely one of those times the saying needed to be put into actions. Maybe he'd arrived at a point to play nice with Stanley.

As Brody put on coffee, he laughed and thought, *Maybe "you can catch more flies with honey than vinegar" was more fitting. Another worn-out cliché that a journalist would avoid like the plague.*

While the coffee brewed, he put up the half-empty liquor bottle and washed out his glass. He was happy to have a glass, because in the mood he had been in the night before, typically he'd be picking up shards all over the floor.

He went to the bathroom to take a shower but found himself scrubbing his head like he'd been out in the dirt for two weeks without any water. He made a note to call the gal who cut his hair and see when she could get him in. That step alone would definitely disqualify him for the joint task force.

In most parts of Texas there were three things you'd rarely find: A barbershop open on Monday, alcohol sold before noon Sunday, and car lots open seven days a week. He knew he could call June at home and she'd open her shop just for him.

It took Brody surprisingly longer to shave his shaggy beard and sideburns than he anticipated, but finally he wiped a clean hand towel over his face. Other than his hair, he hardly recognized himself in the mirror.

What a surprise everyone would have when they held muster on Tuesday morning. Unless they had run into Sylvie or Lola Ruth, nobody but Danny Scott would know Brody had cleaned up because he'd come out from working undercover.

After drinking three mugs of coffee, Brody dressed and headed for the sheriff's department. As he crossed the last cattle guard leaving his ranch, he'd had time to think about maybe stepping out of his comfort zone and running a small cow-calf operation on his land. He had an old bunkhouse where he could put up a couple of hired hands. He could get that housekeeper he'd thought about and add cook to the job description. That was, if he wanted to go back into ranching.

Before he knew it, he had crossed the railroad tracks and had entered the city limits. He stopped by the sheriff's office to see if anybody had an update on Deuce.

He also wanted to know if they'd gotten anywhere with the investigation and if Tommy was a person of interest. Until Deuce returned, Brody didn't trust anybody with the investigative material he had. If he did, he might wake up one morning with a knife in his back.

Nothing about Deuce's condition sounded positive. Brody knew if the trauma team had flown his friend to Lubbock it wasn't a good sign, but he'd get excellent treatment for his head injury. The only other thing he learned, as he anticipated, was that Danny Scott was still drivin' the "I" wagon.

Brody looked at his watch. It was between breakfast run and lunchtime at his sister's cafe. Typically, Stanley cut the brisket, ham, and ribs on Monday about this time, so possibly Brody would have an opportunity to talk with his sister alone.

Play nice. Play nice. He had to keep reminding himself. Regardless of what buttons Stanley pushed, Brody would just bear it and go on. He'd had to do that a zillion times as a cop, so he'd treat this like any other investigation.

He parked in his usual place and came in the back door. As he had anticipated, Stanley stood at the butcher block, cutting meat. He didn't even look up when his brother-in-law walked in.

Brody reached over and picked up a slice of brisket from the serving warmer pan. "Hi, old man. Smells good. I don't know how you cut the slices so perfect. I used to think you all used a meat slicer before I found out you do it all by hand." He took a bite. "Really great flavor."

"You want a roll to go around that meat?" Stanley reached up on the shelf and took one from under the cellophane wrap and handed it to Brody. "Freshly made."

"Thanks, man. Is my sister out front?"

"Yep. Get you a cup of coffee. I owe you a big apology because I dropped your special mug the other day. I'll find one to replace it." Stanley began chopping the part of the beef that most people thought was undesirable but adds that recognizable flavor to chopped brisket sandwiches.

"Thanks, but you don't have to. Everyone has slippery hands every now and again. Brody strolled into the dining room, got some coffee, and took a seat at the table where Winnie was sorting flatware.

"Good to see you, big brother." She put a handful of iced teaspoons upside-down in a holder. "But I think if you want any woman to look at you twice you need to get that ugly mop on your head cut. I'm surprised that Avery allowed you to kiss her more than once—"

"You saw that?" Brody's hand shot to his chest.

"Of course, you may not have had time to stop by, but I've kept an eye on you. She's sure cute." With a damp cloth, she rubbed a spoon and put it in the holder.

"So you know her?" Adrenaline rushed through his body.

"Well, kinda. She's with Mesa LeDoux when I see her mostly. For some reason Avery doesn't sound right, but that's the name I was told. I don't know if she's local, but until a couple of weeks ago I hadn't seen her around for years."

His luck had just run out. Brody thought for sure he was about to find out Avery's last name and then could locate her. He reminded himself for

the umpteenth time that she might well be an out-of-town visitor who had
come to Kasota Springs just for the festival.

Brody nodded his head toward the kitchen. "Why's he in such a happy
mood?" He deliberately raised his eyebrow.

"Don't know, but it's nice. I didn't give him any last night, if that's what
the raised eyebrow meant."

They shared a laugh.

"Maybe he's still sorry about breaking your cup. It'd been a long day,
actually three days, because we had to shop, cook, and get ready for the
catering, plus keep the doors open here. I know he felt bad about your cup."

"It upset me, just because you'd given it to me years ago." He took a
sip of coffee and sat his standard-issue café cup down. "I have something
we need to discuss."

"What in the world could be that serious?" She began filling the napkin
holders. "Are you getting married? Oh no, getting a haircut?"

"Maybe letting that hole in your ear grow up," Stanley said from the
doorway. "Never thought a grown man should have any ear pierced."

"No wonder you two are so good together. A true Dean Martin and
Jerry Lewis act." He looked from his sister to his brother-in-law and back
but didn't see any response on their faces.

Finally, Stanley said, "Join us and we'll be the Marx brothers. Wasn't
there three of them?"

"I think so, but I do have something serious to discuss. Since Deuce
is so badly injured and they don't know when he'll return to the sheriff's
department, I've agreed to step away from the JTF and come back here
for a while." Again, he gauged actions for any clue as to how they felt.
"Actually, Deuce and I discussed the move at the festival and I made a
pretty firm commitment to him."

Winnie responded first. "I totally agree. The sheriff's department
needs you, and it's a whole lot less dangerous here than working nights
and looking for God only knows what or who." She started another napkin
holder. "And I don't even want to know what you do." She raised her hand,
as to say *stop*. "And, no, I don't care whether it's undercover for the county
or under your personal covers."

All three chuckled, causing Brody to think that maybe this cat and
mouse game might be working.

"What are you gonna do with *your* house?" Stanley put way too much
emphasis on *your* for Brody's liking. But then ever since Winnie's and
Brody's mother had passed away and left the house in Amarillo to him

and the life insurance policy to her, there had always been a chill in the air when the subject came up.

One time Stanley told Brody that Winnie was still trying to accept that he got a two-hundred-thousand-dollar house, while his sister only got a fifty-thousand-dollar life insurance policy. Brody didn't believe him then, and things hadn't changed an iota.

"I heard that Danny Scott is going to be named interim sheriff." Winnie broke the silence and turned back to sorting flatware. "Do you want to work for him?"

"Technically, at the moment, I'd have no choice but to follow his lead. I told Deuce the afternoon before he got hurt that I'd make the change and move back to Kasota Springs. You know the VanZant family.... A promise to a friend is a promise come a drought or an overabundance of spring rain."

"I agree with you," Stanley said. "I'll be glad to help you out when you get ready to move." From the sideboard, he brought over several trays of salt and pepper shakers.

"I'm not sure when, if ever, I'll put the home on the market to sell. I'm going to spend most of my time at the ranch. It's closer, and as Lola Ruth Hicks reminded me, 'The price of gas is going up.' You gotta trust a gal like Miss Hicks." Brody reached over and pulled a tray of salt shakers and a heavy box of salt to him. "When I'm not in Amarillo I can always get Mrs. Otis to watch the house for me."

"I have to go into town a couple of times a week for supplies; I can check on your mail. Still got your post office box?" Stanley asked.

"Sure do." Brody opened the remainder of the saltshakers. "You still have the keys to the house and PO box, don't you, Winnie?"

"Yes. It's in my top left-hand dresser drawer underneath some jewelry boxes. So it's safe and one thing you won't have to worry about, but I do want you to know where the keys to both the house and mailbox are," said Winnie.

"Thanks," Brody said.

Standing with his arms across this chest, Stanley said, "If I can't check the post office box, I can get Tommy to do it."

"I don't think so, Stanley, but thanks for the offer. There's never any mail that's worth a trip to the post office. I'll be flexible enough to go, although I'll spend most of my time around here."

"So you'll be able to keep an eye on my brother. He seems to entice you so much." Out of the blue, Stanley's tone turned sarcastic and his words reeked with insult.

"Please, Stanley, don't start it again," Winnie pleaded.

"Oh, I'm sorry, dear. I'm sure Brody knew I was kidding, right?" He looked into Brody's eyes without any emotion.

Under the table, Brody clinched his fist so tight that he could have cut off circulation to his fingers. "Of course. I couldn't have a better brother-in-law. I'd be pleased as punch to have a brother like you to help me out, if I were Tommy." Brody went back to his chore.

The hot swell in Brody's stomach almost made him want to vomit for telling such a lie.

He got up and set the finished trays of salt shakers on the shelf. "Gotta go." Brody leaned over to kiss his sister's head. "Love you, little sis." He turned to face Stanley. "How's your brother? Understand he had a cold or a touch of the flu yesterday."

"He's none of your concern. He's doing fine and you need to focus on real criminals, not a kid like my brother." Stanley's mocking words followed him into the kitchen.

Play nice! Play nice!

"Stanley, if you all need anything with Tommy, don't hesitate letting me know."

"You'll be the first to know." Sarcasm imbedded itself in Stanley's tone.

Well, the visit proved one thing. If Brody were in Tommy's shoes, he'd be thankful to have a cunning liar of a brother to help him out by fibbing for him all the way to the core. The biggest benefit? He could get stoned and along the way try to wipe out the sheriff and his brother would look the other way or maybe drive him home.

It was always convenient to have a family member like Stanley Mitchell on your side.

Chapter 10

Avery stood on the porch with her arms clutching her waist as if trying to hold everything together. She had so many feelings running through her that she didn't know whether to run or stay.

If she didn't return to her old job in Houston, she definitely would always feel she hadn't faced her feelings of guilt for her partner's death. Everyone would think she'd been hiding from the reality that it was her fault Lee was shot and killed.

She began jogging her favorite course: West Main along the railroad tracks until she crossed over to the Dairy Queen and hit the road leading to FM208 near Mesa's ranch.

Ever since she'd been allowed to run without having an adult with her, she'd never deviated from her path.

Just the idea of getting out into the fresh spring air lightened her mood a bit as thoughts of her childhood took over. Before she had run as exercise, she had been allowed to play in the town square or on the Sullivan Ranch, where it wasn't much fun to dodge pump jacks and drilling rigs, not to mention a hungry rattlesnake or two.

One piece of her father's advice always remained front and center. After they went out of the cow-calf business, he'd tell her it was easier to cash a check from an oil and gas outfit or an energy company than chase crazy ballsy bulls all over the place.

That memory made her laugh aloud. It wasn't until she was eight or nine that she asked him what the difference was between bulls with horns and ballsy bulls. She was particularly interested in knowing about bulls without horns. What were they called? Her father's explanation confused her more until she was quite a bit older and sat down with the ranch foreman and he explained *everything* to her. Even jogging with the wind to her back, she knew her face turned beet red.

But Avery still had decisions to make. Go back to Houston or return to the warm arms of the town she was born in. Even if she could only get a job at the Dairy Queen or work for Clara at Pumpkin's, at least she'd have money to take care of her immediate needs. She briefly thought about the Ol' Hickory Inn, which served barbecue, but she'd have to draw the line on that. She didn't eat beef, which was almost a crime in Texas, and she didn't even know the owners. She mentally added that to the cluster of things she needed to find out about.

That left little doubt she had let her job take over her family life. Her parents hadn't even asked how long she'd been in town. They just presumed she'd arrived after they had left for Dallas, and she had let it stand that way.

Returning to the matter at hand, Avery figured that since the Ol' Hickory Inn was out, any of the remainder of options would work until she could find a better-paying job.

No doubt her parents would not only allow her to move back home temporarily but encourage her to never move out. She had her own car and plenty of money in savings plus some investments. She'd gotten her good business and financial sense from her father, certainly not her mother.

Before she realized how far she'd run, she was even with a gigantic wind turbine. She had crossed over FM208 and headed for open prairie without giving it much notice. She would just run the barbed wire fence line, where a path had been formed over the years, and circle back, watching carefully for prairie dog holes. She could make a choice then whether to go see Lola Ruth and get a glass of tea or head back to town.

In the distance, she saw a few feet of yellow crime scene tape flapping in the wind. Now she knew for a fact this was the area where the sheriff had been injured.

Although she was a little winded, her headache had ceased and thoughts had cleared. She felt like she'd had a gallon of new life pumped into her. That was, if new life came in gallons.

Flashing off the brilliant sunrays, a dark amber glass caught her eye. She squatted and looked at the vial without touching it. The label was face up and more faded than legible, but she could see a date of 1963 and Teg Tegler III DVM. She knew right away the thick prescription bottle had come from the Jacks Bluff's infirmary because there had been a Tegler working for the ranch since the late 1800s. She didn't know what the bottle was doing out there. But since it was fairly close to where Deuce had been hurt and it hadn't been out in the elements very long, she certainly didn't want to handle the bottle without gloves. She took three clean tissues, securely wrapped the vial and put it in the pocket of her running shorts. Luck was on her side, because she had selected shorts with zipper pockets.

Suddenly, she heard someone running behind her. She was on private property, so there were few people who liked to dodge mesquite and yucca enough to go through that area. Most, if not all, would be on horseback. Avery had her own path.

She made an effort to stay calm, but when she thought back to the fact this area lay exactly where Deuce had been hurt, chills ran up and down her spine. And now to have someone following her.

The cautious side of Avery kicked in. She slowed down and listened carefully.

A man, by the sound of the shoes—big ones—slowed.

Her next option, speed up and watch for an exit or a stand of trees to hide in. Mesquite would hurt like hell, but it was better than death. Most ranches in the panhandle of Texas had been owned by the same families for generations, so few had other type of trees unless they were around old abandoned homesteads or ranch foremen's camps. Since she hadn't run this path for some time, except for the last two weeks while she stayed with Mesa, she had to really observe everything around her.

The person chasing her closed in.

Perspiration ran over her shoulders and down her back.

Her only other choice was to circle back and take him down like a professional. Spying a small arroyo running beneath the bottom row of barbed wire, she went down on her knees, then her belly, and crawled under it before she circled back. She hid behind a stand of mesquite trees with her back to the path until she heard him nearing the dry crossing.

At just the right time, she rolled into the ravine, but with the depth of the gully, the barbed wire post obstructed her vision. Hoping not to be seen, she ducked until he passed. All she could see were running shoes, men's extra large, if she were a betting woman.

Avery lagged behind the man and couldn't see any more than she could while in the gulch. She lunged, hitting him in the middle of the back with one shoulder. He fell to his knees. As she applied pressure to the middle of his back, he lay facedown with her straddling him.

As fast as a camera flash, from behind she simultaneously slid her left arm under his arm and crossed his chest while her other arm came over his shoulder and she locked her fingers together as tightly as possible. She had him totally under control. Her knees and arms were out of his reach and she was on his back. One tight squeeze and he'd be temporarily out like a light.

"What do you want with me, you bastard?" Avery almost yelled, wishing she had a third hand to slug him with.

Suddenly, with a full body press he flipped and straddled her, holding her hands above her head. His knees were tight against her hips.

She stared into Brody's crystal-blue eyes. A flush of adrenaline gushed through her body like she'd never experienced before, even when she had taken down a criminal.

"I'd like the same answer, but I wouldn't add bastard to the end." He rolled over, taking her with him. Their faces, lips, were only a breath apart. "I presume you didn't realize that I had circled back at the curve when I saw you shimmy under the barbed wire?"

"I guess you're a better cop that I thought you were."

As hard as she tried, she couldn't ignore the feel of his well-developed, muscular body against hers. She'd try another approach since he didn't respond to her statement—which could have been taken as a compliment or an insult, depending on his mood. It was very obvious he hadn't thought her takedown was all that cute. "Would you please let me go and I'll explain the reason behind my actions?"

She could tell by the look on his face he wasn't interested in listening to any explanation. After all, she had played it very loose with the procedure on that particular hold. She knew he was muscular, but it'd been months since she had been forced to use that maneuver, and he wasn't exactly a hundred-pound elf either.

Brody jumped to his feet and put out a hand for hers.

Avery looked at his palm, to his face, and back down before allowing him to assist her to her feet.

A smile that could brighten a rainy day settled over his face. "I know you figured that once I got your hand in mine there are a number of pretty vicious holds I could pull on you as payback. Right?" The warmth in his voice overshadowed his smile.

"I've...I've been around the office and seen posters and sat in on presentations about various holds, but I've never performed any except at the gym with other novices." She began dusting off the dirt and prairie grass from her clothes and knees...and prayed he didn't see the deception.

"Remind me, if I ever find an error on anything you type for me, to redo it myself before asking you. I'd probably be through the window and over by the playground on the square before I could say *please*," he gleefully said. "For Harris County to have you at a desk job instead of out in the field is their loss. Most men without training couldn't have done what you did." He wiped blood from an elbow. "I guess you don't have a Kleenex?" "No, I'm sorry." She dropped her arm to her side to make sure the medicine bottle was still intact. As much as she wanted to give him the tissue, she couldn't. Not without disturbing the bottle and taking a chance of contaminating any evidence, if in fact there was something of significance. "Here, turn around." She took his elbow—covered with a fairly good degree of road rash—and pulled her blouse hem up to help clean the abrasion.

"If you start for my other wrist, I'm out of here." Brody chuckled.

"Don't tempt me, but I'd have to have handcuffs on me and I don't." She lowered her blouse. At least that was the truth. "Okay, you can turn around. I do want to say I'm sorry. Living in a big, crowded city like Houston, I keep my eyes and ears open at all times. Plus, the tales the deputies tell don't help either." Suddenly she realized she'd dished out a little too much information, so she added, "I guess that's the Texas Ranger blood that runs through my veins, having them as a grandfather and great-grandfather. This is private property, so I didn't anticipate anybody following me."

"Let's get things straight. One, I was *not* following you. I didn't even see a car, yours or anyone else's. And, secondly, I'm a county deputy and have access to every inch of Bonita County if justified." The tensing of his jaw displayed his deep displeasure with her accusation. "This is also a crime scene area, if you didn't notice some leftover yellow tape, which I pulled down and stuffed in my pocket, if you'd like to see it."

"I'm sorry. I didn't know it was you or I wouldn't have been scared." She put out her right hand. "Friends?" He took it and they shared a good ol' fashioned Texas handshake.

Before she realized what had occurred, he drew her to him. With one arm around her waist, he pulled her closer. With his other hand, he pushed back the hair from around her face, gingerly removed three or four pieces of grass, and lowered his lips to hers then pulled back.

Avery looked into his eyes. They were the eyes of a dream, an emotion she had not felt until recently. Like the bright, strong, Texas sunshine raining down on them, her desire overpowered her resistance.

His mouth swooped down and captured hers, leaving her mouth burning with fire. Shock waves rushed through her body. His moist, firm lips demanded a response. Something she was eager to explore. She returned his kiss, savoring the sweetness.

Leaning back, she said, "Is that the last of the round of kisses from the festival or is this the beginning of another set?" She slid her arms from around his neck and settled her hands on his chest.

"Whatever you want, Scarlett."

Her answer was simple. Standing face-to-face, she buried her forehead in his neck and breathed a kiss. Her lips found their way instinctively to his. Warm and sweet. She slid her hand over his chest then locked her fingers around his neck. Her answer was sealed with a fiery, passionate kiss.

Brody released her and took her hand, no doubt reading her response exactly the way she meant it.

"Can I buy you some lunch?" Brody asked.

"I'm sorry, I really can't. I've got to be in Amarillo to catch the late plane to Houston."

Before she could say anything else, he said, "I hope your next trip here is long before next year's festival."

"I can assure you of that. I've got to run over and see Mesa before I leave." She had to use her tip-toes to give him a kiss on the forehead. "I'll see you soon, Mr. Blackbeard."

Knowing his truck must be parked quite a ways south of them, she began jogging north. At the first cattle guard, she slipped between a huge stand of cottonwoods and waited until she heard his truck engine fire up as he headed back to the highway. She began jogging toward the Jacks Bluff headquarters.

Now it seemed she had a third equation in her decisions whether to stay or go.

Go back to Houston and continue what she'd been doing for nearly ten years.

Or...

Stay in Kasota Springs with loving parents who still didn't have all the answers as to why she needed time away from Houston.

And probably the most sweet-sour of all...Brody VanZant. He was too professional to push her so much, but she wasn't sure how many times she could be in his arms without blabbing the whole truth about what had brought her back to Kasota Springs for a few weeks.

Once he learned what had happened in Houston, he wouldn't want anything to do with her and she'd have another broken heart to deal with... both by her own doing.

Chapter 11

With only a towel wrapped around his waist, Brody sat on the bench in the sheriff's department locker room, rubbing his neck while he rolled his shoulders. It was hard for him to believe it'd been two weeks since Deuce had been nearly killed and there had been no announcement of who would be named as interim sheriff, although rumors flew around town like fruit flies.

With Chief Deputy Scott in charge, Brody stayed away from the sheriff's department as much as possible, preferring to spend time out on the streets so he didn't have to listen to Scott. He had had a meeting with the head of the joint task force in Amarillo about the changes needed, particularly Brody not taking on any new assignments until further word.

In no time, he was dressed, and couldn't help but take a second look in the mirror at his new clean-shaven look. He checked his watch. He needed to hurry to the hospital, see Deuce, and get back to town before his shift started. Allowing for the fairly long drive each way, he'd have about an hour or so to spend with Deuce and Rainey.

He grabbed his keys and rushed to his county unit, where he headed toward I-40. The thought crossed his mind that typically after a good run he'd feel better, but for some reason he didn't today.

It'd been several weeks since Deuce had major surgery. Brody had seen him almost every day since the injury, but today compared to others was so different.

Not only had the drive given him the opportunity to think about whether to continue honoring his commitment to Deuce, in view of the rumors that he'd be working for Danny Scott, but he also couldn't help but think about his brother-in-law and that damnable brother of his.

When Brody wanted to think good thoughts, he let his mind wander to Avery and the two weeks since he'd seen her. She had said she had to catch a plane for Houston the day of their takedown, which always made him laugh.

Although it was her takedown, he out-maneuvered her, so he continued to think of the whole event as *their* takedown. No wonder it brought him out of a bad mood. Just the thoughts of Avery's smile, kisses, and even her sassy, sexy mouth seemed to do the job.

He also continued to visit with Lola Ruth Johnson to see what was going on with her and Mesa. Which, of course, translated into *had Mesa heard from Avery?* He got the same answer each time that Mesa was helping out on a horse rescue ranch. Lola Ruth promised to tell her he'd been by if she called.

Usually while visiting Lola Ruth, he'd eat a peach-apricot fried pie and drink coffee. Lola Ruth always reminded him that she'd quit frying them in lard years ago. It always made a confession come to mind; one of the first signs of being guilty was letting the investigator know what they haven't done. But Lola Ruth Hicks could convince a scarecrow he was human any day.

The one problem? Every time he'd ask more about Avery, Lola Ruth would either change the subject or she'd act like she hadn't heard, which he attributed to a tad of memory loss due to her age. Seemingly nobody at the sheriff's department knew of an Avery from Kasota Springs, since they hadn't mentioned her. As much as he had a yearning to do so, he wasn't ready to make an inquiry…not yet.

Damn it, he still didn't know Avery's full name, and he was an investigator! Brody wanted to laugh aloud because he knew if Deuce could respond he'd let loose with some profanity-laced inside-joke.

With all of his thoughts, good and bad, time flew by and before he knew it he sat beside Deuce, holding his friend's limp hand and talking nonsense to him and Rainey.

Rainey and Brody looked up as the door eased open and Deuce's neurologist walked in and greeted them.

"Oh, I hope you have some good news from the recent tests." Rainey searched the doctor's face with eyes that screamed she hadn't had a wink of sleep in weeks, which Brody figured she hadn't. She pulled out of her chair and straightened her back.

"I am sorry, Mrs. Cowan.…"

Brody stood up, circled the bed, and stood close to Rainey, slipping his arm around her shoulders. Over his career, he'd been with people who had received bad news, and many types of unexpected reactions took over. He wanted to be there for his friend's wife.

The doctor took a few minutes to do the typical examination—checking the eyes, listening to the heartbeat, and looking in Deuce's ears—while he talked.

Once he was finished, the worst began.

The words *freak accident...possibly never using his legs again* ran through Brody's mind like a malfunctioning Taser.

He tried to take in every word, while keeping an eye on Rainey who was becoming more pale by the second. She closed her eyes, grabbed Brody's arm, and began to fall. He caught her and eased her into a chair.

"As you will recall, I told you from the beginning that we would have to wait for the swelling to subside and him to recover from the surgery before we'd have any long-term prognosis." The doc flipped up pages in Deuce's chart. "Apparently his head took the blow precisely at the one spot that put all the force on the lower cervical vertebras, which were seriously damaged. He is paralyzed, but it's from the waist down at this point. I am quite confident he will eventually regain usage of his upper body and possibly have full functionality of his whole body. Time will tell." He flipped to another page. "We did not see anything that indicated he cannot recover from the medically induced coma, but unfortunately, I cannot promise a positive outcome. The last thing you need is false hope, but let's just keep positive." He closed the chart. "The other thing I want you to begin thinking about is what rehab center you want your husband to go to when it's time. There is a lot of thought that needs to go into such a decision, so I want you to have plenty of time to think it through and check your options."

Deuce's doctor shook Brody's hand and laid his other on Rainey's shoulder. "Mrs. Cowan, you know you can call me at any time. Night or day. The nurses know how to get in touch with me twenty-four seven." He said a good-bye and walked out the door.

After a few minutes of private reflection to allow the surgeon's news to soak in, Brody said, "Rainey, let's go downstairs and get some coffee. If I have to drink another cup out of that vending machine, I think I might toss my cookies."

All the way to the hospital cafeteria Rainey apologized for not being strong. He wanted to tell her that if it hadn't been for his need to keep her from collapsing, he would have done so and she would have had one hell of a time picking him up off the floor.

After he got Rainey settled, he purchased two coffees and Danish rolls. It ended up being futile as they both only picked at their food.

Deuce knew she'd have a ton of time over the weeks to think about what the doctor just confirmed and she didn't need Deuce's I-know-how-you-feel lecture, because she'd get enough from other people.

He felt sure she didn't need his input into a rehab center because no doubt she'd want her husband at the Kasota Springs Rehab and Nursing Home where his mother resided.

"You know, you guys had the best wedding this part of the country has ever seen?" Brody said, trying to lighten the mood by talking about good memories Rainey and Deuce shared.

Her blank face lightened up a bit. "For sure. Not many couples are married in the Alzheimer Unit of a nursing home. I remember how good-looking Deuce was clad in his sheriff's uniform." She stopped and took a deep breath. "It was memorable for sure with me in a dress from the 19th century selected by my maid-of-honor, Sylvie, being hosted by my mother-in-law-to-be, and being presided over by a nursing home chaplain."

"Well, don't forget how excited Deuce's mother was that she could see her *special young man* and you get married while watching her son play football on the wide-screen television that you all donated to the Alzheimer's unit." Brody took a sip of coffee, then continued.

"I can still see her sitting with her earphones on watching the DVD, which of course she didn't know it was a fifteen-year-old game. And she sipped that strawberry soda like it was four fingers of Black Jack on ice." Brody laughed to himself. "And you and Deuce were saying your *I do*'s in front of forty patients who were there for a dozen different types of parties, just depending on the day they thought it was."

They joined into something similar to a laugh but very lackluster. His heart had broken for the families and caretakers, but he'd never say that to Rainey. She had enough on her plate.

Rainey stared ahead with a slight smile on her lips. "But that's what we wanted. Having his mother and her friends there was very important to us. The ceremony was unusual, unforgettable. A wonderful day." Tears overtook her and flowed down her cheeks. She wiped them away with a napkin. "And don't forget we had the county deputies in uniform. Poor Captain Chalmers thought they were there for him as part of his unit during the Korean War."

Brody cut in, "I personally think he thought they were there praying that Deuce wouldn't bolt because Captain Chalmers has had a crush on you since the day you all met."

They shared a genuine laugh. More tears ran down her face. Whether they were happy or sad tears, Brody didn't know, but he did know the memories were heartwarming.

Rainey continued to watch the entrance to the cafeteria.

Brody couldn't stand it any longer and as much as he hated to invade her privacy, he finally asked, "Who are you watching for?"

"Sylvie. She called me a couple of hours ago. I told her of my fears that Deuce might never walk again from what I've observed." She lowered her head, as she spread her fingers on the table. "Even if he can walk eventually the rehab will be very lengthy. Hey, let's go back upstairs in case she gets here."

Rainey and Brody got up and walked toward the elevator. "Brody, you have no idea how much your friendship to Deuce and me means. I know if he could speak, he'd tell you the same thing. I'm so happy that he brought your friendship to Kasota Springs."

About the time they reached the floor, Brody's phone rang. Once he saw the caller was Danny Scott, he mouthed an excuse to Rainey.

She waved and went into Deuce's room, while Brody answered the phone. "VanZant," he said, while thinking that she probably needed time alone with Deuce anyway. "Slow down, Scott. I can barely understand what you're saying."

He sat in a chair in a vending machine area near Deuce's room and listened. If Brody had had privacy he would have flipped on the speakerphone so he could have kept count of the *I*'s and *mine*s while Scott told him about everything the doctor had said. *Rumors sure do run wild.*

"Okay, I'll be back as soon as I can. I've got to make sure Sylvie or someone gets here to take care of Rainey. She shouldn't be left alone right now." He stopped and listened and knew Scott was rolling his eyes at the ceiling. "Okay, as much as I want to show total support for the department, if I don't make the press conference, it won't be the end of the world. I think the county commissioners can handle putting the Heart of Bravery on you as the interim sheriff without my presence. Deuce and Rainey are my concern right now." Brody started to hang up then thought to ask, "Scott, how did you hear that you had been named the interim sheriff?"

Danny's reply didn't particularly surprise Brody.

"Hum, Sylvie for one."

"Isn't that sort of a rumor?"

Scott countered rather loudly, "It isn't rumor. The mayor's secretary called and asked for me specifically to be there and to contact you and tell you what the final prognosis is on Deuce—"

"I was with Rainey when she got it directly from the doctor—"

"...and that he wouldn't be back, or at least anytime soon, so they'd be naming an interim sheriff at one o'clock here in the office and hold a presser an hour later, so it can make the early news. She specifically said the commissioners don't want a lot of rumors flying around."

"Makes sense—"

"And I'm the next in line for the job, and I am the most qualified, and I'm..."

"Hey, Scott, don't think you can hear me because we've got a bad connection here in the hospital, but if you can, I'll be back as soon as possible. Scott?" He waited, perfectly able to hear Danny Scott but not sure he could stand to hear another "I."

"If you can hear me, Scott, I'll be back as soon as possible," he lied.

Brody ended the call.

Damn, he hated to do something so unethical to a fellow deputy, but Brody was barely able to breathe, and no doubt his blood pressure was rising by the minute. Hell, fire and brimstone, if he could do something, anything at all for Deuce, he undoubtedly would feel better. A dense fog of uneasiness about the future shrouded him.

Running came to mind. If he could run—run as far away as possible, and at the same time he wanted to protect Rainey since Deuce couldn't. As hard as he tried, he couldn't let go of the sensation that he was responsible for Deuce's situation either directly or indirectly.

If he could do it all over again, he would have never agreed to Deuce's interrogation of Tommy.

Brody saw the men's room sign and went inside to wash his hands.

When he returned to the vending machine area, for one of the few times in his life, he was pleased to see Sylvie. He would be able to get back to the office in time for whatever asinine ceremony the commissioners wanted to hold but it was his job to be there. He also needed to change into his dress uniform. The weight of his longtime friendship with Deuce was on one shoulder while his responsibilities in the political scene of the sheriff's department weighed down his other shoulder.

If Danny Scott wanted to throw his newly found authority around and make sure everyone knew who was the new boss, likely Brody would be back working undercover before the sun went down.

"Oh, Lieutenant VanZant, I'm so happy to see you," Sylvie said in a velvety, Southern voice. She rushed out of her seat, circled the table, and threw her arms around his neck, then retreated like she'd done something wrong. "I'm so sorry, I'm just glad to see you." She glanced down at her iPhone.

Other than the black mascara accenting the tears in her eyes, Sylvie looked like she always had when he'd seen her with Thelma . . . June Cleaver style. "Don't worry about it. I can use a hug from just about anybody right now." He smiled for her benefit, certainly not his. After knocking lightly, Brody held Deuce's door open for Sylvie.

"Thank you. I brought some clothes." She took Rainey's hand and looked up at Brody. "I'm sure you know that she's rented a hotel room near the hospital, but I don't think she's spent a night there. If it wasn't for the ladies from Kasota Springs, including your sister, coming over and sitting beside Sheriff Cowan, Rainey would never get any rest." She patted Rainey's hand. "Isn't that right, honey?"

Staring into space, Rainey nodded.

Brody didn't want to touch Rainey, fearing Sylvie would pass the friendly gesture along the rumor mill that he was trying to make a pass at Deuce's wife.

To hell with the rumor mill!

Slowly, Brody walked around Sylvie, patted her on the back, and said, "Thank you. Your friendship means a lot." When he reached Rainey, he put his hands on her shoulders and leaned over and kissed the crown of her head. "Please don't hesitate to call me or anybody in the sheriff's department if you need anything. I mean anything at all."

Brody rounded the bed, looked at Sylvie, smiled and said, "You, too, Sylvie. I know you're under a lot of pressure."

She got up and hugged him again then stepped back. "Good luck to you. I heard that your meeting today is to announce the interim sheriff. Heard it was Danny Scott. Well, I personally heard it was *Danny*, and the only deputy with that name is the chief deputy, which makes sense. Where does that leave you, Brody?" Her eyes looked like a poor little puppy wanting a doggie treat.

"Let's go out in the hall to talk," said Brody.

With his back against the hall wall, he said, "I guess exactly where I've been all along. I've always been with Bonita County, although I was on loan to the joint task force. I promised Deuce I'd return full time to Kasota Springs, so I presume I'll continue unless Scott doesn't need me." He bit his lower lip. "I'm sorry I have to leave, but I have to get back. If you don't mind, Sylvie, I'd like to take a minute to go back into Deuce's room."

He'd only taken a couple of steps when Rainey appeared. She nodded then said, "Thank you for being such a loyal friend to Deuce and to me. He may not respond, the doctor said, but they believe he can hear and his brain possibly gets the information but just can't process it. They truly believe there's a chance he'll come out of the coma, but the damage that was done is a coin toss. Thank you for coming, Brody." She addressed Sylvie more than Brody then bit her lip. "If Deuce could talk, he'd tell both of you how much he loves you guys."

A thought hit Brody just as he opened Deuce's door. He turned back. "Hey, Sylvie, where did you hear about what the doctor said today?"

Rainey spoke up. "From me. Why?"

"I was just wondering how it got to Danny Scott so fast."

Then it was time for Sylvie to speak up. "He's really concerned about Deuce. You can tell by the amount of calls he makes to me to check on how Deuce is doing. Everybody needs a friend like that."

"You are right about that." He looked from the teary eyes of Rainey back to the somewhat cheery face of Sylvie. "I'm gonna go in and say good-bye to Deuce then get back to Kasota Springs."

He slowly walked to Deuce's room with several additional thoughts stacked on those already piled high in his mind.

It took everything in him to go back in to see Deuce, but building up courage, he pushed the door open. He took the chair next to the bed, pulling it as close as possible and still allowing for his long legs.

"Hey, pard," he said as if he expected a return greeting. "I guess all cards will be on the table this afternoon when I get back to the office. I've been hearing for weeks now that Danny Scott will be your replacement until you get off your lazy butt and back to work." He took Deuce's limp hand. "You know I like Dan—well most of the time—but I might not be able to keep my promise to you to work out of Kasota Springs. I've been on a leave, so today is the day I have to let the captain over special crimes know whether I'll work out of there or stick around here. I'm afraid if you don't wake up or give me some sign that I need to stick it out here, I might well have to return to the big city."

Brody closed his eyes and said a prayer for Deuce and added a line or two for his own needs, never letting go of his friend's hand.

"Amen." Brody squeezed Deuce's hand. To Brody's surprise, as he opened his eyes, he would swear he felt a light squeeze from the sheriff.

Brody squeezed again, just in case it was a knee-jerk reaction, but to his disappointment there was no response.

As much as he wanted to step outside and scream to both women that he had felt movement, he knew it could be as little as a nerve reaction that meant nothing or it could be a sign that Deuce was unconsciously responding to things around him. He didn't want to give Rainey false hope.

Stepping to the nurses' station, he motioned for Deuce's nurse to walk with him out of view of the vending machine area. He told her what had happened and that it might well have been his own reaction or prayers Deuce responded to but he felt it was real. Like an idiot, he explained that as a peace officer he had EMT training. She smiled nicely, as if to say, *Duh,* then thanked him for not getting everyone in an uproar and their hopes up too much. She ended by saying she'd notify the doctor immediately.

After thanking the nurse, he looked back over his shoulder.

Rainey sat with her head resting in her folded arms on the table.

Sylvie was texting to beat the band.

Exiting the elevator, he headed toward the hospital parking lot and then turned into the closest Quick Stop. After purchasing a bottle of water, he began his trek back to Kasota Springs.

The return trip gave him plenty of time to think.

By the time he pulled into town, a zillion thoughts had gone through his head. Brody decided it all boiled down to the fact that just the thought of any type of response from his friend made it possible for Brody to find the internal answer to the question that had been bothering him.

A friend was a friend to the core and a friend would do what was necessary to help the other one, regardless of the discomfort and inconvenience that might get in the way of the promise.

True friendships came with unwritten promises, and by damn he'd keep his to Deuce.

When Brody crossed the railroad tracks leading into town, he had made a decision. All that needed to be done was a call to let everyone know he would continue to be employed as a detective by Bonita County. He checked the time. If he hurried, he could catch a cup of coffee at Pumpkin's Café then head to the locker room to change into his uniform so he'd be on time for the meeting at the sheriff's department. He'd never had to wear his dress uniform except for a parade or a formal event. As a detective, he typically wore regular street clothes, which consisted of a suit, white shirt, and dark tie. Of course, when he was undercover, everything from his hair to his shoes had to fit in with what he was investigating.

Something was up, because he'd never had to wear his uniform for a departmental meeting.

No doubt the decision had been made, and he had to get all dressed up for the world to know that Danny Scott had been selected the interim sheriff—and he and the other deputies were being used as a nice backdrop, all dressed up in brown for the announcement.

Chapter 12

Avery sat in the corner of Pumpkin's Café and watched the front door screen. She'd been home from Houston not long, and the majority of her time had been spent stowed away in her father's study or his law office conference room, drinking hot tea and cussing and discussing the sometimes not mutually agreeable aspects of her new job.

The café screen slammed, and she looked up. A couple of workers came in and slipped onto stools at the lunch bar.

She glanced back at the café door and wished she could have had time to find Brody VanZant before the formal meeting at the sheriff's department. Her shoulders slumped.

If only she could have had the opportunity to explain why she had been gone and what job she'd accepted and the reason.

She'd even called the sheriff's department but didn't dare leave a message.

One thing Avery didn't want was for him to learn all or part of the truth from the gossip and the media. Typically, they were never accurate, but just the main part that would be true likely would sever their friendship forever. He'd never trust her again.

In addition, there was the reason she had deliberately kept her last name a secret. He'd likely understand why she'd do it to the public, but not him. She didn't know his background except he was a deputy and his sister and family owned the BBQ café. That was all she knew about him. As far as her reason to be reluctant to give her last name, first off if he was really interested in her, he could contact Mesa and find out.

Secondly, and most likely, he wasn't interested in her beyond a few kisses at a festival. Oh, and she didn't want to forget she'd brought him down with a rather difficult hold that led to some fantastic kissing that made the ones in the park child's play.

All of her thoughts boiled down to one. She'd been used too many times because she came from one of the affluent, founding families of Kasota Springs.

Avery stared out the window and watched every parking space around the square fill up.

Gossip lines and news media weren't what she wanted. But from the looks of the TV station vans and other vehicles with the logo, every news organization within three hundred miles had come to town. News representatives with mics and cameras were standing everywhere although it would be a while before the press conference.

Unfortunately, the dress uniforms in Bonita County were tan shirts, black ties, and black pants, while everything she had in her closet was just the opposite. Earlier when she went by her house, a package awaited her with an authorized dress uniform for Bonita County. It hung in a locker in the dressing room.

As hard as she tried to focus on today and not the time since she had left for Houston, she could only think about the past. Much of it way beyond the time she'd been gone, much of it back to when her partner had been killed and her part in it, but all of it ended up with Brody.

When she left for Houston and told her dad that if he found a job for her that'd be good, she didn't care even if it was at one of the cafés, the DQ, or his office. Avery just needed a job when she returned. Nowhere in her imagination did she ever believe the job would be in the sheriff's department, although she was more than qualified.

She noticed Brody's county vehicle drive up and park at the side of the courthouse. It was about a half an hour before the meeting of all of the sheriff's department employees with the county commissioners and her father.

VanZant walked directly toward Pumpkin's Café. Avery looked around to find a back exit out of the cafe when she realized he had opened the screen door and walked in.

The thought of leaving vanished as she looked up, mesmerized by Brody in his uniform. Up to now, she'd only seen him in his running clothes and costume as a pirate.

As hard as she tried, her gaze remained on the strappingly built, clean-shaven man. She'd recognized he worked out and was well built, but his long hair and unshaven look had masqueraded much of his awesome looks.

Pulling her hands to her cheeks, she prayed he didn't see her because they didn't have time to clear the air before they had to go into one of the hardest meetings she'd ever been to in her life. Luckily, she was in street clothes, but that created another problem, because she had to get to the sheriff's department ladies' restroom and change clothes before the meeting.

Her mouth dried and her heart beat faster as he noticed her and walked directly toward her.

"Good morning, Avery. Could I sit and have a cup of coffee with you?"

Avery swallowed hard and barely nodded as he slipped into the seat across from her.

The owner, Miss Clara, was right on the spot with a mug of coffee. "Can I get you anything else, Mr. Hunk of Burnin' Love?"

"This will do me fine, darlin'." He slipped her a five. "This should cover our tab."

Clara lowered her head, probably to cover her smile, and scurried her round little body off to fill other customers' cups.

"I'm glad to see you, Avery." He sipped at his coffee. "At least we're in a place you're not likely to try a takedown on me." A jovial laugh came from deep inside. The words were strong and sexual. How could two weeks make such a difference in a man?

"I'm glad to see you. I've tried to contact you, but—"

"I never got a message." A frown crept over his eyebrows.

"I didn't leave a message. It was kinda an afterthought." She twisted her cup. "I mean, I thought if you weren't busy, we might have coffee and talk. Now here we are."

Brody's phone rang. "I'm sorry," he said as he answered.

Avery tried not to listen to his conversation and let her mind wander to her feeling stupid and insecure, which typically wasn't one of her problems—or at least not until she had let her partner get killed to save her. Why today? Likely because Brody and the whole Panhandle would know she had joined the Bonita County Sheriff's Department, and not everyone would be happy, especially Danny Scott.

Being that just about everything was available on the internet, there was little doubt that her becoming a part of the department would bring up her past with her previous job. There'd be questions she'd prefer not to answer. Whether they were asked today or later, she must tell Brody the full truth before he got shards of the truth, which never pieced together as the full and reasonable fact.

She must tell Brody first. She owed it to him.

After sliding his phone back into his pocket, he said, "I'm so sorry, Avery, but I've got to get over to the office right now. Danny Scott wants to talk to me because he's sure he's being named the interim sheriff and I'm sure he wants to make certain I'm on his side. We've worked together a long time. I would have thought by now he'd know that although I don't always like his approach to things, I'll respect him as the interim sheriff."

She wanted to stand up and scream, "No, don't go yet! You need to know the truth!" but she knew she'd wasted too much time and it was much too late to explain anything to him.

Brody scooted from his bench seat, laid his hand on hers, and said, "Hey, maybe when this circus is over, we can have coffee. Even dinner?"

She gave him a weak smile.

His fingers squeezed hers. "See you later."

Pulling to his full six-foot, four-inch height, he shot her a final sexy-as-hell smile and headed for the door.

Avery ducked her head and rested her forehead in her hands.

Was she ready for professional rebellion?

She couldn't watch him walk away and only whispered into her hands, "I doubt if you'll want to even talk to me by dinner time."

* * * *

Brody headed for the courthouse, although he could barely work his way through the crowd of reporters, photographers, and live news media trucks and setups. He couldn't remember the last time he had had microphones thrust at him with questions flying around.

"Lieutenant VanZant, do you know the purpose of today's press conference?" asked a local reporter who Brody actually trusted, but in fairness he couldn't answer her truthfully.

"Gail, I have no idea, but if I did, you know I couldn't divulge it." He deliberately shot her a smile that might suggest forgiveness.

Brody squirreled through the crowd and made it to the open space around the side to the back of the building and went directly up to the hall leading to the back conference room of the sheriff's department where all of his cohorts were gathered around the two six-foot tables.

After taking or giving a fist bump, handshake, or slap on the back from nearly everybody there, he took a seat between Chief Deputy Danny Scott and Deputy Eddie Jessup, who typically worked dispatch along with Thelma and Raylynn, aside from other office duties.

Once settled in, Danny leaned into Brody and said, "Well, it's time, so get used to this, VanZant. I promise I'll give you any case you want because you've always had my back." He twisted the cap off the pen laid out for each person. "Hey, there's Thelma Crawford over there," Scott said as if Brody didn't know her. Then Scott said, "It's just unusual that she'd be here."

Jessup walked over to the water supply and grabbed a couple of bottles, stopping along the way to talk.

The deputy put a bottle in front of Brody. He accepted and thanked him. Brody took a plate of brownies and lemon bars of some sort being passed around. He felt like he needed the caffeine in the chocolate, so he took one along with a napkin.

"What's she doing wearing a polo with the sheriff's department emblem?" Danny squinted, obviously trying to make sure which county's logo Thelma wore. "That's Bonita County for sure." He accepted the plate, ignored the refreshments and passed it to the next person.

What didn't get past Brody, as a detective accustomed to keeping a lookout on his surrounds, was that the whole Commissioners Court sat on one side of the table across from them, quietly observing everyone.

Danny Scott leaned toward Brody and whispered, "Thelma is definitely wearing our county logo on her shirt." He took a drink of water and glanced over at the commissioners. "She can't do that. As the interim sheriff, I'd be the one to hire and make changes in our uniform, not the commissioners. There are tests she'd have to take, like anybody else. She's worked in the office most of the time, so I doubt she's kept up her qualification on the gun range." He folded his arms over his chest. "Something isn't right. And where is the mayor?" Danny said in a sarcastic tone.

"Except for his height and size, I wouldn't know him if he came and sat down beside me. Just don't forget I've spent most of my time in Amarillo, so I've had little if any contact with him. I know he's a really big man and he and his wife are descendants of two of the founding families."

Although it was obvious Danny was getting more annoyed, even aggravated, as they waited, Brody felt like two cocked Glocks were precariously handcuffed to each shoulder and aimed at his temples. His back felt tight, but he sat up straight as he should in the presence of his superiors.

"The mayor is Ira Humphrey." Danny loosened his collar and pulled his tie down about an inch.

"I know that, but like I said I don't know a thing about him. The only reason I know who the men over at the other table facing us are is because I can read their guest badges." Brody downed a couple of swallows of water.

The door opened, and two men entered and took a vacant seat with the county commissioners.

To Brody's surprise the third person to come in was Avery, looking really good but puzzling the hell out of him as to why she was dressed in a tan dress shirt with fitted black pants and of course a holster with no service weapon, two sets of handcuffs, and two flashlights. She sat to the right of the big man who Brody was fairly sure was the mayor.

Avery pushed her paper and pencil aside and immediately began eying the room, one person at a time. When she came to Brody her gaze froze on his.

He stared back, puzzled as hell as to why she wore a dress uniform when she supposedly was a clerk of some sort in Houston.

The extremely big man, probably two inches over Brody, began the meeting. In a deep voice, he said, "Ladies and gentlemen, I'm Mayor Ira Humphrey. Most of you know me, but I realize Kasota Springs is one of the biggest small towns in the Panhandle, so not everybody knows one another...."

He went on to explain why they were gathered—to name the new interim sheriff. Brody tuned out the rest of the foreplay to the meeting because other than the name of the new sheriff, he pretty much knew about everything. He'd visited Deuce and Rainey almost every day and probably knew more about Deuce's prognosis than anybody else in the room.

Brody glanced at Danny, who was either scared or in shock by the look on his face and his folded arms over his chest.

"We have Raylynn up front to answer the phone and if there are any emergencies, she'll text or call one of us, depending on the type of call, so there's no reason to be concerned when everyone is together," the mayor continued. "I'd like to recognize Chief Deputy Danny Scott, who has done a rather grand job at keeping the department running during Sheriff Cowan's tragedy and leave of absence." He turned his head to the left then to the right as he concluded, "The county commissioners, county judge, and as mayor, I promise on their behalf we will provide any and all resources necessary to find the person or persons who caused such severe injuries to Sheriff Cowan. Whatever you need, we'll make sure you have it, whether it's equipment, employees, or finances...it'll be there for *our* sheriff's department."

In the far distance, Brody heard the phone ring, distracting him from what he almost could consider a political whistle-stop than anything else.

"As we looked at each and every candidate and considered every employee, it became apparent that Avery..."

Avery stood up and took her place next to the mayor.

Danny Scott looked at his phone then slipped a note over to Brody,: "Son-of-a-bitch! I'm out of here." Scott got to his feet, and not bothering to push his chair to the table, he stalked out and slammed the outer door.

Nearly everyone stared at the empty seat, as Brody slid the note into his pocket.

Mayor Humphrey continued, "Yes, in full disclosure, many of you may remember my only daughter as Danielle Humphrey, but the department she previously worked for thought Avery was easier to keep her separated from the male Dannys, so Danielle and Dannie went by the wayside. Thus Dannie, as only her family and a few of her close friends know her, became known as Avery. I guess to be completely correct she was Lt. Detective Avery Humphrey, who we've named as interim sheriff until either Sheriff Cowan returns or the next election, whichever comes first. I'm pleased to introduce...."

Brody's whole body tensed with shock and his heart beat out of control. *Now I know why she wanted to talk to me at Pumpkin's.*

When he looked up, Avery stood at full attention with her hands behind her back. She had just begun to speak, and he hadn't heard a word until now. "I've spent several days going over the personnel management manual particularly written for the sheriff's department, and although I've only spoken with the commissioners, county judge, and the um, well, mayor—" She stopped and cleared her throat. "I must apologize, but I've never thought of my father as the mayor. He's just Dad to me..."

Some giggled.

Some laughed out loud.

Some showed no emotion.

"I promise that I'll do the best job possible. My experience has taught me the importance of cooperate and communicate; therefore, I will be holding individual meetings with each deputy to find out what we can do together to make our jobs easier and what your needs are. We will also be discussing each of the active cases and work in teams to get them solved as quickly as possible. We will continue working any cold cases there might be. I am committed to the town I grew up in and the people I love and care about." She looked straight at Brody.

From inside his jacket, Brody's phone vibrated, and he read the text message from Danny Scott. "Code 2 at Pumpkin's." Brody immediate decoded to *Urgent, no lights or siren;* in other words, be discreet.

Brody couldn't keep from staring at Avery. Her gaze met his. He looked back at his text message. Although he wanted to stay, he had no choice but to go. Danny needed him pretty damn bad or he would have never disturbed Brody in such an important meeting. He lifted his phone and pointed to it, letting her know he had an urgent call. He had no choice but to wait for the right opportunity to leave, so his departure didn't seem rebellious.

Avery acknowledge his gesture, but said, "We're so short on time today to answer your questions, but beginning in the morning, I'll have a private meeting with each employee of the department to discuss our future. Please make note of any questions you have and we'll discuss them." She glanced over at her father and said, "Mr. Mayor will conclude this meeting."

"Ladies and gentlemen." the mayor's strong voice echoed off the wall. "The commissioners, Judge Humphries, and I will be holding a press conference for the media and members of our community immediately following this meeting. We welcome each of you to stand on the steps of the courthouse as a symbol of unity and a welcome to our new interim sheriff." He smiled down at Avery.

After returning the gesture addressed directly to her father, she stiffened as she glanced Brody's way, obviously not missing him getting out of his seat. As quietly as possible he pushed his chair into place and walked out.

As he closed the door behind him, another text message arrived from Danny Scott: "Meet me at Pumpkin's ASAP."

Once out of hearing range, Brody slammed his fist on the wall. "If it wasn't enough the bastard hadn't made a fool of himself, he's succeeding in making me look like a total jerkass," he said slowly under his breath.

Thrusting his chest out and taking several deep breaths, he turned his focus back to the new sheriff.

Damn, Avery was stronger than I ever imagined. Stood straight and sure conveyed herself as a tough leader.

Damn it to hell, she was his new boss, and the sheriff's department had an enforceable nepotism policy—or that's what he remembered from their personnel manual, which was as old as the battle cry "Remember the Alamo!" But, then he didn't want a show of favoritism; he wanted to kiss her all the way from one evening to the following morning.

Brody walked to the front office to find out what in the hell was so important that Danny Scott called him out of the meeting—making him look bad, really terrible in the eyes of the new interim sheriff, as well as the city commissioners. Hell, the whole community.

Chapter 13

Brody exited the back of the building in an effort to avoid the mob of news media, but it didn't help. The group that gathered in what was supposed to be a secured area tossed questions at him like bullets in a shootout. He wished he had a sign that read "No Comment."

He got around the structure, but Danny's unit was not parked in the lot. His was easy to recognize because it was the new Tahoe Police Pursuit Vehicle, which was ordered for the sheriff. At the time it was Deuce; now Brody couldn't help but wonder how Avery would feel repossessing the PPV from Scott. No doubt that wasn't even on her agenda.

As he walked to Pumpkin's Café, he deliberately pursed his lips and allowed a smile to come to his face, thinking about long-legged Avery climbing into the vehicle. He imagined her cute butt as the fabric of her tactical pants pressed against her skin.

What in the hell is wrong with me! I'm worrying about the new sheriff's backside when I need to be concerned about protecting her. I've got to find out why she kept the truth from me. One day she was an office worker and the next qualified to be interim sheriff.

Isn't omission the same as a lie?

Brody forced his mind to return to serious business and stow away Avery's and his issues for later. He'd only known her for a few weeks, but to be honest, he'd kissed her as many times as weeks he'd really gotten to know her. Or as many weeks as he thought he knew her, but obviously his calculations were wrong.

Whatever the crisis was that drew Danny out of the meeting and then calling for Brody must have been urgent, especially since Danny Scott didn't wait on Brody. Typically, he would have asked the relief dispatcher if any emergency calls had come in, but he figured Scott knew what he was doing. After all, being the chief deputy and second in command gave him latitude others didn't have. Everyone noticed he had left, and he'd be the talk of the town. Scott liked that stature but had no idea that it wasn't always positive.

Brody was professional enough not to make an ass out of himself by walking out regardless of whether he liked the announcement or not.

Frankly, other than Avery hiding pertinent personal facts, such as her full name and family affiliation, Brody had no objection to the appointment.

Not willing to work back through the gaggle of geese that were called news media, Brody sighed. Every reporter had at least one other person with them plus a cameraman, so they didn't miss any angle of activity. Brody made his way to the west side of the square where both Pumpkin's Café and his sister's place sat like bookends to keep the block standing up straight.

For a small town Brody found it amazing that the news about Deuce and naming a new sheriff was so big in the Four Corners states that touched the Texas Panhandle.

Thinking back, discounting the fire at the train depot that housed Rainey's antique shop two years ago, nothing of interest had happened in Kasota Springs in years. That case was closed and the varmint, who had wanted the property to add to his so he'd have all the land adjoining his to make a big sale to the new GreenMart, was serving time in an eight-by-ten cell down at the state penitentiary in Huntsville. If he was lucky his cellmate hadn't made Hunter into his bitch.

As Brody neared Pumpkin's Café, the owner scared the living hell out of him when she flung the screen door open, blocking his way, and tossed a chef's apron at him.

"Give me your Stetson and put this on. Keep your eyes glued to the floor and follow my lead. I'll be walking fast." Once they entered the café, Pumpkin turned and yelled back at him, "It's about time you got here. You're already late for your shift, so get your sorry butt back there before I fire you just to have something to do." Pumpkin turned to him and said loud enough that everyone had no trouble hearing, "How many times have I told you that you can't wear a hat in a house, especially in the kitchen? You're worse than my fifth—or maybe it was my sixth?—husband. Geeze, get to work." She swung through the saloon doors leading to the back of the café and let them go, almost hitting Brody in the chest.

Once he was out of view of the main eating area, he couldn't help but glance around and no doubt if he'd come in with full tactical gear on, nobody would have noticed. They were all staring down at their food probably trying to ignore Pumpkin's outburst. If he'd been a patron, he'd be doing the same thing. There was not a face in the crowd he recognized. Brody followed Pumpkin to the far back of the café.

"It's about time you got here. Scott called and said you two were meeting here." She rubbed her hands on her apron. "If we weren't so busy, I'd love to catch up on what's going on."

"Thank you," Brody said, setting the apron on the sideboard. "I thought I was going to get eaten alive out there. Anybody wearing a uniform of any kind is subject to interrogation by the news media. Better make sure the UPS man doesn't try to stop."

They shared a low laugh, but Brody's was very stilted with a false undertone and he knew it.

"I'll get you some coffee. Be right back."

In a few minutes, which didn't even allow Brody the opportunity to reevaluate what had just happened, she returned with a mug and a carafe. Pumpkin pulled the folding door to, making the area fairly private.

"If you're wondering about my charade. Your sister called and said to catch you if I could. Their place is full of all kind of folks trying to make the six o'clock newscast with a breaking story. Every TV personality and journalists from Oklahoma City to Lubbock have people here." She put her hands on her ample hips. "They are bombarding her with questions. She wants to close, but Stanley sees it as an opportunity to make a lot of money. I didn't think appointing an interim sheriff was such a big deal."

"Neither did I, but every news outlet has been following Deuce's injuries—or attempted murder depending on how they view it—almost daily. Do I need to go down to the café to protect my sister?"

"No. She's got Stanley and as I said, he still has his loud, obnoxious mouth—and people wonder where Tommy got his. I guess this is the biggest thing that has happened since the fire in Rainey's antique shop."

Brody took a big gulp of hot coffee. "Have you seen Danny Scott?"

"No. Just his call." She refilled his coffee cup. "Gotta get back to work." She took two steps then turned and threw him a kiss. "I'm so glad to see you. I heard you're moving back to the ol' home place. I sure got lots of memories from the ol' WBarT when my mama cooked for those good-lookin' cowboys. That's the reason I've had so many husbands, I think." She let out a heartwarming laugh and took off for the kitchen.

"You're always welcome to come back to work at the ranch anytime, Pumpkin."

Waiting on Danny gave Brody time to reflect. The biggest question that kept resurfacing.... Why had Avery felt the need to lie to him? Obviously, no clerk, even in a big county, qualified to be sheriff.

But, if this were a regular case, he'd have to put all the evidence in order like a Sudoku puzzle, one number at a time until they all fit without jumping to conclusions. Jumping will always send a detective into deep water or a concrete staircase.

Maybe the old adage was true and the key to why he was mistrusting at the moment. *The longer you're undercover, the longer it takes you to remember who you are.* Brody might well fit that scenario. He wasn't sure why he was where he was, but he'd always trusted the Good Lord to show him the way.

Suddenly, the door on this side of the swinging doors opened and Danny Scott almost ran into the table with Pumpkin behind him. He threw his apron on the back of a chair and turned around and addressed the owner. "What in the hell?"

"I'm doing what I was asked. I've got work to do, so Brody will fill you in." She walked toward the door and over her shoulder said, "I'll bring you a cup of coffee in a minute." She left the tiny room.

Danny said, "Thanks." A weird noise came from his throat, as he sagged against the wall.

"Hey, here's some coffee." Brody pulled up from his chair and got a fresh mug. "This is strong and just what you need right now."

"Damn it to hell and back, what I need now is a bottle of Jack Daniel's and the job I deserve. I worked my ass off for it and went to a lot of trouble to make it happen." He almost stumbled to the chair and plopped down. "I mean how hard I worked because I wanted it." He rolled the cup between his chubby hands. "Thanks for the coffee and letting me vent."

"Hey, you're still chief deputy, and I can always go back to the task force if it doesn't work out." Brody took a drink. "I have my own issues with our new sheriff." He broke eye contact with Danny. The last thing Brody needed were questions about Avery and him.

"Yeah, I guess this is a good lesson in not letting gossip get in the way of the truth." A stony expression filled Danny's face.

"I don't understand." Brody squared his shoulders as he waited for the answer.

"Someone, and I can't tell you who but it was someone I trusted, told me that she overheard one of the commissioners talking to the mayor about 'Danny' becoming the new sheriff. To me that made me the only choice and it was all tied up with a nice tidy bow. Then at the meeting

I found out that the mayor's daughter was the person they were talking about. Avery Danielle—"

Brody interrupted him. "I guess I don't understand. I've had a few conversations with her since I returned to Kasota Springs, and she introduced herself as Avery. Looking back I see that she avoided giving me her last name. Of course, I would have suspected her as Ira Humphrey's daughter."

Brody wanted to cuss a blue streak for being so dumb.

"Yeah, only those very close around her call her Dannie." He pinched his lips together. "Everyone in school called her Danielle because her prim and proper mother thought that was more fitting for a girl of her stature."

Brody did as he always did when cornered and needing time to analyze things: he changed the subject to business. "And, where in the hell were you when you called me out of the meeting? By the way, it makes both of us look like very sour grapes...rotten grapes, not just sour." He gritted his teeth. "I knew it wasn't too serious if your Tahoe was already back, but I did get out as quickly as possible. So what was so important that you had to leave so suddenly?"

"I had good reason and I don't like your insinuations. Trust me, I'm sure Avery, oops—the sheriff—will understand."

"It has to be pretty damn serious to justify your behavior." Brody arched an eyebrow.

Danny put a packet of creamer in his coffee. "The relief dispatcher notified me that they needed an ambulance out at the Jacks Bluff, so of course that meant us, too."

"What in the hell happened?" Brody's neck stiffened and he felt his muscle strain. He knew that the strong-willed ladies of the ranch wouldn't call an ambulance unless it was a dire emergency.

"The person who called in specifically asked that her request be done discreetly and she did not want our new sheriff to know about the call. She'd tell her later. Which told me it was someone close to Avery, oops, the sheriff."

"Then why in the hell didn't you wait on me?"

"Well, uh, I didn't have time. I saw the ambulance coming toward the DQ, so I stopped to see what was going on. You and I both know...." Danny cleared his throat and sweat began to appear on his forehead.

"I know. They'd never call unless it was extremely serious. You did the right thing, Scott." He took a sip of coffee. "So what happened?"

It didn't take Scott long to explain that Mrs. Johnson, the matriarch of the LeDoux family, had fallen and Lola Ruth panicked, as did the foreman, and she made the call. In character Granny Johnson let the paramedics put on a bandage, signed a medical release that she refused to go to the hospital, and got in her car to drive to Amarillo for a meeting about the Panhandle Livestock Association turning one hundred years old.

As Danny explained, by the time he had some news for Brody there was no reason to call except to tell him to meet him at Pumpkin's. The crowd was then beginning to disperse, so Danny had headed over to the café, taking the back way.

He was interrupted once by Pumpkin, who brought both of them a piece of her famous chocolate cake. Out of courtesy Brody ate it, although each bite filled him with guilt, since Pumpkin and his sister had a running feud about whose cake was the best. He could bet his badge that Pumpkin got the recipe while working on the WBarT with her mother. The truth would probably never be known.

A vibration, indicating a text, came from his pocket. He pulled his phone out and read the short message twice.

Definitely it came from the last person he thought he'd hear from today. It read simply:

Meet me @ I-40 truck stop n 30? k?

Chapter 14

As a professional, Avery knew if she and Brody were to work together, she had no choice but to find him and explain things.

In all of her years in law enforcement, she'd rarely felt uncomfortable in any operation, but as she entered the truck stop fully dressed in her uniform, an unknown one to boot for the area, about a quarter of the patrons hurried up with their meal, paid, and left. This sure wasn't the type of truck stop she was accustomed to. Obviously privately owned, but doing a big business with truckers, although the gas prices were higher than the one farther down the road. This immediately sent up a flag that she needed to investigate the business, but that was far down on her list of priorities.

Since she hadn't eaten much of anything, she ordered a cheese omelet with toast, along with a glass of iced tea.

Out of the corner of her eye, she saw Brody come in. He almost took her breath away with his good looks. There was just something about a uniform that set most women's heart aflutter and Avery was no different.... Except she was his boss and couldn't allow any feelings to develop, although there were already the makings of a lot of them inside of her.

He looked around, squared his shoulders with purpose, avoided looking at Avery, and walked directly over to a young, rough-looking yet pretty young woman sitting in a booth. He slid in across from her and said very little. She seemed to do the majority of the talking.

Suddenly, the woman jerked up her excessively ornate and obviously cheap purse and almost cleared off the table getting out of the booth. She leaned over to pull down the hem of her much-too-short skirt. Avery was certain everyone in the café could see all the way to her toes from the opening in the bodice of her dress—or what she probably called a dress.

The woman looked at the floor and in a voice shrill enough to be heard in the square in town, said, "Okay, Mr. Sheriffman, I wasn't doing a damn thing wrong. Just having coffee. I can't believe you'd make a pass at me all decked out in your uniform. So, I'll get on my way. I don't do favors for pigs." She stumbled toward the front door, deliberately, if Avery had to make a guess.

Brody slid from the booth. "And I mean it. If I see you here again, I promise I'm going to arrest you for loitering if I can't prove anything else. You hear me!"

"Go fu..." The woman was too far out the door to make out her words, but again, Avery knew exactly what she had said without hearing it. She'd heard the phrase way too many times in her career.

Brody stood with his arms crossed until the woman got in her car and pulled away from the café, letting gravel fly. Then he walked over to Avery. "You wanna talk to me?" He put his hands on either corner of the table and leaned down and looked her sharply in the eyes. He radiated a vitality that drew her to him like a magnet. She prayed the observant man didn't see straight through her.

"Yes, yes I do." She could barely get the words out. "Have a seat, please. We have a number of things to discuss, especially since you had to leave the commissioners' meeting so quickly." She tried to sound confident, yet calm and not too bossy.

He exchanged one booth seat for another.

Avery tried to clear her mind, but it didn't work. So far, she had seen Brody in a pirate's uniform with most of his bronzed, hard muscles exposed; regular clothes that made him look sexy as hell; running shorts and tee that needed no explanation; but now in his uniform, she didn't know exactly what to think. All of her feelings were way too naughty to quickly push to the back of her mind since she had business to conduct with the tall, dark-haired, handsome man with one ear pierced and needing a shave.

One thought did stick in her mind: she'd kissed him with a full beard and a late evening shadow, but she wondered how his midday need of a shave would feel.

Back to business, lady!

"You wanted to see me?" Brody asked again. His gaze darted to the clock on the wall.

Avery couldn't help but follow his gaze. The clock was a Coca-Cola antique identical to the one of the many cafés.

"I think we need to talk." She took a sip of iced tea.

"Before you begin, I'm the one who needs to explain having to leave the meeting—"

"I know why Danny Scott would, because I'm sure he is rather POed that he didn't get the job as sheriff, but I didn't expect it from you." She shook her head in disbelief. "But I did see you motion to your phone."

"With all of the hullabaloo, I'm sure you didn't realize, nor should you have known, Danny got a call to go out to the Jacks Bluff for a medical emergency. He texted me to meet him outside, but I didn't know who was involved or where the emergency was—"

"What happened?" The words flowed out fast and furious. Something sour hit her stomach. This was the first time she'd become aware of anything at the ranch. Although Granny was still tough as leather strop, she was advancing in age and anything could have happened.

"It ended up being nothing serious." Brody went on to explain the situation.

By the time he'd finished, Avery's stomach had settled and her heartbeat had returned to normal. It was obvious Brody knew she was like part of the LeDoux-Johnson family, and she appreciated his sensitivity.

"That's good that you didn't have to wade yourself back through all the people, and I'm thankful for Pumpkin's help." She selected a small packet of strawberry jam, then put it back in the bowl. "There are a number of things we need to discuss concerning changes in the office, but aren't you going to eat?" She motioned for the tall, skinny waitress, who obviously preferred yakking with a truck driver to taking care of other customers.

"No. I'm not hungry. We've got a lot to talk about, so I'll just watch you fiddle with your late lunch or early dinner." He laughed richly, as if sincerely amused at himself. "We both have a lot of questions, so I'll answer one I know you're dying to find out about."

The waitress brought him a glass of ice water.

"Oh no, you're not going to upstage me." She laid down her fork. "The girl you ran out of here is a Lot Lizard, and if you can indulge me, she's likely your or someone else's CI. Right?"

"How'd you know she was a confidential informant?"

"It doesn't take someone running undercover ops to see it all over her. She stumbled out like a very bad actor in a stage play, so I suggest if she wants to make everyone around believe she's high that she take a few hours and observe true druggies. She had a good voice for the job and made up her face to look like she'd used a lot of bad stuff. But no, Brody, that isn't what I want to talk about." She paused with her fork halfway to her mouth then laid it down. "But I am interested in knowing if you truly plan to stay in Kasota Springs with the changes. Or are you staying here but going back on the multi-county joint task force?" She added a tad of pepper to her omelet.

"What do you want?" Brody took a drink of water.

"That's part of what needs to be settled. I'll be talking with each employee, and I've had a week to think about the department as a whole. Which isn't that long, I'm sure you're thinking. That's why I need your help. I have some ideas, but I truly need your opinion. I trust you."

She could almost read his mind by the look on his face. "You trust me so much that you couldn't tell me the truth about how you can be qualified to be the sheriff!"

Avery drew her attention back to the matter at hand and placed her hands flat on the table.

"Here are my thoughts. First off, we'll have one cruiser out on the streets, especially at night. In nice weather, if a couple of deputies want to pair up and be bicycle patrol, that's fine. I want the department to be friendly and our citizens to know our faces. On the flip side, I don't think I have to tell you because you've lived it; if a rowdy knows he can trust a deputy, he's more likely to turn on another bad guy."

"Sounds like a great start." Brody took a sip of water. "So, what's next?"

"I'm pairing Scott with Deputy Jessup, until Rocky Robertson arrives. Then I'll pair Scott with Rocky. I've heard nothing but good things about Robertson. I'm not sure, but I've heard he'll be here any day, and he does not want to do undercover or human trafficking, so he'll be perfect to work with Scott."

"You're right about that because it's the reason Rocky left the California Highway Patrol to become a private detective."

"I read his email exchanges with Deuce, and it's a possibility he'd go undercover, but not with a unit, just the county." She picked up a piece of dry whole-wheat toast.

"Then where do I fit in?"

Avery hesitated, not sure how he would take her next comment. She hoped she showed confidence when she said, "It isn't fair to demote Danny Scott, unless he does something to make it impossible to keep his rank, so I'm making you a special investigator. Lieutenant, major crime detective if you wish, and you and I will work together solving old cases. We'll pull the others in as needed. When I say old, I mean anything that hasn't been solved or is about to be solved as of today. I'll be going through every file." She laughed softly. "Thank goodness this is a small county. And, before you ask, I made sure you'd taken and passed the test for the position. As a matter of protocol, you've come up the ranks in order and excel in the qualifications."

She could tell by the look on Brody's face and the way he touched his throat that her announcement had come completely unexpected. Add the lack of an immediate verbal comeback and there was no doubt in her in mind he needed to think about the proposal. He was that kind of lawman.

"If you need time to think about it—"

"No, it isn't that. I want the new rank, if nothing more than to find out who assaulted Deuce and left him for dead or if in fact he simply fell. I think we all want that solved."

"I know I do and I barely knew him. His case is number one on my list," she said. "By the way, Deuce had already sent in paperwork to keep you as a Bonita County deputy."

"That's good. We talked that day and I told him I wanted to stay in Kasota Springs, since my undercover stint was over." He took another drink of water. "I've also spent a lot of hours involving drugs coming through the area, and I'd like to see that through. By the way, Victoria, but you can call her Vicky or Vic, is my CI posing as a Lot Lizard. She told me she's on the verge of finding out who the middleman is in the trafficking of a lot of drugs. We know they're coming across the border through the Mexican cartel, but have dozens of leads on how they are getting on to Dallas or up North."

Avery placed the toast back on the plate. "Well, that just got moved to number two on my list. The easy part is over. We've got some other things to talk about, and I have no doubt they are all personal, beginning with why I didn't give you my full name and job in Houston. But if you don't believe anything I say, please trust me that I did not come to town to become the sheriff. Needless to say, I didn't know Deuce would get hurt. I came for some R&R. That's all. Simply to get away from the big city and do some self-reflecting."

"I believe you." The look in his eyes confirmed he was being honest.

"You do?" She surprised herself by giving him such a stupid response. Damn it to hell, she should have acted sharp enough to expect he'd say that. No doubt her unexpected reply wasn't missed by someone like Brody VanZant, especially since she was hiding the real reason she needed R&R. She'd stick with her story until she was ready to tell Brody the whole truth about why she left Houston. That information would take more time than they had at the moment, plus they needed to be in a more private setting.

She didn't have much time to come clean with Broday.

On the other hand, with a little bit of time and a computer, all he'd have to do was search the internet for her name and he could read all the ugly details himself. Fortunately, the local news organizations hadn't as yet found out about Lee being shot, since Houston was the biggest city in Texas with a population over two million occupants, plus being a little over six hundred miles south of the Panhandle. But time wasn't on her side and she knew it.

Brody's voice broke into her thoughts. "Let's get out of this place. I don't like to be seen here much, as you can imagine. Let's go to Pumpkin's. She has a private room where we can talk. Things have probably settled down by now, but park in the back. I just need to get out of this place."

In less than twenty minutes he had paid the bill and they drove to Pumpkin's, which gave Avery plenty of time to think about what she planned to say to Brody—and at the same time, she couldn't help but analyze how smoothly their talk had gone. Or had she missed something?

They had barely taken a seat at the little table hidden in the back of the café when the ol' bar type swingin' door opened and Pumpkin waddled through. "Sorry, long day," she muttered.

Walking directly to Brody, she sat down two glasses of ice water with a glass of tea. She got a set of keys out of her patchwork-printed smock pocket and held her hand out toward Brody. "These are to my pickup parked in the back. Use it..." She turned slightly to meet Avery's gaze then continued, "Both of you go somewhere but without your county hoot-mobiles. The town is still in a flurry, full of people, and the minute they see you two, the questions will fly. New ones, since they've had time to think up more. Many are broadcasting direct from here. So they might be around until late newscasts are taped."

Brody accepted the key ring and pulled a key from his wallet. "Here is mine." He eyed Avery. "Not my official unit, of course. But you know where I keep my pickup, in case you need it before I get back. I'll leave the department's vehicles parked in the back, if it's okay." He turned to Avery with a questioning look in his eyes. "I presume your family is having a big get-together for you."

"Yes." For a minute, Avery didn't know how to respond. She knew what she wanted to ask but wasn't sure how it would be taken. "But they are planning on a simple dinner. We're probably the only family in this part of Texas who has dinner instead of supper, but once you get to know my mother—" Avery cut herself off.

Forge on girlfriend...forge on!

Avery gathered her thoughts. "This might seem a little forward, but would you like to come to Mother's dinner tonight, as my guest?" She hesitated. "Now, I know all about the nepotism policy, as they call it, but having dinner with the mayor and his family after a day like today isn't the same as falling into...uh, something that would come under the department's policy, which by the way is as out of date as a Prairie Schooner." She felt a flush come to her cheeks and knew she was talking him to death, but finally continued, "Hell's bells and cockle shells, do you feel comfortable accepting my invitation or not?"

"Definitely would be nice, but I've got to go to the hospital and check on Deuce. If it's acceptable to be fashionably late, I'd accept."

Pumpkin intervened, "That'll give me and Mama a chance to clear up the ranch house a bit, since you said you're going to be sticking around." She turned and took a couple of steps toward the swinging door, laughing.

"I know exactly how much whiskey I have in the kitchen of the headquarters, so if there's more than two glasses gone, I'll know it," Brody shouted after her.

All three chuckled, as Pumpkin slipped out and returned to the kitchen.

"Okay, I have two questions. First, I had no idea Clara, or Pumpkin as you all call her, was a friend. And secondly, what kind of whiskey do you drink?"

"Second question first. Jack Daniel's. But I can buy something, if you like. I can see you as a champagne or fine wine type lady." He grinned.

"No. Now don't get me wrong, I've had my share in the past." She lowered her head, trying to stay on topic. "But that's history."

"I see, then the first question. Her mama, Abby, cooked at the WBarT for years. Pumpkin grew up there. Of course that was long before I bought it. The Jenkins and Sullivan families had it before I bought the land. And you were too young to probably even know the story," Brody said.

"I bet you didn't know that Mother was a Sullivan? My grandmother didn't like the ranch life, so she sorta forced PawPa to sell the whole dang thing to the people you likely bought it from or maybe even your family. PawPa wouldn't split it up. All of the range land or none. Small world. You'll have something to talk to Mother about."

"It is indeed a small world, in more ways than one."

Avery took a minute or two to reflect on his words.

Brody seemed to realize her needs, as he sipped on his ice water, while she drank another glass of tea.

Breaking the silence, Brody asked, "Do you have time to go visit Rainey and Deuce with me?" Noise from the dining area filtered through the air.

Although being physically tired as she had been in a long time, she wanted more time with Brody. "I'll go if you'll agree to make it a business trip. We can talk about the cases we need to deal with, so don't forget to bring a notebook." She smiled and slid Pumpkin's keys his direction. "Deal?" Just the thought of spending time in a car with this good-looking, suave rogue created a burning sensation in her stomach and made her heart speed up.

"Deal." He picked up the keys, got up from his chair, and helped her out of hers. They headed for Pumpkin's Chevy Equinox and he opened the passenger door for Dannie and ambled around to his side and got seated.

He inserted the key in the ignition. "One thing I want to get straight. If we're going to work closely together and try to be friends too, no secrets. None whatsoever. Especially about cases."

"I totally agree." Well, lie number one slipped from her tongue, but she promised herself she'd begin being honest by coming clean about the bottle she'd found not far from where Deuce lay on his deathbed. But, after all, at the time she hadn't been a part of the case, just a plain ol' citizen. In the event it was important to the case, to keep the chain of custody, she had put the bottle in a plastic bag, along with the Kleenex, and locked it in a filing cabinet in the mayor's office. She'd only moved it a day or two ago, under the supervision of her father, to the locked gun cabinet in Deuce's office. She'd taken it out, after she was named sheriff, in the event time allowed for her to bring it up for discuss with Brody.

Shivers ran down her spine. This was the first issue, but there was certainly one promise she couldn't make...telling him why she had left Houston. Or not any time soon, unless he asked, of course. Then she'd explain everything he needed to know. Officer involved shootings weren't unheard of and were more frequent than the public knew, but being involved in one was an altogether different matter. She took a deep breath and made an asserted effort to bring her thoughts back to their discussion. "Yes, sir. I totally agree. The last thing we need is to be forced to bring in an arbitrator to resolve our lies, particularly anything that causes us to bring in the Texas Rangers." She fingered the gold stud earring she was wearing. "I love the rangers, but I don't want them nosing around in the department's business, unless it's absolutely necessary."

The special ring she'd assigned to her father on her iPhone sounded from her purse. "Excuse me." Without hesitation, she grabbed it. "Hi, Dad."

Dannie listened intently to what her father had to say before commenting. "That's fine. I know how fragile Mama can be at times and this was a very stressful day. Even yesterday was preparing for today, so I understand."

Same story...different chapter!

After a while, she finally said, "Yes. Yes, Dad, tomorrow would be great. And I'm bringing a guest." She raised a questioning eyebrow at Brody, as he stared across at her and nodded his head. "It's a surprise, but you'll be pleased. Actually, I'm kinda glad for the reprieve from the festivities because not only am I tired but I also need to do some more things at the office." She giggled softly. Her dad was not going to get his way this time, and she needed to make sure she was on record that she now ran the sheriff's department and he was mayor. "No, Dad, I'm not redecorating and not no but hell no to an interior decorator. I don't care if it's in the budget or not, the office is staying exactly like it is in the event Deuce returns. Every paperclip will be in the same place." She laughed a little louder this time. "You're too funny, Dad. I know that isn't possible. Don't wait up for me tonight." She laid her free hand on the dashboard and responded, "No, I haven't filled you in on all the changes I plan to make and frankly don't plan to, but I've got to go over some more case files. You know, get my stuff in order, because I want to be like a little mother duck and have her ducklings right where they belong."

She glanced over at Brody, who winked.

"Love you, too, Dad, and please give Mother the attention she needs, not that you don't. An irregular mammograph is nothing to be ashamed of. I know she's been feeling bad but once her treatment is over, she'll be back to zip-lining in no time. I promise. Bye and kisses to Mama." She put her phone back in her purse, then continued addressing Brody, as if there had not been a distraction. "I guess you heard that. You're not going to have to face a million questions from my father about everything from your heritage to whether you wear tighty whities or boxers."

Brody didn't answer. Silence settled around them like smog on the Gulf.

To her surprise, he finally responded. "Tighty whities."

"That's more than I wanted to know."

"Uh, but you said your dad would need the information, so thought I'd give you a heads-up. Plus, you know how awful boxers look under tactical pants."

"Stop!" She pulled her hand up like a crossing guard.

They both shook with laughter.

Although it was hard for her to come up with the right words, she finally decided how to broach the subject of her and her father, as mayor.

"Brody," she looked over at him, although he kept his eyes on the road. "My father can be a little, well let's just say...." The last word she wanted to use was controlling, so she began over, "My father can be presumptuous and brash. Some of it's because of his size and loud voice, some just comes naturally. He would have probably been a general, if he'd stayed in the service. But his heart is in the right place. He stretches the limits sometimes if he thinks he needs to and certainly will step over the boundaries, but besides his family, the citizens of Bonita County are his primary concern."

"I can see that. My dad wanted me to play football, whether I wanted to or not. Then he wanted me to go into law enforcement. He didn't recognize boundaries either. But you know what? He was right. He pushed and pushed and I'm a better man for it."

Dannie pulled at the seatbelt. "I can see his obvious influence in you, and I don't even know him."

After what seemed like a decade of silence, she finally scrounged up the courage to ask, "I'm sure you heard that Mama isn't feeling well and we've decided to call off the celebration tonight, but would you like to come with me tomorrow, Brody?" She twisted her lips from side to side. "I could use a detail, I mean an escort. You've never met anyone quite like my folks, I can promise you."

"Since you've agreed to be my bodyguard, if Sylvie is visiting Rainey, I guess I can be your escort tomorrow."

Putting her index finger near her mouth, she acted as if having to think it over. "I agree, but I have one question. Can you give me a definition of nepotism?"

Avery laughed when Brody quoted, "It's a noun, meaning we can't have a family relationship, as in business and politics."

"Hum," she said as she tried again to loosen the seatbelt a tad. "We'd better speed it up a little, so you won't get me home so late that Daddy has to read the nepotism manual, as he interrupts it."

"We don't have a full manual on that.... Do we?"

She smiled and said, "No. The county manual and the sheriff's department manual are vastly different, as I found out. I think we both agree that the policy was written when the county was established about a century and a half ago. I think they confused fraternizing with nepotism."

"So we can fraternize, as long as it doesn't get serious? Sounds like it's all in the interpretation."

Chapter 15

The drive back from Lubbock seemed a great deal shorter than the one coming in from Kasota Springs, or at least Brody thought so. Partly because of the news that Deuce's latest tests had indicated a noticeable improvement of his frontal lobe area. The best news of all: once they took him out of the medically induced coma, there was a very real possibility he would regain some, if not all, of his memory. It'd be a slow recovery and no doubt he'd likely have some aftereffects from the type of injury he had sustained, but he could function better than they had first thought.

Only time would tell!

With a little nudge from Brody, Rainey had agreed to leave her husband's side and go with Avery to the cafeteria for something to eat. Avery reported that the ever-watchful wife seemed less stressed than she had in prior visits.

Brody leaned a little forward toward the wheel and pressed this thumbs against one another. "Did Rainey bring up anything about you being appointed interim sheriff in Deuce's place?"

"No, because she's been pretty shielded from the town's news. Even Sylvie, as curious as she is, seems to have realized that right now isn't the time to burden Rainey with problems. It'll devastate Deuce and ultimately Rainey if he can't return to the sheriff's department." She raised her shoulder to loosen the seatbelt a tad then continued, "But, I can assure you if there's any job he can do, he'll remain on the payroll. Rainey did tell me that Sylvie is doing an excellent job running the antique store. She's even letting Sylvie do the books and purchasing."

"A lot of people think because Sylvie has allowed men to use her, and for whatever reason she's caught up in the fifties, that she's dumb. She is anything but featherbrained," Brody said.

"I agree. Rainey told me that the doctors have asked what nursing home she wants Deuce to go to when he's ready for rehab."

"Of course she said Kasota's center. He'll be with his mother. Although the long-term rehab is separate from the Alzheimer's unit, it'll be best for both of them to know they are near one another."

Brody nodded in agreement.

"Plus, Rainey said something interesting. Once he's moved, she's going to focus mainly on her law practice."

"What about her antique store?"

"Sylvie has proven she can handle it, and they've talked about expanding the business into a vintage type store for clothes, which is gaining popularity. The younger generation loves the retro look. Vintage chic, I think it's called. Thinking of clothes reminds me. Thank you for suggesting that we go by my house so I could change out of my dress uniform. That kept Rainey from asking questions."

"If you'd been in uniform, Rainey wouldn't have had to ask anything since she's married to your predecessor plus she was with the L.A. DA's office for a number of years. She knows what every insignia on a uniform means."

Avery took a notebook out of her purse and read some pages. "I didn't eat much lunch, so why don't we go by the DQ and pick up some food and then go over some files at the office? I have a few questions and have barely had time to read the case records thoroughly and make notes. I would really like to get into them. Especially Deuce's and the one you're working on. How about it?"

"Only if you buy the burgers."

"Salad for me." She twisted her mouth and narrowed her brow. "We said no secrets. I'm kinda a phony vegetarian. I don't eat red meat but love omelets and fish, which makes me a fraud."

"So, you eat salads and stir them around like you did the last time you ordered one?"

"That kinda comes with being a fake vegetarian. I know that's strange, being born and raised in beef country." She shifted her left shoulder against the seat belt, and quickly seemed to change the subject. "Thanks again for stopping by my house and letting me change clothes. This outfit is so much more comfortable and it didn't scream to Rainey that I'm now with the sheriff's department. And I'm glad we took Clara's vehicle, too."

"You're welcome, but I have a question. Do you have a grudge against Pumpkin's seatbelt or what?"

"Well, remember men and women are made differently—"

"Oh man, can I ever tell you were a detective. Right?"

"Right. I have something to ask you." She opened her handbag, rummaged around a bit and pulled out a plastic bag. "What does this look like to you?"

Avery held the bottle where he could see it, yet keep his eyes on the road.

"Without an examination, it looks like inside is an old medicine bottle."

"It is. Now before you get mad at me, when I found it I didn't know any of the specifics involving Deuce's case. No suspects nor any of the circumstances. I guess the cop in me made me want to keep this bottle, since I'm familiar with the product that was in it."

Brody glanced over at her. "Don't stop now. Where did you find it?"

"Remember when we ran across one another jogging?"

"You mean when you thought I was a stalker and took me down?"

"That's it. The bottle is from the Jacks Bluff vet back in the 1960s, and it had PCP in it, but liquid instead of powder. At the time it was just strange being out there. That's the main reason I decided to keep it and took care not to contaminate it. It wasn't like the bottle had been tossed out and disposed of inappropriately. No vet would ever be that careless. As you know in the sixties they used it as a general anesthetic for humans and tranquilizer for animals, and today—"

"Almost no animals, but mostly as angel dust, ecstasy, and a ton of other names depending on whether it's wet or dust." A weird feeling rushed all over Brody, knowing it could be that Tommy had stolen the powder and put water in it so he could drink the concoction, because he likely wouldn't have the paraphernalia or time to shoot up or snort it. "I hope to hell you kept a clean chain of custody."

"Trust me. I didn't. I'll tell you later," she said.

Brody didn't even want to think the thoughts he was having, because they pointed directly to Tommy as the number one person of interest in Deuce's case. Brody had to remind himself that his loyalty to the citizens and the oath administered to him took precedence over what he wanted the truth to be and what it appeared to prove out. No doubt by now Avery knew that Tommy was Brody's sister's brother-in-law.

He knew the bottle needed to be tested for trace evidence, but at the moment he wasn't sure it was evidence regardless of what his gut told him. Since the bottle was in her possession, he'd let her make the call, although if Tommy had drunk from the bottle they'd find his DNA as well as fingerprints.

There was no choice to be made. He handed the bottle back to Avery without asking what she planned to do with it. Sometimes in life it was better not to know than to know.

"Avery, if I may call you that—"

"Of course."

"It's early yet. Let's stop by the Jacks Bluff and talk with the vet about the bottle. Teg Tegler, isn't that his name?" He felt like a blunt force instrument hit him squarely between the eyes as he waited for her response.

"Yes, and I think that's a good idea." She bit her lip. "Please remember that I wasn't even an officer of the law at the time and had no duty to turn in a bottle just because I found it. I didn't even know the facts surrounding Deuce's assault. I just kept the bottle because it's over fifty years old and an antique. I wasn't even a deputy in any county of Texas. I was on a leave of absence."

"If it's not too personal, for what?"

"I'm not quite ready to talk about it, but I promise..." Avery turned her upper body to face him. "I give you my word when I'm ready to discuss it, you'll be the first I call. And you can rule out anything illegal."

"Like shooting your partner?" He laughed, but noticed she lowered her head and not another word was said for the longest time. Finally, after going over everything he said that could have upset her, he said, "I apologize for whatever I said that disturbed you."

"It's okay. I'm thinking about Deuce and Rainey, that's all."

Brody saw by the slack expression with slightly wet, dull eyes that she was holding back tears and he knew it had nothing to do with Deuce and Rainey.

In less than forty-five minutes they pulled into the circular drive at the Jacks Bluff. An old, vintage pickup was parked at the end of the drive, and an ancient oil derrick stood as a tall, petrous reminder of yesteryear.

Almost before Brody cut off the engine, Avery unbuckled her seatbelt and said, "That old F-110 belongs to Granny Johnson. She has a brand new Caddy and a couple of new pickups in the garage, but she uses them for funerals and church only. This one's for ranching."

Brody reached Avery's side of the vehicle and opened the door for her before she had time to get out by herself.

"We definitely need to stop by and see either Granny or Lola Ruth before we go out to talk with Teg or Chase. Chase is their foreman." She straightened her shirt. "By the way, Teg is fourth-generation Tegler to have worked at this ranch. Sometimes he's called Four, but most people call him Teg now that his father has passed away. Plus, plan on spending some time in the house, because I'm bettin' Lola Ruth won't stand for you leaving until she feeds you. Both of the ladies, Granny and Lola Ruth, have deep-rooted Texas southern hospitality."

Before they could get around to the back door, Lola Ruth came out and greeted them like she hadn't seen either one for months.

Short, round, and always wearing an apron, she hugged both of them with a true Texas welcome. "I haven't seen you all since yesterday. We're so excited about Avery being named sheriff—"

Avery interrupted, "Interim sheriff."

Lola Ruth batted her eyes through her heavy, black-rimmed glasses then continued, "Well, interim sheriff...but we barely got home before Granny and I let out a hoot and a holler that I bet they heard all the way down in Austin." Lola Ruth held on to Avery like she was a kitten that might run away if she loosened her grip a tad.

"I'm so glad to officially meet you, Deputy VanZant. I know we've talked but a person doesn't know somebody until they sit down and have coffee with them. Talkin' on the side of the road doesn't count." She let go of Avery and grabbed Brody by the elbow. "Got a pot of coffee I just fixed and fresh peach-apricot fried pies I made this morning." Over her shoulder she said to Avery, "Plenty of iced tea, too."

Brody held the back screen for the ladies and then entered.

"Granny isn't here right now. She went with Chase out to the pasture where she has a bull she wanted him to look at."

Lola Ruth scurried around the kitchen, fixing the drinks and putting pies on plates, while she talked. "I haven't seen you out here shooting for a few days." She addressed Avery.

"No. I've been busy getting up to speed on things in the department. When Deuce comes back, I want him to be able to just walk in and take over." Avery took a seat at the table and motioned to Brody by raising her eyebrows as if to say *this is a lost cause, so enjoy the coffee and fried pies!*

After eating two pies and drinking two cups of coffee, Brody wiped his mouth on a cloth napkin and said, "Lola Ruth, I apologize because I feel like I made a pig out of myself, but those were the best pies I've ever eaten. I might just drop by every day to check on you two ladies." He smiled at Avery, who had a pleased look on her face. "On county business, of course, but if you have coffee and fried pies, it certainly wouldn't be gentlemanly of me not to come inside and check on you all."

"What's your favorite pie?" Lola Ruth asked.

"Ma'am, whatever you have, I'm sure would make me happy. But those peach-apricot I just ate might well be my favorite."

In a bubbly and light voice, Avery said, "He's a charmer, isn't he?"

"Sure enough is. Now whatcha two come all the way out here for?"

Avery took the lead. "We'd like to talk with Teg for a few minutes, if he isn't too busy." She wiped her fingers on her napkin. "It's about the kid who was trespassing on the ranch the night Deuce was injured."

"Are you sure you all don't want another cup of coffee or glass of tea?"

"No, ma'am, but thanks for asking. It's been a pleasure, Lola Ruth, but we need to get with Teg and head back to town. We've got a lot of work to do." Avery hugged the older woman and kissed her on the cheek.

After Brody thanked her again for the hospitality, Avery walked her to the door and gave her another hug. "Thank you. Tell Granny that we came by and are sorry we missed her, but we'll be back. I want to catch up with her and find out how it went with the neglected horses Mesa is bringing back."

Brody put on his Stetson and tipped it to Lola Ruth, then followed Avery out the door and across the graveled path to the barn.

He spied Teg Tegler in a stall that housed a pretty little deep-red blood bay, about the time the vet saw the lawmen. "Hey, what brings you all out in these parts of the woods?" He took off his gloves and walked their way, shaking hands with Brody and then said, "I'd hug you, gal, but don't want to ruin those sparklin' clean duds you have on."

"I don't care." She hugged him anyway. "We need your help. It's about the night the stables were broken into. Can you give us a quick rundown on what happened?"

"Sure. Take a seat." He motioned to bales of hay stacked near the entrance. "I can't give you exact times, but it was long after Mrs. Johnson and Lola Ruth got back from the festival and that was not long after it closed down. They'd taken a cab and had someone break down their booth and bring stuff back, so they got here after the fireworks, I remember that." He twisted his lips. "Guess that'd be one or so in the morning."

"Were you in the main house or your place?" Avery asked.

"Mine. That's why I know it was pretty late. I saw a shadow running from the barn back toward the west pasture. He was tall and lanky. Didn't see his face, so I don't know who it was. Later I heard it might be Tommy Mitchell—"

Brody broke in. "Who'd you hear that from, Teg?"

"Deputy Scott. He was out here that night after it was called in. By the time he got here, I couldn't find anything missing. I'd already talked to Mrs. Johnson and Mesa. They both said they didn't want charges filed. That whoever it was probably was just pilfering." He leaned against the railing of a stall. "So the whole issue was basically dropped."

Avery pulled the bottle from her purse. "Recognize this?" She handed the plastic wrapped bag to him. "If you need a better look at the bottle, you'll need plastic gloves."

"Yep, and I don't need any gloves to know what it is. That's what the little jackass took. Damn it!" Teg turned his back to them and under his breath he used a couple of cuss words then turned back to them. "I should have known it was gone, but since we don't use PCP any longer it never crossed my mind. I should have destroyed it a long time ago, but it's one of my dad's bottles and I think I just didn't want to get rid of it and pushed it around on the shelf for years." He moved to better light and read the label. "Yep, it's from the 1960s, but wouldn't have had the liquid in it. It was powder." He handed the bottle back to Avery. "Yep, that's what the little bastard was lookin' for. With liquid added, it's a strong drug, but snorted or smoked with other drugs it can take effect within two to three minutes. That's why vets liked to use it on big animals. They're hard enough to handle without being injured." He pounded his elbow against a bale of hay. "Typically, this whole place is locked up tighter than a drum, but since the cowboys were bringing back in the rough stock from the rodeo, I'd left the side door to my office unlocked for their convenience in getting the bulls back in their stalls." He lowered his brow. "It was my responsibility. Damn it to hell and back again, I should have destroyed that bottle years ago or at least had it locked up in the medical supply closet."

"Don't be too hard on yourself, Teg. A drug addict will find a fix one way or another." Damn, Brody hated the thoughts that were running wild through his mind. "Then Deputy Scott didn't come here directly after you all called the sheriff's department?"

The vet addressed Brody. "I didn't see anybody, but that doesn't mean he didn't talk with Mesa or Mrs. Johnson. The only deputy I saw that night was you when you came up the road, turned off your lights, parked, and then walked up here. Circled the headquarters, the bunkhouse, barn, and corral, then walked back to your pickup. But that was hours after the incident."

"That I did. You should be a deputy. I was sent out to check on your welfare and the lights were out in the headquarters and all of the outer buildings, so after I circled the main house, I went back to where the search party had organized." He looked over at Avery. "This was after the search and rescue was well underway."

"Maybe Deputy Scott talked with Chase, our foreman, but I doubt Scott could have gotten by without me seeing him. After I called in the break-in, and I guess we can't call it that, because we weren't actually totally locked up—"

"Trespassing or burglary, at best," Avery said.

"Anyway, I headed out to the east pasture toward I-40 in case the kid ran that way. Chase said he couldn't see which direction the jackass—excuse me, ma'am—went but I thought it was west, not east, although I think I maybe thought the kid had double-backed."

"So, you ended up going east and Scott found Mitchell over by the west pasture. Interesting," Avery blurted out before continuing, "Thanks so much, Teg. After Deputy VanZant sampled Lola Ruth's fried pies, I think you'll see more of him." She snickered and elbowed Brody good-naturedly.

Brody shook hands with the vet. "Sorry, but I have one more question. Where did you hear the name of the guy Scott picked up?"

"Oh, I remember it very clearly. I was lookin' for a mama cow who just gave birth out in the west pasture and I saw Danny Scott out there. He said he was lookin' over things in daylight. I asked him if they had any leads, and he said that it was a kid who just got out of the hoosegow and I put two and two together. I think Stanley Mitchell's brother is the only one around who fits that bill. Thanks for coming out."

"Thanks, Teg. You helped us a lot."

Avery and Brody walked to Pumpkin's vehicle.

Absentmindedly, he opened the door for Avery, but he had more questions than ever about Tommy. He hadn't been privy to the report written up by Chief Deputy Scott, although he'd mentioned it to Danny. Brody's memory of the night didn't coincide with those of the veterinarian, who to Brody's knowledge didn't have a rooster in the fight.

Since the bottle was nearly sixty years old, no doubt it wouldn't have been missed if the vet had used it himself. Brody couldn't think of a reason for it to have been tossed in an open field by anyone. But Brody was still perplexed as to why Scott was on the Jacks Bluff property the next day, long after Deuce was found.

In Brody's estimations, unless Chase were to tell them another version of the incident, which he doubted, both Teg and Chase Slade could be ruled out as having anything to do with the bottle or Deuce.

Unfortunately, the more info gathered the more light seemed to be shed on Tommy Mitchell, which bothered Brody greatly. He didn't think the kid was a criminal; he just needed guidance and maturity. He also knew Winnie did everything she could to mother the young man, but no doubt in Brody's mind, his sister was hiding something within the family unit. It could be nothing more serious than her being a little ashamed of Tommy's reputation in town.

Brody needed some big brother-little sister time, but without Stanley lurking around. How Brody would accomplish that could be tricky at best.

However, his biggest heartburn right now was how in the smothering hell was he going to tell Avery what he found at his sister's house on the night Deuce was injured, much less explain away Stanley's actions at the café after Tommy had been let loose from Deuce's investigation?

How could he be critical of Avery's withholding the bottle she found when she wasn't even a department employee, when he hadn't had the opportunity to fill her in on his own private investigation of a family member? She'd kept the chain of command by locking up the evidence much like he did by putting his letter in Scott's desk for the records and mailing himself a copy.

What he knew, and had to be truthful about, would likely send Tommy Mitchell right off probation and directly to prison for many moons, if the timeline matched. But that might well be a big *if.*

The last thing Brody wanted was to have mistrust between him and Avery, but it looked like that might happen, once he told her about his investigation.

Brody had to think through everything and see what Danny Scott had put in the official records before he talked any more about Tommy. To find just the right time to tell Avery the truth...But when?

He doubted Deuce had had an opportunity to do little more than make notes about Tommy, if even that, since at the time Tommy's trespassing had seemed totally insignificant. Also to be taken into consideration—the owners of the Jacks Bluff didn't want charges filed.

When Brody had the opportunity and there were fewer time restraints on the new interim sheriff, he'd fill her in. He guessed he could wait until she fired him, once she found out about his unauthorized investigation, to start looking in the want ads for a rent-a-cop in security at the GreenMart.

Once he told Avery the truth, his career would be worth about eight bucks an hour at best.

Chapter 16

What Avery had just experienced set her brain in an uncontrollable spin. She desperately tried to mentally match the information she'd read in the case file with the sketchy timeline she'd created and what she'd just heard.

Brody shut the passenger door. She closed her eyes, leaned her head back, and tried to force the investigative information into some kind of order. It was like playing Scrabble and suddenly learning that you couldn't use vowels. She stared into the reflective blue, orange, and red colors of the late evening Texas sunset.

She and Brody had plenty of time to get something to drink before they went into the office. That would give her an opportunity to think about Deuce's assault. Two heads were always better than one. No truer cliché fit how she felt.

Tommy Mitchell was on her screen. But nowhere in the handwritten notes that she'd quickly scanned that morning before the press conference had she seen anything about what the vet had told them. Of course, now she had the answer...Scott definitely had not talked with anyone at the Jacks Bluff the night Deuce was injured. So, he didn't have anything to write down. The information was crucial to the whole chronology of the investigation. Who—and at what time—had he talked to at the ranch, should have been part of the case notes.

But she could hardly wait to find Scott's notes written up that night. The chief deputy had had a huge burden placed on his shoulders, which was a lot for a small town where very little violence took place. Then he had to become accustomed to his surprise at her being named interim sheriff, when it was obvious to everyone in the department that he anticipated getting the job. To a degree she could internally rationalize the chief deputy's actions, or rather lack of action.

Overshadowing her thoughts, she heard Brody ask if she'd still like to pick up something at Dairy Queen and eat at the office.

"I'm actually full, but a Butterfinger Blizzard sounds good," she said. No doubt he recognized her lack of enthusiasm.

"A Blizzard sounds good. Afterwards, we can go directly to the office and eat out of the coupon queen's baskets of goodies. Thelma saves us a lot of money using coupons."

His iPhone buzzed, indicating a text. He pulled to the side of the road, read the message, and placed the phone on his seat next to his hip.

"How about we stop by the office, so I can change clothes, and have a bite to eat at the truck stop instead?" He glanced at her. "They have an excellent cheese omelet." He teased. "It was my CI from her burner phone. She wants to see me at the truck stop east of town and specifically asked that you come along."

"Has she already heard I was named the interim sheriff?" That was the only reason Avery could think of for such a request.

Very little was said on the short ride back to the courthouse except for discussing their Texas Ranger relatives. It was obvious to Avery that Brody had avoided discussing his family, except for the little bit he'd shared earlier about his father and that he had to take care of his little sister. But then they hadn't had much time to talk. She did learn that his grandfather had been a Texas Ranger, but he never mentioned what his father did for a living.

The lawmen were greeted by the night dispatcher, Thelma, and Deputy Jessup before Brody headed to the locker room.

After returning the bottle in the evidence locker and logging in the time, date, and her initials, Avery went back up front. She told Thelma that she and Brody had an appointment but didn't volunteer any specifics.

When Avery saw Brody come out of the locker room dressed in civilian clothes, she couldn't help but draw in a deep breath. With tight Wrangler jeans on that fit like the gloves they wore to investigate a scene and a starched white cowboy-cut shirt that fit him about the same, a warm glow flooded her body. He wore his usual cowboy boots and Stetson.

He headed out the back toward the parking lot.

Suddenly, she realized she had not allowed thoughts of Houston and her partner's murder to be the norm for her instead of the exception. However, nary a day passed without her thinking about the incident, but much of the horrific part had begun taking a backseat to the good memories—probably because of how busy she had been. She closed her eyes and couldn't help but think that the word *incident* seemed way too inconsequential for such an earthshaking event in their lives. And she'd still have to testify in the trial, if the perp was ever found and arrested.

One thing for certain, she'd never allow herself to become close to another partner. Never again. Even if he wore tight-fittin' jeans.

Avery went out the front, waving at Thelma, who was on the phone. She rounded the building to where Brody waited for her.

"We need to change cars. Mine is—"

"I'm only three blocks from here on Arrington Street. Will that be faster?"

"Sure."

In just a few minutes, he pulled up in front of her parents' house. She had already found car keys, and before he could get close enough to open the door for her, she tossed the keychain to him and headed to a fiftieth anniversary white Mustang.

"You drive, since we're on a date." She laughed out loud, thinking about the untruthfulness of her statement.

"It's been a while since I've driven a Mustang on a stakeout, but then this really isn't one, just a meeting." There was something warm and enchanting in his words, not to mention the smile he gave her. "I figured we'd take one of the unmarked cars."

"Yeah, I know we both loved Pumpkin's Equinox so much that I can almost see tears in your eyes because you are forced to drive my car."

"Who can turn down a Mustang?" He wiped away a fake tear.

She waited until they were pretty far away from her parents' house before asking about his CI. He filled her in, reminding her that this particular CI was only one of several around since he'd been involved in the special crimes unit and spent a lot of his time undercover. He figured the call was about the drug traffic but couldn't guarantee it. Since Avery hadn't been around town much as an adult, few transient people stopping off I-40 or truck drivers would put two and two together and realize they were both from the sheriff's department.

Sure enough when they arrived at their destination, the CI had parked her car far from the door.

When they entered, out of the corner of Avery's eye she spied Vicky sitting in the same booth as earlier in the day.

With his hand flat on the middle of Avery's back, Brody guided her to a corner table where they could see Vicky but she couldn't see them. The booth was only steps away from the cash register, just as he had been instructed.

Brody pulled out two menus that were squeezed between the wall and the napkin holder. "Whatcha want, honey?" He smiled at her with one of those type of smiles that would melt a woman's heart when it was ten degrees below zero.

"I think I only want some iced tea. How about you, sweet thing?"

"Coffee." He folded up his menu, then hers. "You'll be sorry that you missed the omelet."

Before they could order, Vicky walked up to the cash register, laid out some ones, then as if she'd just noticed Brody and Avery, she stepped over to their table. Laying her hands flat on the edge, she spoke loud enough that the traffic on I-40 was drowned out. "Mr. Sheriffman, I know you said you'd find something to haul me in on but sticking around here watching is a waste of taxpayers' money. So get off my case, or I'll call your boss, the mayor, or somebody about how you're mistreating me. I'm just a girl making an honest living, that's all, and you're invading my privacy." The more she talked the closer her right hand slid toward Brody's. "I might hire a lawyer and sue somebody, so get off my case. I don't have anything to hide." She turned to Avery. "I don't know how you can stand to be around this jerk except he must have something somewhere you like a whole lot." As any good undercover cop would do, she dropped her eyes to his lap.

Vicky stumbled around much better than earlier in the day before she ran into the front door being opened by a truck driver, who profusely apologized then asked to help her to her car.

Avery lowered her voice to a whisper, "And what was that all about?"

Brody barely opened his left hand enough so she could see the piece of paper. He stuffed the note in his pants pocket. He waited long enough for the waitress to set glasses of water in front of them. He then told her they weren't quite ready to order yet. When she was out of earshot, he said to Avery, "If you'll excuse me, I'll be back in a minute." He scooted out of the booth and went into the nearby men's room.

A number of thoughts passed through Avery's mind, but one thing was certain: Brody's CI wouldn't have gone to all this trouble without important information about a case.

Avery saw Brody exit the restroom entrance and obvious to her, he saw everything around him without turning his head. Brody neared the table but didn't sit down, just leaned in and said in a very low voice, "Looks like this could be the break we've been waiting for. I've got work to do tonight, so if you're tired I can take you home." He took a sip of water. "I've got to meet her at the roadside park east of here."

"No way am I staying behind. Not after the smile Vicky gave you." She shot him a meek and shy smile of her own. "I've been out of the field way too long. Between meeting with Teg and this, my heart is beating out of control and my adrenaline is rushing like Niagara Falls."

"Are you sure you don't want to eat? Our meeting isn't for another forty-five minutes." He dropped some cash on the table. "And it isn't that far."

"I couldn't eat a bite. Let's just go out there and walk around a bit. Get the lay of the land. That's what I like to do when I'm meeting someone, even a CI who I trust, in an area I'm not familiar with." She latched on to Brody's arm. "Our housekeeper and cook, Jennie, will have plenty of leftovers. By the stature of my father, it's plain he was raised not to leave any food on his plate." She allowed a trace of laughter in her voice.

She got to the car first and opened his door for him. In return, he shot her a wicked smile that set her blood boiling.

The way he settled into the driver's bucket seat definitely made her acutely conscious of his tall, athletic physique. A build she'd expect from a college football player who kept himself in great physical shape. When he shifted his arms to turn on the engine, the rich outline of his shoulder strained against the fabric of his shirt. She couldn't help but wonder if his broad shoulders ever got tired of the burden they carried.

She rounded the car and got in.

Just to stay busy, Avery riffled through her purse. She couldn't help but think that one of the first things she had been taught in the academy was to meet any confidential informant in the most public place as possible or somewhere you designate, that you're familiar with and is not secluded. After all, every CI had a history, which typically made the majority not always the most trustworthy people on this earth. On the other side of the coin, each handler had to know their CI very well and trust them totally while staying alert to their every move and every word that came out of their mouth.

Not much unlike the way she had to have faith in Brody.

Avery had to trust Brody enough to believe he knew what he was doing to agree to meet Vicky at a place of her choice...in a highway rest stop surrounded with trees and brush.

Shortly they were on the road to being part of a huge drug bust or being set up.

Chills ran through her veins at the choice.

Chapter 17

Once Brody pulled into the lot of the roadside park, with better lighting than most GreenMarts, he and Avery settled on one of the concrete benches. He sat facing the traffic, leaned back with both elbows on the picnic table, and stretched his legs out in front of him.

As he'd expect, Avery opted to use a cop's training and instinct and sat next to him facing the path that ran along a small stream. She didn't fool him in the least; she was doing exactly as one officer would do for another...always having the other's back.

Neither said anything for the longest time, but he got the impression that Avery might finally be decompressing and putting her very long, busy day behind her.

"This really is quiet and peaceful, although I feel guilty knowing we're working a case," she finally said. "How did you get involved with this CI?"

"It's kinda a long story. She's actually now an undercover cop, but that came after she was arrested for being in a car with under an ounce of marijuana on her. Not enough to send her to the hoosegow except for one night, but enough to cause her plenty of grief. She swore she didn't know she had it and I believed her." He roped his arms to his side and looked up at Avery, the prettiest woman he believed he'd ever seen.

Back to business, mister!

"Anyway, I was convinced she was set up. I saw something in her and we worked out a deal with the DA. Her records were sealed and she became my CI. Since the offense was not only minor but sealed as a juvenile, she later applied to the police academy—and with a lot of politicking, she became a valuable asset to the department."

"So you call her a CI, although she's really a UC." She shook her head as if she didn't believe him and moved around to straddle the bench.

"Now before you start in on me, that's what she wants when she's working out in the field. She doesn't want to be referred to as an undercover cop. So far it's served the special task force very well in the case called *Harbor Crew*. That's the code name given to the cartel moving drugs up from Mexico. We know they are coming across I-40, which of course runs coast to coast, but we can't put all the pieces together. We're getting closer." He shrugged.

"What makes you think that?"

"As you know, the interstate branches off east of here going up north or eastwardly to Dallas, thus leading to a number of major drug hub cities. A thoroughfare to many distribution points."

"Do you think someone local is a middleman to the big fish in this part of Texas?" She rested her hand on his knee.

"Don't know." Just the heat from her palm through the denim of his jeans might as well be a scorching iron on his skin. He gathered his thoughts, which was harder than he thought it'd be. "If you have any ideas, let me know. This is such a big business that we know it's taking a lot of brainpower and manipulation behind it. No dummy is running this part of the operation. It's much too complicated." He needed to think, so to pass the time, he smiled at Avery. "Hey, tell me more about yourself."

"Of course. I haven't been back in town except for a few days here and there since I left for college. The area has changed so much that I hardly know anyone. After Daddy spent a zillion dollars for me to get an Ivy League education and I turned around and went into law enforcement, Mama's never been all that happy with me. She certainly has never mistreated me or anything. I love her with all my heart and soul, but being a cop isn't what she envisioned for her cute little debutante in a tutu." She curled his fingers into fists and then stretched them out before laying her hand back on his knee.

"Let's go for a walk." He got up and put out his hand and took hers to help her up but never let go. They sauntered down a path along a small stream. "You know that we can't always please our folks, so we've got to do what we know is best for us in our heart. I'm gonna tell you something, I've never confessed to anyone. Sometimes I feel like Tarzan after I've done something really worthwhile to prevent a murder or arrest a group on organized crime charges. Or even simply when we close a case and I know nobody else will get hurt, plus we are successful in getting drugs or weapons off the street." He dropped her hand and rolled both hands into fists, pounded his chest, and bellowed out, "Me Tarzan, you Jane."

His antics sent Avery laughing so hard that she leaned down and placed her hands on her knees. Then she suddenly stood upright and beat her chest. "No. Me Sheriff Tarzan, you—oops, Jane doesn't sound right. How about you John?" She laughed so much that she stumbled on a rock, and he caught her around the waist before she hit the ground.

Pulling her into his arms and giving his heart a chance to settle down, he said, "Okay, John is fine with me."

With all the laughter gone from her, and he suspected a tad of being embarrassed that she had nearly fallen as well, she whispered, "No, you Tarzan because you saved me."

Before he knew what was happening he pulled her tighter against him, drilling her ample breasts into his chest. Being as she was almost as tall as him, they were nearly eye to eye, and he saw what he hoped was a wish for a kiss. He was more than ready to oblige the lady.

Slowly she ran a finger along his lower lip before extending all of her fingers over his five o'clock shadow, caressing it like she would a baby's cheek. Her touch was soft, desirable, making the air around them feel like they were on a Gulf beach on a hundred-degree day instead of along a small stream in the Texas Panhandle.

Brody allowed himself the luxury of a chain of kisses down her neck. Ending up capturing her lips, he pulled her closer, tighter. Undoubtedly, she was one of the sexiest women he'd ever met in his life.

As he parted her lips, her hands imprisoned the back of his head. He glided his fingers down her back and planted his hand firmly on her behind, bringing her to him and his show of desire. He devoured her mouth with deep, sweeping strokes of his tongue. She joined hers to his and their tongues danced as their bodies melted together in a sacred union.

In the distance, he heard the sound of a car engine as it turned into the parking lot. No doubt Vicky had arrived for their meeting.

He let go of Avery and kissed her lightly on her forehead. "I'm sorry. I shouldn't have done that."

As she straightened her blouse and ran her fingers through her hair, she said, "No reason to be sorry. I contributed my share. However, I think we both need to review the department's so-called policy on nepotism." She raised an eyebrow and kissed him on the cheek. "That's pretty far down on my list of priorities right now. But we can't make a habit of this."

"To hell with nepotism. That was business, the other half of a kiss you still owed me from the Spring Festival." He lied like a driver being pulled over for a DUI. But oh well, a falsehood was little repentance for his enjoyment. And, he had taken pleasure in their few minutes together, if her body wasn't telling an untruth.

"You're lying." She gave him a light slug to the upper arm. "It's called n-e-p-o-t-i-s-m! Circumstances have changed since the festival."

He chose to act like he ignored the meaning behind her comments, although he'd thought about the policy he presumed was discussed in the meeting Scott had called him out of. He wondered if a kiss was part of favoritism, so he said, "That's a pretty embroidered eyelet blouse you have on."

"I've never known a man who used the words 'embroidered' and 'eyelet' together or even separate. Most don't know embroidery from fishing line," she said as they walked toward the bench where Vicky had settled in.

"You've never raised a little sister without a mother to help out, have you?"

"No. I'm an only child, but that seems to be something I'd like to hear about when we do have show-and-tell time."

They reached Vicky before he could think of a comeback except *to hell with the telling, let's go to the showing!*

Vicky stood up and turned their direction.

"Glad to get your note, Vicky," Brody said, then raised an arm toward Avery. "I don't think you've officially met Sheriff Humphrey."

Vicky extended her hand, "Nice to meet you, Sheriff."

As they shook hands, Avery said, "I'm the interim sheriff and will be until either Deuce gets to where he can return as sheriff or the next election. Please call me Avery. I'd appreciate it."

"Thanks, Avery. I've heard a lot about you from those around town and trust me you no doubt will be a major asset to Bonita County. The county would have never hired you if you didn't know what you are doing."

"Brody filled me in on you, and I believe you are a true success story yourself," Avery said.

Brody enjoyed the sensual, yet proficient smile the sheriff gave him.

"Okay, enough of the *I'll up you and you can up me* stuff. I'm dying to find out what you know, Vic." He shot a smile to one lady, then the other.

Brody took a seat next to Vicky, while Avery sat across the concrete table. A soft breath of a warm breeze favored them.

"I've been hanging around that truck stop for a couple of months now, and something isn't right but I can't put my finger on it yet. Maybe you can, since you have family in the catering business."

"I don't spend a lot of time around them, but what seems out of order? I can always find out from my sister," Brody said.

He glanced across the table. Avery's eyebrows knitted together, and she gave him a questioning look. It was apparent that she didn't realize his sister and brother-in-law owned the Ol' Hickory Inn, but then she didn't eat meat, so she probably had never even shown her face inside the cafe—not to mention the fact they'd moved their operation to Kasota Springs from Amarillo only a few years back.

Brody knew he frowned at his thoughts but couldn't help himself. He was digging as fast as he could through a pile of information that seemed insurmountable.

But what about Deuce's file about Tommy, if he'd had time to write up notes?

There should have been handwritten information inside about Deuce interrogating Tommy Mitchell. Regular protocol would call for writing up such notes. Deuce surely had put in the fact that Tommy was related, although not by blood, to a member of the sheriff's department. On the other hand, with what had gone on that night, it was certainly possible he had written up the notes but never made it to the file before he left to get some fresh air.

Brody rubbed his chin and felt a breath-taking tightness in his chest. He stared at the ground and his thoughts froze in his brain. Lifting his head, he watched the highway traffic. His mind raced, searching for answers that would be acceptable to Avery.

A thought finally seeped through: If that were the case, why hadn't Chief Deputy Scott logged in the notes after the search had concluded and he went back to the office?

Or maybe Danny had been too busy taking over and pounding his chest like Brody had just done trying to be Tarzan, making sure everyone knew the county was in good hands—his hands. Take care of minuscule things like case notes would not have been his priority.

Vicky went on, "Are you listening, Brody?"

"Oh yeah, I'm right with you."

"All in all I've been a believable Lot Lizard, but of course my price is too high or the timing inconvenient for the drivers. I make sure of that." She laughed good-naturedly. "There's one tractor-trailer that perplexes me, and the driver stays away from me like I've got the plague. He drives for what appears a legit company, ABC Smith and Jones out of California. Transports mostly food supplier products, along with some things from a furniture company coming out of Mexico. Everything has been checked out, but the driver always parks far away from the café, gets his order to go, and almost races back to his cab."

"No co-driver?" Brody asked. "And the officers in Laredo or any of the places the rig could be entering the US are very thorough at confiscating drugs coming out of Mexico."

"They are." She bit on her lip. "The dude stands around, eats, and drinks his coffee. I've gone out to talk to him, but he brushes me away with a story about being married, although he doesn't wear a ring. Nobody around seems to even know his name. He's there generally on Thursday."

Vic took a deep breath, then continued, "Somewhere between twenty minutes after he eats, but sometimes over an hour, an unmarked white van parks on the other side of his trailer and the big rig driver pulls out a number of boxes with the same logo as on the side of the trailer from his load and transfers them to the van. At first I thought it was just a driver ripping off his company, but they never exchange any money that I could see. The driver of the white van seems to make an effort to stay in the shadows, out of sight." She took a drink of water from a plastic bottle. "I have more in the car, if you'd like some?"

Avery and Brody shook their heads and thanked her.

The break gave Brody a chance to ask a couple of questions. "Vic, how about license plates? Are they always the same? And the Permanent Trailer ID?"

"Always muddied up. Looks like the truck drove through a pasture full of bull...." She looked over at Avery and said, "Bull manure, or a wet cotton field."

"It's okay to say bullshit. I'm from here and remember dancing to the 'Cotton-Eyed Joe,' one of the best line-dance songs ever written," Avery said.

All three laughed.

Vicky took another swig of water. "I'm surprised the guys who patrol the interstate haven't stopped him for the corroded plates, which makes me believe he messes them up before he stops at the Kasota Truck Stop and cleans them up before he gets back on I-40. When the van gets there, it seems that another person, not always the same, distracts me about being a Lot Lizard, wanting directions, or something that keeps me from getting a view of the license plate or which way the van goes. There are no owner signs or anything to connect the van to any business. He must drive some back route to the southeast or I'd see him. If I ever get where I could get a good view of the van's plates, they are also messed up and I can never see enough of the driver to even tell you more than he's Caucasian, relatively tall, and middle-aged, I'd say."

Believing he'd have his answers to the question he and Vicky had been working on, Brody felt frustrated and had no idea where to turn, but it'd hail volcanic rocks in the Panhandle before he'd admit it to anyone but himself.

"Vic, if you think of anything else, you have my number, and the only other person in this county who knows who you are is Avery, so you can contact her through the department if I'm not available. Thanks for coming and I'll make sure the boss lady here gets your contact information." He hugged Vicky, and she extended her hand to Avery.

Avery stepped forward and gave Vicky a hug. "I look forward to working with you."

"Me, too." Vicky waved. She scurried to her car, looked around her, got in, and drove back to the west, likely Amarillo.

"Let's get out of here." Brody noticed Avery shivering, and he removed his cowboy-cut jacket and put it over her shoulders. He couldn't turn down the opportunity to keep his arms around her longer than he should.

Part of his confidential informant's report fell into place like a good line dance. Other parts unsettled Brody to the point of frustration and added more questions than answers.

When they got near the car, Avery tossed him the keys. "You drive. I think the realization of what I've gotten myself into just hit me. We may be a small town, but there is a lot to digest when it comes to crime." She tightened his jacket around her. "And I thought Houston was bad."

"I know you're tired, so just close your eyes and we'll be at your folks' house in no time." Brody didn't have a chance to open the passenger door for her.

"No. I have things to work on." She pulled the seat belt on and laid her head on the neck rest.

He couldn't be certain if she was fighting sleep or trying to figure out the same things he had on his mind.... Like how in the world did she *not* know about Tommy.

"Just drop me off at the office. I have some things we discovered today that are really bothering me. I know I won't sleep thinking about them. You can leave my car in the drive and drop the keys in the mailbox, unless there's a light on in the kitchen; then you can give them to Jennie."

"Need some help? I've got probably a lot of the same questions," Brody asked.

"Sure. How about changing cars first?"

Brody wasn't certain her "sure" was a positive "sure, I need your help" or "sure, I'm fixin' to kick your ass from the Panhandle to the Gulf of Mexico and back for not telling me that Tommy is a relative"—but then how could she have read the whole file and not known it? He'd been working under the assumption she knew about his family connections from the official file, although neither of them had mentioned it.

He'd even made sure his unofficial investigation information was left in Scott's desk to cover himself, in the event Mesa or Granny Johnson decided to file charges on Tommy for trespassing. Brody had even gone to the extent of mailing a copy to himself for protection.

The trip back to the Humphrey house gave Brody time to give more thought to a few specific pieces of intel Vicky had given them. Add on the information he and Avery learned at the Jacks Bluff, and they now had more loose ends than a weaver without a loom.

Right now one of his biggest questions lay heavy on Brody's mind. Why in the blue blazes would a semi-truck coming out of Laredo on the Mexican border going to Dallas not use I-35 North directly to Dallas, or even if the driver had other stops, why bypass I-10 and I-20 and go out of his way to run on I-40?

The coffee wasn't *that* good at the Kasota Truck Stop!

Chapter 18

Beneath a full Strawberry Moon of June, Brody drove into the back parking lot of the courthouse. He didn't slow down enough going through the street's gutter, and Avery came fully alert.

"Wow." She straightened upright. "Did our street department lift the curb while we were gone?

They shared a deep jovial laugh and got out of the car.

Brody rang the night bell to the rear entrance of the sheriff's department.

Thelma Crawford unlatched the door and greeted them. "I didn't anticipate seeing you all back tonight. It's so quiet I can even hear the gnats hit on the windows."

"That's the kind of night we wish we could have all of the time, but unfortunately, that isn't the way it works," Brody said. He placed his hand lightly in the middle of Avery's back, as any gentleman would.

The interim sheriff added, "Thelma, since Raylynn will come on duty as dispatcher shortly, why don't you go on home?"

"No. I'm fine, plus I need the hours."

"You'll get paid for your whole shift," Avery assured her. "Plus we plan on working for quite a while, and if a call comes in before Raylynn arrives, we can take it. There's really no problem, so please go home."

Brody interceded, "That way we can raid your goody boxes." He smiled at her. "You have no idea how much we appreciate you getting snacks for the department."

Thelma returned the smile. "Collecting coupons is one of my hobbies, and I'm glad to get us some snacks." She picked up her purse and thanked them before she exited through the back door with Brody by her side.

Preparing himself to face his boss, Brody walked back in and followed the scent of fresh coffee grounds to Avery's office.

He stood at the door watching Avery put grounds in the filter to start coffee. Her hotpot steamed, no doubt in preparation for her tea. Guess she anticipated he'd stick around long enough to drink a whole carafe of coffee.

Looking up, she quietly said, "I'm gonna add an extra scoop since it's so late. We need the caffeine." She added more coffee and pushed start before turning to him. "Okay, we promised no lies. So, I'll admit, I lost track because I was thinking about everything that went on today."

"Thanks. Now I have to ask, Sheriff Humphrey, do I sit down so we can talk or lean over to make it easier for you to kick my ass?"

When she didn't respond immediately, Brody took his badge from his inside pocket and removed his service revolver from the holster. He put them in the middle of her desk, where she had butcher paper with colored sticky notes all over it.

"I guess I have my answer," he said before he turned toward her door.

"Although I like the kick in the ass idea, we have work to do, so until I fill in the gaps and make sure the case isn't compromised, please don't pull that stunt about taking off your gun and badge. That's only done in movies and on television. I have a lot of questions. The least important right now is Tommy Mitchell, although you should have told me from the start he was part of your family. At the moment, you are the only person in this department that I totally trust."

Brody found the muscles in his neck and arms turning rigid, and his posture stiffened, while a heavy sensation hit his stomach. He knew this was not the end of the subject, but he had to think through his fuzzy thoughts and keep his mind on whatever kind of weird drawing or map of events she had on the table.

Before she changed her mind, he quickly put his Glock in his holster and his badge back where it belonged.

She spoke first. "I should have asked more questions, and I presume that you figured I knew your family or at least the information was in the case notes." Avery looked up at him with confidence that he'd not seen before. She touched her fingers together, forming a steeple, and flexed them. "Am I wrong or are the notes?"

"Both." He half sat and half stood, learning on the edge of her desk. "I presumed the information was in the file, and since you were born and raised here, I figured someone—especially Danny Scott—would have told you that Tommy was related to me. I would have advised you, if I'd known you didn't have all the facts."

"That's why I trust you, Brody. Either I wasn't given all of the notes, or the evidence file isn't complete, which is a huge problem. And it would have had to have been before anybody knew I got the job." She looked up at him, obviously waiting on his response.

"Definitely left out. Scott brought Tommy in after picking him up near where Deuce was eventually located. This was after the call from the Jacks Bluff that someone was seen in the veterinarian's treatment area," Brody added.

"That's in the notes, but between that information and the search for Deuce is totally blank, as if it had never existed." Avery pointed to a blank area on the timeline.

Avery continued, "You know what...we've had more information and misinformation dumped on us today than probably what the garbage men left at the landfill. So, how about we fix our drinks, talk a while and then head for home? Begin all over again tomorrow. Whatcha think?" Avery lifted herself out of her chair, stepped over to the coffee pot, and poured him a hefty mug of the hot liquid. "No sugar, as I recall."

"That's right, and going home sounds good to me. My mind is fuzzy." He accepted the cup. "Where's your tea?"

"Right here." She sat back down and put her cup on the desk. "Orange and Spice Decaf Herbal Tea."

Raylynn lightly knocked on the door and stuck her head in. "I'm here. Thelma called and said she was leaving a tad early, so since I was ready I came on in. You need anything?"

"Thanks, Raylynn, I appreciate you, but I think we're in good shape."

"Fresh coffee is made," Avery said. "Thanks but I brought something from home." She closed the door.

Brody took a big swig of coffee, and he thought its strength was about to knock him over. He swallowed then said, "That'll sure put lead in my pencil." He felt his face turning red, and it wasn't from the heat of the coffee either. He should have never said anything as uncouth to his boss.

"Well, then you'll be prepared to write a letter tonight." She smiled at him and raised a questioning yet quizzical eyebrow.

Quickly, Brody changed the subject to avoid any further embarrassment. "Let's get out of here. It's been a long day for both of us."

"Frankly, I have to agree with you. I didn't realize exactly how tired I was until I sat down and sorta relaxed." She walked to the counter and turned off the coffee pot. Picking up her purse with a silver Star of Texas on the side, she asked, "Ready?"

"Just about." Out of courtesy, he took another swallow of coffee. "And to help you out from now on, I'll make the coffee."

Only moments later, Brody pulled into the Humphreys' driveway and turned off the engine. "Wake up, you sleepyhead, you're home."

Without a response, he gently touched her arm and unbuckled her seatbelt. Avery leaned into his shoulder and rested her head. He shook her again with no reaction, so he gingerly lifted her head back on the neck rest and got out. "You can go into a deep sleep faster than anyone I know," he whispered.

Avery woke long enough to get out of the car with his help and mumble an apology.

The backdoor leading to the mudroom was open, so he held her tighter around the waist. She laid her head on his shoulder and he helped her up the stairs.

The screen door flew open and a woman came rushing out. Although she wasn't much over five feet tall, she slipped her arm around the other side of Avery's waist.

"I've never known Dannie to drink. Not even in her college days," the woman said then continued, "I'm Jennie, the family housemaid. You're Deputy VanZant, aren't you?"

"Yes, ma'am. I'd shake your hand, but Avery is kinda in the way," he replied to the attractive, middle-aged woman.

"Thank you for taking care of her. Is she sick?" Jennie used her right hand and lifted Avery's chin. "She looks exhausted. I knew this job wouldn't be good for her. I just knew it, after everything she has been through." They left the kitchen and headed toward the staircase. "Her room is upstairs, second on the right. I just knew it was too much, after...."

"Ma'am, she isn't sick or even had anything to drink. I don't know what time she got up, but she was in the office when I got there and it's really late. We've had a long, hard day. After her swearing-in, we immediately began working on cases then drove over and saw Deuce, so she's been on her feet for hours. She's exhausted is all."

"And, she was up early and said she was going into the office and get ready for her swearing-in. And, even for her, it was early-thirty," Jennie said.

They entered a bedroom of white lace and embroidery just like he had imagined after she described her mother's disappointment. Her words "*a room fitting for a cute little debutante in a tutu*" came back to him.

Jennie and Brody got Avery to the bed and he held her upright while the maid removed his jacket from Avery and pulled back the covers.

"Thank you so much, Deputy Van—"

"Please call me Brody."

As they laid Avery on the bed the strangest thoughts came to Brody. Something he hadn't thought about for years—Cinderella and how many times he'd read it to Winnie in order to get her to sleep, particular after they lost their father to a drunk driver while he was on duty as a Texas Ranger. Then their mother took to her room, too sick to take care of her four-year-old daughter and twelve-year-old son. But those were memories he tried to push to the back of his mind. If it hadn't been for his father's death in the line of duty, and football, he would have probably never bonded with Deuce Cowan, who had lost his Denton County sheriff father in the same manner.

Jennie's soft voice broke into Brody's thoughts. "I thank you so much for your help, but I can handle her from here. I know her parents appreciate you, too. Please come back."

"You are welcome. She just needs a little rest and then she'll be a ball of fire by tomorrow, I'm bettin'."

Looking up at him, Jennie smiled. "I think you really know her well. Also, I'm going to make what we call party chicken around here for tomorrow, and I understand you'll be our guest. I hope you like chicken."

"That I do, ma'am." Brody accepted his jacket from Jennie. "I can see she's in good hands, so I'll say goodnight and be on my way."

He wanted so badly to kiss Avery, at least on the forehead, but that would be against all protocol.

Instead, he picked up her pink music box with a white rose on top and turned it on. He also took a long look at a picture of her in her sheriff's uniform. He had to look twice because he couldn't help but think that her hair must grow faster than his. In the picture her hair was extremely short and colored differently. She didn't even look like the woman in the bed he stood next to.

Brody walked down the hall with not only the sound of the *Blue Danube* coming from Avery's room but with six words that stuck in his brain: *after everything she has been through.*

Chapter 19

Avery woke the next morning to the smell of coffee brewing and hot cinnamon buns that only Jennie could make. Avery rolled over into the face of the brilliant rising sun, slightly shadowed by the church bell tower.

After the luxury of a morning shower and washing her hair, which was getting longer by the day, she dressed, put on a light application of make-up, added a pair of tiny gold stud earrings, and headed downstairs.

"Good morning, darling." Her father's booming voice filled the dining room. Before she could respond, he added, "I heard you come in last night, but I was reading in the study so I wouldn't bother your mother. Did you sleep well?"

"Yes, Daddy, I did, but I have to admit I was tired." She added a package of the green stuff to the cup of coffee Jennie placed in front of her. "Thanks, Miss Jennie."

"You're welcome, sweetie." Jennie turned to face Avery's father. "I met Deputy VanZant last night." She bit at her lip as if she'd spoken out of turn.

Avery stirred her coffee. "He brought me home after we took care of some business that had to wait until my swearing-in was over."

"He's so nice and even walked her up to the house, so she'd be safe," Jennie added.

"That's nice." Avery's father balanced his elbows on the table, "What case were you working on, Dannie?"

"Now, Daddy, when I agreed to the job as interim sheriff, I made it abundantly clear that I'd take care of the county's sheriff's department and you'd take care of the town's and county's business. What we're working on is not up for discussion." Avery lifted her chin, feeling proud for standing up to her father on behalf of herself and the sheriff's department. "Please pass the butter."

"You're right, darling. I apologize. It's just that I've always been the one in charge and I'm finding it hard to not overstep boundaries. I'll do much better. I promise." He took a gulp of coffee. "Jennie, did Kathleen talk with you about tonight?"

"Yes, sir, when I went upstairs to take her a breakfast tray."

"What's wrong?" Avery interrupted. "Daddy, Mother usually comes down and joins you for breakfast."

"She's fine. The trip took a lot out of her and her energy level has been pretty low ever since," her father answered. "I'm sorry, sweetheart, but we need to cancel dinner tonight again. Not only is your mother not up to par, but she has a meeting this afternoon for our Relay for Life. It's likely to run longer than expected. I hope you don't mind."

"Of course, I don't mind. That's a good cause and frankly, I wanted to stay late at the office because I've got a lot on my mind. An endless amount of work to do." Avery added a small pad of butter to her cinnamon roll.

"I know one person who'll be unhappy. Deputy VanZant said he loves chicken, and that's what I planned," Jennie inserted.

"I'll handle Brody." Avery smiled to herself, thinking about the hot cop.

After a second cup of coffee, scrambled eggs, and finishing off her cinnamon roll, Avery said good-bye to her father and kissed him on the forehead then hugged Miss Jennie, the woman who had been with the family since before Avery was born.

She left for the office in probably the oldest vehicle in the county's fleet, but she didn't mind. Now wasn't the time to pull rank. Not after only twenty-four hours on the job, on top of the disarray that had occurred with Deuce being out for two months already.

Thoughts of a more suitable county vehicle crossed Avery's mind. Deuce's crew-cab was still in the county's impoundment area in case they needed to check for any additional trace evidence. That was, if they ever narrowed down the suspect list.

In less than five minutes, she pulled into the parking lot at the same time as Brody.

After they had exchanged greetings, she said, "Brody, thanks for making sure I got home safe." They walked to the entrance at the back of the sheriff's department. "I hate to even tell you this, but we've got to cancel dinner tonight again. Mother has a meeting in Amarillo."

"That's no problem." He had a very serious look on his face. She bet she could win a bucket-load of cash if she put money on him losing sleep over what they had learned the evening before from his CI. "What are your plans for today?"

"I was going to ask you the same thing." She turned to face him. "I have something I want you to look at, if you have time. It's on Deuce's case."

"Sure. As soon as I check for messages with dispatch and my phone, I'll come to your office."

"No. I want to meet you on the second floor in the vacant interrogation room. Alone, nobody else with you, please. I've not shared this with anybody and don't want to until we're finished with it."

By the questioning look in his eyes, she felt she owed him more of an explanation. She rubbed the back of her neck and said, "You won't be sorry, or at least I hope you won't."

* * * *

Brody stared directly at her face, and the early morning sun shone against her green eyes, making them sparkle like emeralds.

"I have my reasons," she said.

He opened the door for her and couldn't help but think that the woman not only looked strong and feisty but also was as pretty as anything he'd ever seen in his life. The thought of holding her in his arms and making love in a field of beautiful Texas Bluebonnets crossed his mind. He attempted to erase the vision as quickly as it flashed before his eyes.

Dummy, there are no Bluebonnets in the Texas Panhandle!

After checking in, Brody did as he was asked.

When he opened the door to the vacant and large conference room turned into an extra interrogation room, sometimes referred to as their third interrogation room. It hadn't been used in years to his knowledge. As he entered, shock couldn't even begin to describe how he felt. On the large conference room table, Avery had laid out cards with names, times, locations, and evidence written on them and had them taped to a five-foot piece of butcher paper. Not only were index cards used, but colored ones to boot. *Now, this is one organized lady.*

"Come on in. I began a timeline of events based on the case file. I did most of the work in my bedroom at home a couple of days ago, but I want to see what you think." She smoothed the paper like she might a silk scarf and began talking him through her process.

Brody stood behind her, way too close for his comfort, but it was the only way he could see, since she had spread her arms out on the table, leaning in.

There was one thing for certain: this was going to be an emotionally charged exhibit in more ways than one. He looked over her shoulder.

"The festival ended at eleven, and you and Deuce were helping to clean up and take down booths." She pointed to the first card in the left-hand corner, making her bottom press against his.

Brody wasn't sure if he could get through the investigative process without throwing her on the table and taking advantage of his boss. Hell, fire and brimstone, pass the matches.... What was he thinking?

"At 12:32 a.m., according to the dispatcher log, Mesa got a call from her foreman. I can verify that because I was with Mesa and Deuce's wife at the Buckin' Bull Saloon. About the same time Mesa got a call from Deuce." She reached down a little and seemingly didn't realize what she was physically doing to Brody by squirming around.

"Okay, I'm with you so far, and can verify that I was with Deuce until around 3:00 a.m. here in the office," he said.

She took a card out of the pack, wrote the information on it, and began to move things down, having to re-tape the card each time. "I'm sorry this is taking so long, but this is all I had to work with and I really have my reasons for not wanting anyone else involved at this time. Once I agreed to be named to this position, I began working on this project." She exhaled. "I believe I have the only key to this room, or that's what I was told when it was turned over to me. I was warned that it was the only one, so be careful to keep it safe."

"Thelma?" He twisted his head in her direction and leaned against the wall. "You mean Thelma knew you were going to be named the new sheriff?"

The look on her face told him everything. "I didn't have time to lose and she was sworn to secrecy. No doubt she's on our team and can be trusted."

The sheriff continued, "There are now notes in the file that indicate Deuce was interrogating Tommy Mitchell. The file doesn't say who he is, but now I know. You helped by telling me Deuce was here with Mitchell. Two minds are better than one, so don't hesitate speaking out," she said, as if he'd ever not put in his two cents when appropriate. "Who else was here?"

"The night dispatcher, Raylynn. Of course, because of the Spring Festival, Danny Scott and the night deputy, Jessup, were both on duty." He stopped to get his thoughts in order. "They were in and out. I recall one time, Deuce told them to check on the partygoers, so they were both gone for a while—Scott much longer, I'm positive—a whole bunch longer."

Avery looked up, shook her head a tad as if trying to organize the information. "You, Deuce, and Mitchell, along with the dispatcher." She stared at the timeline. "I've already received the information from the helicopter pilot." She continued to look intently. "Surely, Scott used a map for his coordinates during the search."

"He did. I saw it myself." Brody closed his eyes at the thought of having to remember the events of the night. "There was an area he didn't have marked off as being covered. I asked about it and he said he'd forgotten to write who had it covered." His thoughts intensified, and he shivered at them. "The more I think about it, the more I believe it was near, if not exactly, where Deuce was located."

"That's interesting." Avery lowered herself into a straight-back chair and covered her eyes with her hands. "Where could the map be?" Avery almost whispered the question. "And why isn't it in the file?"

The dispatcher's voice interrupted his thoughts. "Detective VanZant, there's someone here to see you." Thelma's voice sounded soft and a bit on the sensual side, not anything like her typical tone over the intercom.

"I can't imagine who it is, but guess I'd best go downstairs and leave you with your thoughts." Brody got up, unlocked the door, and walked downstairs, only to be met by Thelma on the landing.

"What's wrong?" Brody asked, fearing for the worst. "Who wants to see me?" A slight shock ran up and down his spine at the glazed-over look in the dispatcher's eyes.

"Oh..." She swallowed hard. "Nothing's wrong. He's—he's, well, he's absolutely breathtakingly handsome with wide shoulders. Beautiful brown eyes, like the color of a newborn calf. He's so tan, it's ridiculous. Obviously not from this neck of the woods. Dark sun-bleached hair...oh and did I mention he has a service dog with him. His name is—"

"Marion Frances Robertson, 'Rocky' to you.... Our new deputy. And I'm going to recommend to the sheriff that you become a detective the way you can describe someone as well as you did in only a few seconds." Brody shot her a smile, hoping she realized he wasn't chastising her, and headed into the outer office. Over his shoulder he said, "Thanks, Thelma. Appreciate you."

Brody opened the door to the outer offices for Thelma only to come face-to-face with the larger-than-life fugitive specialist and Bonita County's newest recruit, Rocky Robertson. At his heels obediently sat his K-9 multi-purpose dog.

He quickly introduced Rocky and Thelma. The dispatcher returned to her office, and Brody could see redness he'd never seen before on her neck. She was obviously impressed by their newest deputy.

"Hey, you old ton of bricks, I'd come over and give you a shot to the arm and hug, but I'm afraid that Malinois pooch there would make sure I didn't have an arm, or leg for that matter, to hug anybody again." Brody knew better than to make any sudden moves without Rocky giving his service dog the appropriate gesture.

"Happy to be here finally. Glad to introduce you to my best friend, Bruiser." Rocky gave the K-9 on a leash a treat, signaling that everything was okay.

"I didn't expect you until next week. Got a place to stay?"

"Didn't take time to get an apartment, but figure I could do that once I got here. Got all of mine and Bruiser's stuff in the SUV," Rocky said.

"You're more than welcome to stay out at the ranch." Brody reached into his pocket and retrieved a set of keys. At first, he gave consideration to tossing them at Rocky, but on second thought, knowing any unforeseen movements could make Bruiser think his handler was in jeopardy, he laid them on the table. "In between the madness that's been going on, I did find time to make arrangements to get the headquarters cleaned. You'll know my room by the unmade bed, but there are four more to choose from. All clean." Brody leaned on the side of the table. "I don't have a lot of food, but have Bud in the fridge and Black Jack in the cabinet. You probably want to go by the GreenMart to pick up anything you want and I'll reimburse you."

"Thanks, I'll take you up on bunking with you, but I'll pay my own way," Rocky said.

"There's lots of land and a big dog run for Bruiser," Brody replied. "But now we need to get you introduced to the sheriff."

"She's here?"

"Always." Brody walked the few feet to the dispatcher's area and was surprised that the door was closed. He opened it and asked Thelma to page the sheriff. He smiled at himself, just thinking about Avery's surprise at being paged over the intercom for the first time. The offices were so small that a person could holler and be heard in the attic.

Thelma's loud, yet womanly voice boomed throughout the building.

"While we wait for Sheriff Humphrey, let's go into my office." Once Rocky took a seat with Bruiser at his feet, Brody continued, "I'm a little surprised at the K-9." He hesitated then further explained himself. "He's really good-lookin' and obviously he's your pal."

"Deuce authorized him to join the department, and I just presumed you knew. Bruiser is getting up in age, but he's certainly not ready for retirement. As all handlers and dog teams are, we're pretty inseparable, so I bought him. He goes everywhere with me, and if I tried to force him into retirement, I'm afraid he wouldn't make it very long. We've been together for a while now."

"He's good-lookin' for sure." Brody leaned against the credenza. "So, a bounty hunter is now called a fugitive specialist out in California?"

"Only when we are still a part of law enforcement." Rocky let out a deep, jovial laugh that fit his bigger-than-life personality. "After being in the Air Force and then working as a C.O. at Lompoc Federal Prison, I needed to try my wings. You know I don't like to be tied down. Once I worked on Deuce's wife's problem a couple of years back, I got the yearning, so here I am...still in law enforcement. I want the bad guys off the street," Rocky explained.

Sheriff Avery Humphrey knocked and immediately opened the door to Brody's office. After an introduction, she accepted the chair he offered her and the three began a friendly discussion, getting to know one another.

"Your reputation preceded you, Deputy Robertson. As I understand it, Sheriff Cowan hired you and swore you in while he was out in California talking you into coming out to Texas." She smiled then said, "You sure do look like you will fit in, and I have no doubts about your abilities."

"Thank you, Sheriff Humphrey. I already knew Deuce and more about VanZant than I want to know. I feel very welcomed and comfortable."

Avery looked over at the dog. "And what do we call him?"

"Most folks think of him as Killer, but he's Bruiser. A dual-purpose K-9, drugs and tracking; he's so driven and highly motivated that I can use him for other things. He's been known to alert me to a thing before I even knew for sure what we were looking for. He believes he's smarter than his owner."

Bruiser turned his head from side to side as if to say, *You ain't kiddin' me!*

Feeling the vibration of his phone, Brody took it out of his pocket and looked at the caller ID. *Rainey Cowan!*

"Excuse me just a minute, it's Rainey and I think I should take it." He stepped away from his desk and answered.

"Rainey, please Rainey, talk slower. I can't understand you. Please." He stopped and listened intently.

Through her crying, all he could hear was, "Deuce...Deuce. Please come, Brody. I need you. Please, please come."

With that, the phone went dead.

A panic like nothing he'd experienced in a long time flushed through Brody. With a pounding heart and a dry mouth, he managed to get out, "Something is wrong with Deuce. Terribly wrong. We've got to get to Amarillo *now*."

Chapter 20

As if a vampire suddenly sucked all the blood out of Avery, she folded her hands in her lap, not sure what to say. Yet, at the same time, she realized as the interim sheriff she had choices to make.

Pulling up from her chair, she rubbed her hands on her pant legs, and with a dry mouth she looked at Deputy Robertson, who gripped the chair arm. She couldn't help but notice his knuckles were clinched in a fist.

Brody paced, obviously in an effort to calm himself. He glanced up at her with eyes that reeked of pain.

Again, Avery reminded herself that for the time being she was the one in charge and decisions were on the line. The one thing she had no choice in was getting to Amarillo as quickly as possible.

She broke the suffocating silence. "Rocky, I presume Deuce didn't give you a service weapon and badge." She ran her hand down her pant leg again.

"No, ma'am."

"I'll be right back," she said as she exited Brody's office.

In only seconds, she returned with a Glock and his badge and handed them to Rocky Robertson. "Welcome to Bonita County." Her words were very audible, but the concern and worry about Rainey's call and Deuce's condition only made her mouth drier.

"Thank you, Sheriff."

"Interim sheriff, but please call me Avery." She took a dry swallow and focused on Brody. "The three of us will be working very closely together, so I think first names used when we're not in public is just one less thing we need to worry about."

She forced a smile toward Rocky then settled on Brody.

"I'm going to the hospital with you." She held her hand up, stopping any discussion. "Rocky, you are welcome—"

"I was by there on my way in," he said. "So why don't you two go, and if it's okay with you I'll let Thelma introduce me around to the other deputies and fill me in on some of the procedures."

"Sure, Rocky." She pointed to a bookcase outside the dispatcher's office. "The Bonita County Sheriff's Department Procedural Manual is there." She looked over at Brody. "But don't pay any attention to the nepotism section because it's outdated. Thelma can assist you, if you need help. I've got to run upstairs and get my purse and I'll be ready to go."

"Thank you, Sheriff...I mean Avery."

As she walked away, Brody said, "You got the keys to the ranch headquarters, and we'll stay in touch with you. You and Bruiser can get all settled in while we find out what has happened to Deuce." He bit at his lip. "Rocky, I'm gonna level with you. I'm as worried as hell. I'm afraid the news is bad."

"I'm with you and Sheriff Humphrey all the way."

Avery took two more steps and turned out of earshot.

She couldn't help but think the perp-walk from a cell to the area a prisoner is executed couldn't be as long as her and Brody's from the back door of the courthouse through the parking lot.

After closing the passenger door, Avery watched him round the vehicle and wished they both had a cup of strong coffee. No doubt, neither person wanted to carry on an inconsequential conversation while their friend could be dying or, worse yet, had already passed and they weren't there for him or Rainey.

"I'm sorry, Brody, but not only has the call from Rainey consumed me, but I keep going over and over in my mind everything we know about how he was hurt." She rubbed her cheek, again and again, before she continued, "I know I shouldn't be, but Brody, I'm horrified that we might have a murder case on our hands."

"And you don't think that's been on my mind?" he said in a deadpan voice and gripped the wheel tighter. "I'm sorry, that didn't come out the way I meant it."

"You don't need to apologize. I understand and that isn't even fair, because no, I don't understand. I know if Deuce had been a friend of mine as long as he's been one of yours, I'd feel much differently. Trust me...."

She wanted so badly to retract what she had said and change it to *Hell yes, I know exactly what you're going through.*

More thoughts flooded through her. She pulled her uniform jacket over her chest, keeping her arms folded across her body.

Oh my Lord, I'm trying to hide from telling Brody the truth. Eventually, the whole world will know that I got my partner killed, and Brody and I are partners. She hung her head and tightened the grip on her jacket. *I've got to tell him the truth or we can't work together. We promised no secrets, and I'm holding the biggest one of my life deep inside of me—not being truthful to a good man like him. I don't have any choice but to tell him tonight, especially if something happened to Deuce.*

An unnatural silence spread like wildfire in the cab of Brody's pickup.

"I hope you don't mind, but I'm going to lay my head back and rest a little." She hesitated before beginning again. "That is unless you'd like for me to drive. I know you're mentally exhausted."

"Hey, get a little rest, I think we're probably thinking about the same thing."

Don't bet the ranch on that one or you'll be sleeping on a cot in the Bonita County hoosegow!

The mellow music on the radio cradled her thoughts, and she closed her eyes thinking about more things than any one person should have on their mind in a week, much less a day.

Rolling a little to her left side, she watched Brody, who had an unnatural stiffness in his body and a gloomy look on his face. She couldn't help but feel sympathy for the man, who had maneuvered himself into her heart at the right time, making it possible for her to desire moving on with her life.

To break the thought of assuming the worst-case scenario, she straightened up in the passenger seat. "I've been thinking. We've got too big of a timeline to work with on Deuce's accident." She carefully chose the last word, hoping the word she had in mind didn't come true. To be optimistic, she said, "So, when we get back, how about going by the GreenMart and picking up some corkboards where we can lay out everything more clearly. We need to upgrade some things in the office, and that would be a beginning."

"I kinda like your colored cards and sticky notes."

"Don't try to fool me, VanZant, you hate them."

"I wouldn't say hate, but—"

"But...you agree whiteboards would be better." She shot a smile at him, although the seriousness in his eyes was oh so distracting.

"I've got a better idea. I've got several whiteboards stored in my sister's storage building at the café. I'll donate them and you can tape cards, as long as they are colored, and use sticky notes to your heart's desire."

"Sounds good. Let's see how the afternoon goes and then make a decision." She watched a tight smile cross his face. The first real one she'd seen since he'd received the call from Rainey. "Oh, there's the turnoff to the hospital." She picked up her purse, ready to get out as soon as they parked.

In short order and with a weary mind and more concern than she'd felt in a long time, the elevator door opened onto Deuce's floor. With legs that felt hobbled, she walked toward Deuce's room with Brody holding her upper arm.

"When did that happen?" Deuce asked, in a reserved voice, as he pointed to the Lubbock County deputy sitting outside Deuce's door.

"I'm sorry. I should have told you, but after we talked to Teg, I called in a favor. There was so much going on yesterday that I didn't think to tell you. I called Lubbock after you left my house last night. Sorry." She hoped he'd understand, under the circumstances.

They both said hello and Brody shook hands with the deputy.

Avery said, "We'll be here for a while, so why don't you take a break?"

"Yes, ma'am. Thank you, ma'am." The young deputy pulled to his feet and headed toward the stairwell.

Brody knocked softly, and when they didn't hear a response, he slowly opened the door.

Avery said a silent prayer.

The sheriff lay in the same position as the last time they had been there, flat on his back with tubes attached to every part of his body.

Rainey sat in the chair next to his bed holding his hand with her head on his chest. When she heard them, she looked up with unreadable eyes. She put her index finger to her lips, indicating quietness.

Brody half lifted her out of the chair as she collapsed against his chest and broke out crying.

As much as Avery didn't want to think about it, there were a few benefits being in law enforcement provided, and one definitely was knowing the difference in a breathing soul and one who has passed. Deuce's chest heaved in a regular manner. She turned her head away from everything and stared out the window.

Oh, God, please, God, this can't be the time Rainey has to make the decision to turn off the machines keeping him alive. Please, Lord, please!

"Rainey, I know this is hard, but tell me what is going on with Deuce. We're both here for you...and Deuce. Please tell me—" Brody asked in a soft, caring voice.

"Oh Brody, I need your help," Rainey said, still leaning against his chest for support. "I'm so glad you are here."

"I'm glad I am too. Do we need to go outside to talk?" he asked.

"No. Oh, no." She shook her head several times. "No, we've got to stay right here."

Avery tried hard to take long, deep breaths to remain composed. She must be right. No doubt from Rainey's words, the time had come.

"See." Rainey took Deuce's hand and put it in Brody's. "See."

Brody glanced from one woman to another then down at his friend, who tried desperately to open his eyes. "I feel some movement," he said in a low, composed voice.

"Darling, you've got visitors," Rainey said and then continued, "How about you open your eyes and he'll do most of the talking, but now that he knows you can hear him, you can listen." She squeezed her husband's hand with purpose. "Deuce, darlin', please."

"Umm," Deuce replied, opened his eyes slightly and grunted. "Hunka, hunka superstud." He closed his eyes.

"Man, I'm so happy I could pick both of you girls up and kiss you." He smiled at Rainey. "I think I'll just do that."

He pulled Avery to her feet, hugged her, and turned to Rainey where he did the same.

"Brody and Avery, you have no idea how happy I was when they began taking him out of the coma." She returned to her chair, while the others stood on the opposite side of the bed. "I know I was crying when I called, but it wasn't until much later that I realized you likely took the tears wrong. They were of happiness. I wanted to surprise you." She glanced directly at Avery. "I'm so sorry I scared you."

"I wasn't...okay, since we're now officially friends, I was scared, but I certainly wasn't going to allow Mister," she turned to Brody and tilted her head. "What was he saying...*Hunka hunka superstud?*"

"That's a joke between Deuce and me," Brody said.

"Okay, Superstud, how about giving you and the sheriff some time alone." She looked across the bed at Rainey. "How about some coffee?"

"That sounds great. And I apologize for being so emotional. That's not me, but I guess when it comes to someone you love, it's okay."

Avery responded, "More than okay." She grabbed her purse from the nearby window shelf and nodded to Brody before the two women exited.

As she pulled the door to, she glanced up and caught Brody's eye. He smiled at her, and she knew how much he wanted to get them out so he could talk with Deuce alone.

He picked up Deuce's hand once again.

Maybe, just maybe, he'd have some of the answers to fill in the blanks.

* * * *

Once the ladies were gone, Brody laid Deuce's hand on the bed and went around and sat down in Rainey's chair.

"Hey, you ol' SOB, you've scared the livin' hell out of all of us." Brody figured his friend only absorbed bits and pieces of what he said, but he knew he needed to just talk. Talk about anything and everything, so Deuce would stay alert as much as possible. Brody also knew the sheriff likely couldn't answer any questions, but there was one on the tip of Brody's tongue that he had to ask.

Deuce said something so low that Brody couldn't understand him, so he leaned down with his ear close to Deuce's mouth.

"What?"

The word that came out of his friend's raspy throat almost caused Brody to keel over with shock. Sweat surfaced and settled on his forehead. His heart beat out of control—and if the one word meant what Brody thought it meant, the Bonita County Sheriff's Department had a serious problem on its hands.

Continuing to hold Deuce's hand, Brody asked softly, "Is that the person who tried to hurt you?"

"Kill."

"You are certain that it was intentional?" Brody had to make sure he was correct.

Deuce nodded. "Murder. Tried to." He closed his eyes.

Letting go of his hand, Brody slowly lowered himself in the chair, while his mind felt like a zillion butterflies on exhibit at the zoo.

"Oh my God, no." He lowered his head in his hand. "Please God, please. This cannot be."

Chapter 21

Avery and Rainey stepped off the elevator, expressing to one another how happy they felt finding out Deuce was coming out of his medically induced coma successfully. Hot tea and a small serving of apple cobbler, plus their conversation, seemed to do the trick, making them both feel everything was going to be okay.

To Avery's surprise, as they turned toward Deuce's hospital room, she saw Brody plastered against the wall, legs planted wide apart. He held his right arm against his sweaty forehead. He glared into open space then turned on his heels and slammed his fist into the wall.

"What's wrong?" Avery said, then quickly added, "Did something happen to Deuce?" When she was in front of him, she grabbed his arm and pulled him away from the door. "What in the hell happened?" She saw that the veins in his neck quivered, making her own heart pound against her chest. Too many questions came across her mind so fast she didn't know what to ask next, but mustered up, "Is Deuce okay?"

Brody appeared to settle down a bit and said, "He's fine. I just got a call that made me mad. I lost control for a minute, but it's better to hit the wall and pay the damages than to come through the phone and strangle someone."

Avery knew her eyebrows knitted together, and by the relief on Rainey's face, she began to calm down herself.

"I'm going to go on in, if everything is okay." Rainey turned to Brody. "If I can help in any way, just let me know. I appreciate you coming." She laid a hand on his arm. "And, again, I apologize for making it sound like something bad had happened when in truth all of our prayers and wishes were answered."

Not waiting on Brody's response, Rainey smiled at Avery. "And you have no idea how much I appreciate you. The ol' saying *Make new friends, but keep the old* is certainly true." She hugged Avery, then Brody.

Knowing something seriously was wrong with Lt. Detective Brody VanZant, Avery said, "I wonder how long the guard will be gone. I think we need to hit the road. We've got a lot of work to do, and I'm so thankful that Deuce is better." She smiled at Brody, who again stood with his legs planted wide apart. "Do you need to say good-bye to Deuce?"

"No," he snapped at her. "I said adios before I took the, uh, call." His tone came across more calm, but she couldn't see the rationale of his going into a rage in front of others. Those weren't the actions of the lawman she had gotten to know over the last few weeks.

In only minutes the door to the stairwell opened and the deputy returned.

Neither said anything on the walk to Brody's vehicle. Deafening silence filled the truck as they pulled out of the hospital's parking lot.

All Avery thought about was what could have happened to infuriate and hurt Brody so badly. Obviously, he didn't want to share anything with her at the moment. Even little comments she made did not seem to penetrate his thoughts.

"Okay, guy, I don't know what happened, but if it's something I can help with, shoot." She rested her hands in her lap. When he didn't respond, she added, "Is it anything we need to talk about as partners or as a team?"

A long silence followed before he said, "Oh, we need to talk, okay. Until I get my bearings together, I don't want to say anything because it'd be jumping to conclusions." He gripped the steering wheel tighter, much in the same way he did his lips.

"Just answer one question, and I promise to leave you alone." She didn't give him a chance to challenge her. "Is it private or business?"

"Let's just say I learned something that affects both of us. A secret we both suspected but couldn't talk about." He stared ahead at the road. "And I'm mad at myself for not seeing the truth before now."

Avery closed her eyes and tried to swallow, but her mouth felt as dry as the Mojave Desert. *He's found out that I got my partner killed...and he hates me for not trusting him enough to tell him the truth.*

"Okay, let's stop at the Flying R truck stop coming up, so we can talk," she said.

"That's a good idea. I need a cup of coffee since I can't drink on duty." His tone sounded flat and pointed.

After they settled in a booth across from one another, Brody ordered coffee and Avery hot tea. The only sounds being made were the noises of the truck stop.

"Okay. You were right about not trusting anybody in the department. And now I know why." He took the spoon off the saucer and put it on his napkin. "Do you want to go first?"

Not sure whether the words could come out or not, Avery began, "Brody, I'm sorry that I didn't tell you this before now, but I came to Kasota Springs with a heavy heart and very damaged." She couldn't look him straight in the eyes, so she focused on the clock on the wall. "I figured sooner or later you'd learn about what happened in Houston either through gossip or through the internet." She turned her eyes down straight into Brody's face. All she saw was a questioning look in his eyes and a face without any expression.

"I'm not following you, Avery," he said. "I rarely look at the internet, as it has a lot of nonsense and misinformation."

"I understand. There's more to the story than you'd ever read on the internet, and you can't depend on gossip. But, I do want to explain.... I'm guilty. I got my partner killed because he was trying to protect me and I froze. I couldn't get off the shot, and—"

"Avery, I don't know what you're talking about. You're not the problem, and I haven't heard any gossip. Since you started, tell me whatever you want me to know." He got up and moved across to the bench where she sat. Resting his arm across the back, he took her hand. "I'm here for you and always will be."

Her mind went into a whirl and her heart beat out of control. The feel of his hand holding hers seemed to settle her stomach.

For what seemed like an eternity, she told him everything about the death of her partner, Lee. For the first time since the incident, she talked about what happened with emotion but not the feeling of guilt. She spoke to him as one peace officer would to another after a crisis. Almost in a therapeutic way.

After she finished, she turned slightly toward Brody and looked into the most sympathetic eyes she'd ever seen in her life. Suddenly, he lowered his head and kissed her lightly on the lips.

"You have no idea how much it means that you shared your experience, fears, and guilt with me." He kissed her again but this time he lifted her hand to his lips. "You do realize you could have gone through your whole career without divulging any part of Lee's death?"

"Eventually someone would have found out, and then I'd might be fired. From the looks of things, Deuce could be back in the saddle before the next general election. I'm so thrilled." Relief for telling Brody about Lee overwhelmed her, as her heart pounded even harder than when she began her story. "But, I do want to make sure you realize that when I went back to Houston for those two days, although I did need to check on my apartment, I also received my final clearance to go back out in the field. All restrictions were removed and I was deemed able to return to active duty. I'm happy to be interim sheriff, but hope and pray Deuce will return."

Brody kissed her hand again and returned to the bench across from her. "What will you do if that happens?" He didn't wait on a reply. "Can you accept being the second in charge?"

"Well, first off, you're assuming a lot. There's still Chief Deputy Scott in that spot, so I'd be happy being just a deputy."

"You're not going to have to worry about Danny Scott."

Not sure she understood what Brody meant, she turned her head from side to side. "Why wouldn't I have him to worry about?"

Patiently she waited for his response, which took a few seconds, as if he needed to weigh each word carefully. "First off, you may fire me when I tell you what I did—then there will definitely be an opening." He took a gulp of his coffee, which now had to be only lukewarm.

"We promised no secrets, so let loose. Right now I'm still in the position to hire and fire, so don't you dare pull that crap about putting your service weapon and badge on the table. You'd scare the living crap out of the people in here."

"Deuce told me who tried to kill him, and I took some actions you might not approve of, because they should have been your call...not mine."

Avery thought she might choke on her tea. "What in the hell are you talking about?"

His eyes darkened with emotion. "Deuce told me that Danny Scott tried to—"

"Kill him!"

Brody nodded his head then closed his eyes, as if he didn't want to see her expression.

"On my God." She reached for her purse. "I've got to call—"

It was his turn to interrupt her. "No. Let me explain. Scott didn't show up for his shift and nobody, including me, could locate him. Raylynn called and told me. She also said Rocky and Jessup located his county SUV in the parking lot, so they went out to his house. He was nowhere to be found. Mail was there, plus two newspapers and they said the neighbors hadn't seen him for several days. Now this is where I took liberties that should be reserved for you and you alone." Again he took a sip of coffee, probably waiting for her response.

The shock of what Brody had said so far almost made her dizzy. She rubbed her throat, hoping to dislodge the burning sensation she felt before she touched her lips. If she could make it to the ladies' room she would, just to have time to let everything Brody said sink in, but that wasn't possible. She must hear the remainder of what she had to know.

"So what liberties did you take?"

"I know I'm trying to justify going over your head when I shouldn't, but as you know I'm a very proactive type of officer. I saw the time flying by, and we need a search warrant, so I called Judge Humphrey—"

"My Uncle Charles?" She realized her mouth flew open with surprise, but after a quick second thought she realized he'd done what he should have under the circumstances. Rainey didn't need to be upset any more than was necessary.

"Yes, your uncle, but I thought time was of the essence." He looked down at the table and back up at her.

"Okay. Let's not get into the who should have done what. You have that authority and took action when it was timely. So, go on." She crossed her arms across her chest, knowing she should be peeved but wasn't.

"While you and Rainey were gone, Deuce said *Scott* and when I asked him if Scott had hurt him, he whispered, *Murder*. That's when I realized Danny Scott didn't just try to hurt him, but made a deliberate attempt on his life." Brody twisted his coffee cup a tad.

"My mind is going crazy, thinking back over the timeline and the evidence missing from Scott's notes." The desire to get back to Kasota Springs and begin further research began to consume her, but she mustered up, "You did the right thing about getting a search warrant. Let's get out of here before it's too late to go by my uncle's chambers. Guess I need to call him Judge Humphrey henceforth."

"No, I don't think so. He's still your uncle. Just like you told me, what is said behind closed doors and how you address someone in public is different." He pulled some bills from his pants pocket and laid them on the table. "Let's get out of here."

Regardless of how hard Avery tried to digest the information, she felt as trapped as a fly on sticky paper.

"Brody, you realize the word of a person in Deuce's condition isn't enough to file charges or arrest Scott, so we have to have someone, anyone, who might know something. To confirm Deuce's accusation. Or at least have plenty of reason."

"I know."

Once they were on the road, she made two calls. One to her uncle, where she told him they'd be back in town in an hour. The second, using the speakerphone, a conference call with Robertson and Jessup, asking them to begin a search around town for Scott. She made a point not to tell them why. Surprise hit her hard when Jessup said, "I think I know why we can't find him."

"What do you think?" She found it hard to ask the question.

"Sylvie told me that when she was at the hospital earlier, Deuce was being taken out of his coma and had whispered a few words. I don't know why Scott didn't show up for work, but I suspect he's afraid of what might happen to his position once Deuce is able to talk. He likes his job too much—rather, he'd love to have your job. The one he thinks he was passed over for."

"I'm losing you guys, but you might be right. We'll be back in town very soon." She disconnected.

"So? What do you think?" she said again.

"I think they know exactly what is going on." He seemed to have relaxed a bit. "I guess Rocky won't ever forget his first day on the job."

"With his investigative tendencies, he probably had it figured out without a timeline. He's one cool dude," she said before testing the waters. "I've been giving thought to talking to Tommy Mitchell. I believe he knows more than he's telling. Probably is afraid Scott would pull him in as an accomplice. It'd be the word of a kid fresh out of the slammer versus that of a peace officer."

"Remember the whiteboards?" He flashed a whimsical smile at her, obviously changing the subject. "How about after we go pick up the search warrant? I have to sign the affidavit anyway and see what Jessup and Rocky have found out; then we can make a jaunt over to my sister's café. We could go to the storage building and get the boards. It'll also serve as an excuse to talk with Tommy."

"Sounds good to me. I know we've got to get more proof if in fact Scott is involved, or we can't arrest him. I've got so many thoughts running through my head that I can't even think straight." She swallowed hard before continuing, "That's a really good idea. Clearly a new timeline posting from scratch would provide an assurance that we have the right perp." She closed her eyes and in a low voice said, "I never thought I'd ever have to use that word on one of our own. I hope to hell the deputies locate that bastard Danny Scott."

"You've used more profanity today than you have the whole time I've known you."

"You ain't seen nuttin' yet!" A tad of relaxation hit her, but not enough to clear her muddled mind.

Avery's phone began to ring with the tone she'd set for the sheriff's department. Quickly, she grabbed her purse, retrieved the phone, and answered.

After listening to the dispatcher, she said, "Do not under any circumstances let him leave. Take whatever actions necessary to detain him. We'll be there in just a few minutes." The dispatcher acknowledged, then Avery reiterated, "I mean under no circumstance is he to leave."

Chapter 22

Brody wished he and Avery had taken one of the county vehicles with lights, because he would definitely be *lighting 'em up* to get to the office faster...and he hadn't even asked Avery for detail about how Danny Scott had gotten to the office.

His thoughts wandered between Danny Scott and the shocking information that only a couple of words from Deuce confirmed so much.

From the look on Avery's face and the way she fidgeted with her phone, he had little doubt she wanted to be left with her thoughts.

Not able to stand it any longer, he asked, "Scott turned himself in?" Brody tried his hardest to keep his mind on his driving.

"I only wish," she eventually said in a hoarse voice and waited for what seemed like an hour to continue, "Brody, I can't tell you what's going on right now. When we get to the station, you will understand." She crinkled her brow. "It'd be irresponsible of me as interim sheriff to tell you anything right now. You're too close to the investigation, and I can't take a chance on compromising the case until I find out more." She looked straight at him, and he glanced her way. "I'm so sorry; I only wish I could tell you what is going on. Brody, if you don't believe another word I say, please have faith in me that it has nothing to do with trusting you. It's me trying my best to follow the letter of the law."

A painful tightness hit his throat. He opened his mouth but no words came out. He felt a shock of disbelief thinking Avery would cut him out of Scott's investigation.

A weary, tense quietness filled the air in the cab of the pickup, while Brody tried his best to think things through about Scott without dredging up history that would serve no purpose.

The remainder of the drive intensified as Avery pilfered through her purse and applied lipstick but mostly remained silent, looking straight ahead with her hands in her lap.

Once they pulled into the courthouse parking lot, Avery said, "Brody, I don't expect you to understand, but please come with me to get the search warrant for any and all of Scott's property. Plus, you'll have to sign the affidavit, since you heard what Deuce said that implicated Scott."

After picking up the paperwork, Brody and Avery went down the back stairs and walked a few feet toward their department's entrance.

"I know this is strange, but I don't want anyone in the department to know about the warrant, so walking across the hall is out," Avery explained.

The moment they arrived at the sheriff's department, they were met at the back door by Deputy Jessup. "He's in Room One waiting on you."

"No problems detaining him?" Avery asked.

"None." Jessup turned and over his shoulder said, "He was very compliant...to my surprise." He continued toward the main offices.

Feeling exhausted and strained to the limits, not to mention having a roaring headache, Brody asked, "So, what's the plan?"

"Until I find out exactly what he has to say, I'd prefer you not to be in the room. Your presence likely would intimidate him, and he may clam up. Of course, he knows there's a one-way window and all he'll have is my word that whatever he has to say is between the two of us." She looked straight until Brody's eyes and without a word made it clear she expected him to honor her requests. "Our conversation will be recorded, with his permission of course."

To his surprise, the sheriff continued, " Again, I just don't want anything to jeopardize the investigation of Deuce's injury—"

"Attempted murder," he corrected.

"Duly noted." Avery went directly to her office and reappeared with a legal pad, several pencils, and a recorder. "Okay, it's time to you-know-what or get off the pot." She touched Brody's arm as she brushed by him to go down the hall that led to Interrogation Room One.

Brody mulled over Avery's comments and decided he'd watch the interrogation. She had not given him a direct order. He poured a mug of coffee and walked to the observation area that covered the two interrogation rooms. He took a seat, looked up, and nearly dropped his drink.

Sitting across from Avery was none other than Tommy Mitchell.

"What the hell!" A tightness seemed to rush all the way to his toes. He took a deep breath before he looked back into the room.

Brody rubbed the back of his neck and allowed a number of feelings to run wildly throughout his body as well as his mind.

Avery began by introducing herself and obviously made every attempt necessary to make Tommy comfortable.

"I see you have a Coke. Do you need anything else?" She opened her notepad. "Some cheese and crackers, maybe?"

Tommy shook his head and politely said, "No, thank you, ma'am."

Brody shifted in his chair, but to his surprise instead of slumping down like a guilty child, Tommy sat up straight and looked the sheriff directly in her eyes. He folded his hands on the table.

"Sheriff Humphrey, there are some things you need to know, and I think, no, I realize, it's time that I come clean with you."

"Thank you, Mr. Mitchell—"

"Tommy, please, ma'am."

"Okay, Tommy, take your time. As I've explained your rights, this is being recorded with your approval, and you don't have to talk with me without your lawyer being present."

"I don't need one, because I don't think I've done anything wrong except not to tell Sheriff Cowan the truth. You probably don't know, but after I was detained, as you all call it, by Deputy Scott for trespassing on the Jacks Bluff, the sheriff put me through a fierce grilling and what I'd call a talk that really gave me food for thought." He rubbed his forehead. "Sheriff, I don't want to go back on the inside. I've really tried to change my life and do the right thing. I've even got involved with a prison program over at the Clements Unit in Amarillo, so maybe I can make a change in the lives of some of the younger inmates. I owe it all to Sheriff Cowan, and, don't let him know, but the faith that I've seen Brody put in me." He lowered his eyes, obviously in an attempt to hide the tears.

"Tommy, I know it's hard on you to tell me all of this, and I truly appreciate it. I can certainly see you've come to us in good faith. Sure you don't want anything before we begin?"

"No, ma'am. I just want to get this over with."

"Okay, let's get this show on the road." She gave him a sweet, yet professional, smile.

"Ma'am, this is really difficult, but I'll try my best to tell you what you need to know and I'll take whatever punishment I deserve for not coming to you earlier." His shoulders drooped, then he sat up straight. "I was at the café one day cleaning up. Not long before Sheriff Cowan's uh, injury. Deputy Scott came in, and we struck up a conversation. It seemed kinda like he picked me to strike up a conversation. One of the things that stuck in my mind—and certainly I'm one hundred percent responsible for—is that he told me about the PCP kept in the vet's offices at the Jacks Bluff." He began to rock backward and forward.

"Just stay calm, Tommy," Avery said.

"He even told me that generally the vet worked late and that worried him because any person on drugs could get ahold of the old bottle of PCP and it'd cause a serious high. He said he needed to talk to Dr. Tegler about getting it locked up." Tommy swallowed hard. "That stayed on my mind, and at the time marijuana wasn't enough for me, so I picked the night of the festival to go out to the vet's office and get the PCP...."

Brody looked away and put his hands on his knees.

What in the hell is Tommy thinking confessing to Avery...Mesa LeDoux's best friend?

Avery might talk Mrs. Johnson and Mesa into reconsidering and filing charges. After all, Avery needed some marks on the wall to show the citizens she got the job because she was good at what she did, not just because she was the daughter of the mayor and one of the town's founding families.

He looked up and noticed Avery had moved her chair back a tad away from invading Tommy's privacy. Certainly a sign she believed what the kid had to say. Brody exhaled with relief. Maybe it wasn't going in the direction he feared after all.

Tommy spent the next hour explaining how he'd gotten to the ranch, parked his car near where Deuce's unit eventually was found, and walked up the path to the ranch's headquarters. He had waited until he saw Dr. Tegler leave without locking his office, so once the vet was out of sight, Tommy went in and snooped around finally locating the single and oldest bottle, thinking it wouldn't be missed. He added a little water and headed back to his car but not down the dirt road. He took a shortcut and walked toward his car through the west pasture. That's when he had gotten a glimpse of the vet and the ranch foreman and hidden behind several massive Yuccas. In the process, he dropped the bottle of PCP.

"That's when I saw it...." Tommy trailed off.

Avery wrote notes as fast as she could and waited patiently for the young man to continue. When he didn't, she nudged him along. "Tommy, take your time. I realize this is hard. I applaud you for coming in and telling me what happened. So, whenever you're ready, just go ahead. You're not being judged. I promise you." She jotted down another note.

"Ma'am...thank you for being patient with me. This is the hardest thing I've ever done in my life. The first thing I learned being incarcerated, although it was only for a short time, was to never, never, become a snitch, and that's what I'm doing now." He stopped and no doubt had to think the rest of his confession through before he began again.

Finally, Tommy wiped his forehead with a napkin and continued, "When I saw Dr. Tegler and the foreman head back east, I starting running, not taking time to go back for the PCP."

Avery took the bottle she had found out of an evidence envelope and asked Tommy if it was the bottle he had stolen.

"Yes, ma'am, it looked like that one." He squared his shoulders. "That's when I saw Deputy Scott and before I knew it, he had me in handcuffs and took me into town and put me in a cell."

"And, how long did you stay there?"

"Not long because then the sheriff came in and they took me into this room." He placed his hands flat on the table. "That's when the sheriff gave me the talking to. One like I've never had. Then he released me. Since I was so watered off and thought some air would help, plus I needed to pick up my car, I just walked back to where Deputy Scott took me into custody."

"That's really good information, so go on, Tommy."

"Well, as I found out later, thinking I had been arrested, my brother and a friend of his had come out and got my car. That left me with little choice but to walk back to the house. We live on the east side of town." He rubbed the back of his hands and made them into a double fist. "About the time I got to the road that leads up to the Jacks Bluff, I saw Sheriff Cowan drive up and get out of his car. He just stood there and seemed to be observing everything around him. Before I got much farther, I heard a car and noticed Deputy Scott pulled up behind him. I stayed hidden for sure because I didn't know what was going on, but knew I might be in trouble all over again." Tommy shook his head twice.

"Go ahead, Tommy," Avery encouraged him.

Just watching Avery handle Tommy in such a professional manner made Brody proud of the whole sheriff's department, but particularly pleased with the person he had gotten to know as a real, trustworthy woman—someone he found himself caring about.

Hell's bells, I don't care about her; I think I'm falling in love with the woman!

Tommy stretched his back but sat up straight. "I was too far away to hear what they said, but obviously the two men were having words. Deputy Scott really came at the sheriff in a threatening way, and that's when the sheriff pulled out his phone. The deputy grabbed it, threw the thing on the ground, and crushed it with the heel of his boot. Then they really began to fight. When Sheriff Cowan turned to get in his cop car, the deputy hit him in the back of his head with his gun." Tommy slumped in his chair, no doubt trying to find the courage to finish his story.

"Did you see anything else? Maybe how the sheriff got into the ravine?"

"Yes, ma'am. I need a minute." He took a sip of his drink. "Before I could do anything, not that I was inclined to do something, the deputy dragged the sheriff away from their cop cars, and he pulled the sheriff over his shoulders and trudged toward the ravine. I stayed as far back as possible because the last thing I needed was to get picked up, and way back in my mind I knew I'd be blamed for what happened to the sheriff. I got close enough to see Deputy Scott drop the sheriff to the ground and shove him over the edge into the ravine." Tommy lowered his head, as if he couldn't face any more of the night, then said, "Are you going to arrest me for stealing the PCP and not telling you what happened before now?"

"Tommy, right here." Avery pointed at her eyes with her index and middle finger. When he looked up, she continued, "The case against you for the PCP is closed. I have no reason to reopen it and have absolutely no reason to believe Mrs. Johnson or Mesa would change their minds about their decision not to have charges filed. Of course, it'll be up to the DA on any other charges, but it'll be my recommendation that you are not charged with any other offense. Needless to say, I'm taking your word at one hundred percent value." She jotted something on her pad. "But Tommy, please don't take your eyes off me."

The young man slowly lifted his head and looked Avery directly in the eyes. Then she said, "I trust you. Tell me again, but in more detail, how Deputy Scott arrested you, right after you left the vet's office."

"I headed for my car as fast as I could, but before I knew it he was on top of me with his knee in the middle of my back and he really pushed on my neck, crushing my face into the ground—"

She interrupted him. "Two questions. First, for the record, did you take any selfies of your face?"

"Yes, ma'am. They're on my phone. Do you want it?"

"If you don't mind."

He retrieved his iPhone from his shirt pocket and slid it across the table. "The screen is broken because it was in my pocket. Deputy Scott is a big dude."

"Thank you. Most importantly, did he identify himself as a peace officer and tell you to stop? Anything on that line?"

"No. Just all of a sudden he was on top of me and the next thing I knew I was handcuffed and thrown in the back of his cop car," Tommy shifted in his seat. "I don't want to tell you this part, but I think it's really important."

He stopped, cleared his throat, and waited for a long time. "The deputy came by the house the next day, since I was home with a cold, and told me that if I told anybody about what I may or may not have seen that he'd make certain I was sent back to the slammer and he had ways to make it happen." He fidgeted with his soft drink. "Ma'am, he also said if I ever went back to the big house, I'd never see the light of day. He also said that was if he didn't shoot me while I was breaking the law. I had a good idea what he meant, and believe me, ma'am, that's been heavy on my mind. I don't want to go back and do time, but being shot would be worse."

Once he looked away, she said, "Thank you, Tommy, for coming forth and being honest with me. I'll see you are protected, for one thing. In return, the only assurance I need from you is that once Danny Scott has been arrested, and if and when he's charged with causing Sheriff Cowan's injuries—I guess it's now attempted murder—you agree to testify on the state's behalf."

"Yes, ma'am. I promise I will. I want to be a better person." He looked down at his folded hands on the table and said, "Will Brody know what I said?"

Sheriff Humphrey hesitated for only a second. "Yes, Tommy. He's our lead detective, and although he can't handle the case because you are related, while not by blood, he will know about it. Does that create a problem for you?"

"No, ma'am. I really want him to know that I'm trying to change and be as good of a guy as he is. His sister is a wonderful person and has done a lot for me. I'm glad to say Brody is part of my family. Can I go, ma'am? And you don't have to remind me to keep my mouth shut. I've done it this long, so another while won't matter. I really have to get back to the café before my brother beats the living...excuse me, ma'am, I mean crud out of me for being late cleaning up." He stood up, and in a boyish voice, he said, "Thank you, ma'am. I promise to keep my word."

"Again thank you for coming to us as a man." She picked up her pad. "And, yes, you can go, but don't be surprised if you see a deputy about everywhere you turn. He'll likely be out of sight, but remember he's there to protect you. There's something else; if your brother-in-law harms you, please promise to give me or Brody a call."

"Yes, ma'am."

Brody knew it'd take more than a few minutes, maybe even hours, to let what Tommy had said settle in. He stayed put until he heard Avery unlock the interrogation room and the back door to the office close. He had no doubt Tommy had gone out the back way so nobody would see him exiting the front…especially his brother, Stanley.

With more scrambled feelings than eggs on a grill, Brody went directly into his office and closed the door. Looking out on Main Street, he spread his legs apart and let everything he'd just heard rush around in his thoughts. From the facts he'd learned from Deuce to the things Tommy had told Avery—especially the change in demeanor with the kid—all rolled up into one really scattered assortment of thoughts.

He finally heard a light knock at his door, although it barely penetrated is mind. "Come in." He turned away from the window.

Avery stepped across the threshold, closed the door behind her, and leaned against it. She didn't say anything for the longest time. She exhaled deeply, crossed her arms, and finally said, "Now you know why I couldn't let you in the interrogation room." She held her hand up as if to stop him from saying anything. "I know I didn't have to say that because you are a professional and I appreciate you not pushing me with a bunch of questions on the ride back from the hospital."

She took the few steps to stand beside him and touched his arm lightly. "Brody, I know just hearing what you did from Deuce at the hospital had to be hard." Her pressure on his arm intensified, sending hot waves throughout his body.

Brody laid his left hand on hers. "I've heard a lot of confessions and deathbed revelations in my career, but Deuce's was the hardest I've ever experienced. I know you really do care, and I appreciate you."

"I do." She stiffened and took a couple of steps backward, turned, and looked out the window into the main office. "Oh, there's Rocky and Jessup." She rushed to the door and opened it. "Gentlemen, I need you in here, please."

Brody reluctantly moved to his chair behind the desk. He tried unsuccessfully to disengage his muddled thoughts as the two deputies walked in. The one thing he didn't confess to his boss was just how hard Tommy's confession had hit him.

"Did either of you locate Danny Scott?" Avery didn't mince words with unnecessary greetings.

Eddie Jessup spoke first. "No, ma'am. We split up and looked everywhere and talked to just about everyone in town and nobody has seen hide nor hair of him for at least two days."

Rocky added, "That'd be his days off plus today. I didn't get the feeling anyone was avoiding us or trying to alibi for him. From the looks of his house and neighbors, he's probably been gone for a day or two. He may have gone fishing or something and thought today was one of his days off." "No." Avery turned toward Brody. "Everybody sit down." She took a chair across from the others, creating a semi-circle. "We've"—she nodded toward Brody—"got some really bad news." She quickly held her hand up. "Deuce is fine. As a matter of fact, he's coming out of his coma and speaking a little. Not a lot but a few words here and there. He knows everybody now, and when Rainey and I had some tea, she said the hospital's social worker was there today to discuss arrangements to transfer Deuce here to our long-term facility for rehab."

"Praise the Lord." Rocky lowered his head and closed his eyes. Jessup made a similar gesture.

"But, I, well we, have a lot to tell you guys, so everyone will be updated on what is going on. And I don't have to say this, but what we have to tell you stays within these walls." She turned to face Rocky. "I apologize for such a horrid first day on the job, but we're thankful to have you here. Once you've heard everything we have to say, you'll see just how important you are." She gestured toward Jessup. "Both of you. We're a team, and I expect us to work together as one unit for the betterment of Bonita County."

Brody smiled to himself realizing that her *I*'s had turned to *We*'s, which pleased him to no end.

To the obvious surprise of both deputies, Avery filled them in on what had happened at the hospital with Sheriff Cowan and her discussion with Tommy Mitchell.

"I'll have the interview with Tommy, who will be considered as ADHCI#1, transcribed from the tape, and each of you can read it. But here's the pie-in-the-face reality of the situation."

Jessep asked, "Your initials plus CI #1?"

"Yes, that's the way I want our transcriptions labeled from now own, but of course, changing the confidential informant's number." She stopped and looked up. "That's until Deuce is back on the job."

Avery picked up the papers from Brody's desk. "Robertson and Jessup, here's a search warrant for Scott's property. We need anything and everything that pertains to Deuce's attempted murder." She stopped, as if giving thought to her next statement, "We need his computer and any notes that pertain to *anything* that might be considered criminal in nature, particularly if it involves his job." She glanced up at Brody. "I mean anything, including his service weapon and uniforms. It's all in the warrant. In the meantime, I'm going to get an arrest warrant issued and put out an APB on him." She slumped in her chair and looked at Brody with eyes that screamed *help me out.*

"The APB will be for the attempted murder of a peace officer and state that he's armed and considered dangerous—"

Avery interrupted Brody, "And we want him dead or alive."

Chapter 23

Avery shook her head, wanting to reach out to provide comfort to all of the people in the room, particularly Brody, who looked as if he'd lost his last friend. She sighed, frankly feeling much like he seemingly felt. The sensation of falling down a deep tunnel of no return hit her, and she wasn't sure whether she could compartmentalize all of the events of the day. If only it were possible for her to stay still and let the relief sink in.

Jessup and Robertson were halfway out the door, giving both Avery and Brody assurance they'd not only check in with any progress but return to the office as quickly as possible.

Brody sat silently. The look on his face spoke volumes.

She excused herself to allow him time to be alone, then remembered the tape.

"I'm taking the tape to Tonya. She's still on duty, and as the office supervisor, she knows that a CI's identity is not to be revealed. I trust her. Do you?" She reached for the tape on his desk and couldn't help but look at Brody. A pensive, restless expression shrouded his face. No doubt he felt as conflicted with all of the information as she did.

"Lieutenant Detective Brody VanZant, did you hear—"

He turned her way. "I'm sorry. I was lost in my thoughts. And, yes, I totally trust Tonya. She's been here a while and knows the ropes."

"Be back shortly," Avery said, allowing herself to feel sorry for the usually strong lawman while knowing that when something in the line of duty hit home, it was hard to shake off. But at the same time she knew he was a professional and would kick it sooner or later. She certainly planned to be part of his recuperation team.

*I care way too much for him to see how hurt he is and how badly
everything around Deuce, Scott, and Tommy hit him. I truly care.... Lordy,
lordy, I think I'm falling for him, but can't with both of us working side by side.*

Her thoughts dissipated as she walked into Tonya's office. After greeting
her, the sheriff said, "Can you stay late and transcribe a tape for me?"

"Sure." Tonya nearly snatched the recording from Avery. "I'll be glad to."

"Be sure to mark your extra hours on your timecard, because you're
staying late to transcribe something very important. There's one extremely
vital part of this particular interview that I must stress to you as being more
confidential than probably anything you've ever transcribed."

"I understand, Sheriff Humphrey."

"I'm pretty sure you haven't worked with many CI interviews, so I
feel compelled to remind you that under no circumstances is the name of
the person interviewed to be revealed to anyone, even if you think they
are familiar with the case." Avery rocked gently in place. "This is the
first for me in Bonita County, so I feel compelled to be certain that we
both understand the rules. I want to make sure nothing compromises our
investigation and causes problems if and when a case is brought to trial."

Tonya nodded. "Yes, ma'am. I understand completely."

"I've marked the conversation as ADH-CI#1. Do not under any
circumstances use the CI's identity. Redact his name—and any references
to his name, period."

Feeling comfortable Tonya would carry out her instruction to a T, Avery
returned to Brody's office. With a covered mouth and unsteady walk,
allowing all of the information to sink in, she watched him from the door.

His lanky body sagged against the wall, reminding her of how he had
appeared when she and Rainey had stepped off the elevator at the hospital.
With crossed arms and eyes closed, he bowed his head. No doubt he felt
the weight of the day on his shoulders as much if not more than she did.

"Brody, we need to get an arrest warrant issued for Scott. Would you
do it, please?"

"Sure." He went to his desk and booted his laptop. "Won't take long,
since we've got the approval of the DA and your uncle to boot."

"When you're finished, let's go get those boards from storage. I really want
to make certain all of the events involving Scott are documented, and what
better way than starting with fresh eyes and new boards?" she suggested.

He looked up with eyes clearer than she'd seen all day long.

Giving her a thumbs-up, he returned to typing.

In short order, Brody took the printed arrest warrant out of the printer
and handed the pages to Avery. "Best I can do."

"I'll ask Tonya to run this over to Judge Humphrey for his signature. We can then leave them for Robertson and Jessup and head over to your sister's café." She laid her purse in his desk chair and pushed it in. "Should be okay until we get back."

In less than five minutes, Brody removed the keys from his pickup. He and Avery exited the truck, walking toward the back door of the Ol' Hickory Inn.

"Lights are on and the back door is open, so I'm sure Tommy's working." Nodding his head toward the huge steel building, he continued, "Since they use this for storage, I'm sure Tommy has the keys." Brody opened the back screen and hollered, "Sheriff's Department."

Tommy appeared from the front with a mop. He wiped his hands on his brown apron. "You presume I couldn't guess who was here by your voice?" The young man smiled up at them, much as he had during his interview.

"Nope. Gotta give you clear warning who's coming in the back door unless you were expecting us." A laugh came from deep inside Brody. "Got time for us?"

"Always when it comes to the law." Tommy set the mop against the wall. "Want something to drink?"

"No, thank you, Tommy," Avery said.

"We're here on county business. We need the whiteboards I have in the storage building. We can use them over at the office." Brody stepped back a foot's length ahead of Avery, but not where she couldn't see him.

"I wish I could help you guys, but I don't have a key. Stanley keeps things stored out there and nobody but him has one. He said they only got one key when they moved in and he keeps forgetting to get another one made." He pulled an iPhone from his pocket. "This is Winnie's. She had two, so when I told her I'd misplaced mine, she offered to loan this one to me. Want me to call Stanley?" Tommy stepped outside.

"No, don't bother them. It's late, and I know they have to get up early." There was a bit of a discomfort between him and Tommy, but not enough to make their conversation awkward. Brody immediately discounted bringing up the kid's interview with the sheriff and the facts as Brody knew them.

Brody asked, "What all is inside that is so important Stanley keeps the only key?"

"Stuff. I know someone tried to break in a year or so ago, so he's been overly protective ever since then. By stuff, I mean coffee, some commercial-size cans of tomato paste and vegetables that Winnie uses. Paper towels and toilet paper. You know, stuff they use. They keep the bigger things that come by the case out there and then Stanley keeps the shelves inside stocked." He twitched his nose, and continued, "There's really no reason for any of us to have a key, since he keeps everything we need right at hand."

"And you're sure he's the only one with a key." Brody made the statement, but Avery saw his look turn from wondering to suspicion.

Tommy nodded. "Yes, sir."

"Sure is a big storage building for so few items," Avery commented, then added, "Especially with only one person with a key." She wanted to give Stanley the benefit of the doubt. "I'm sure he knows there's a locksmith right on the square. You all must really have a huge business when he can't find time to get a key made."

In a businesslike, yet friendly manner, Brody said, "Since you're a vegetarian, except for eggs and a few other things"—Brody smiled over to Avery—"you have no idea how good their food is." He turned his attention back to Tommy. "What else does he have in there? I'm sure he has their catering truck, but what else?"

"Yes, sir, the catering truck and another van. White."

Without being asked, Tommy continued, "It's a Chevy cargo van. Probably late nineties or early 2000 model, and it's pretty well beat up. It's a panel truck, I guess that's what it's called, and it doesn't have Hickory Inn Catering on it like the big one does."

"Hum, I didn't know that." Brody's face screamed of surprise, yet he continued, "Matches my whiteboards, huh?"

"Whiteboards, like both of the white vans." Tommy let out an easy, comfortable laugh. "Let's walk around to the backside and see if by any chance he left it unlocked." Tommy began to amble in that direction. "But it's very unlikely."

Sure as shootin', the entrance had a padlock on the door.

"That's new." Tommy pointed at the latch.

Out of the silence of the setting sun, a hardened, ruthless male voice boomed out.

"What in the hell is the sheriff's department doing nosing around on my property?" Stanley lowered the baseball bat he held close to his side.

Avery fought the raw impulse to knock the arrogant expression off his face. She had to breathe in and out slowly to overcome her urge.

Stanley grabbed Tommy's T-shirt and pulled him around to face him. He shoved the young man toward the back door. "Get the hell out of here and get back to work before I kick your sorry, lazy ass from here to Dallas and back—and don't ever let me find you out here again." He rolled up his sleeve and lifted the bat only an inch. Avery didn't miss the threatening gesture. She was certain Brody felt the same, if not stronger, about the warning.

Just as Avery expected, Brody stepped between the two men. "Stanley Mitchell, we're not here for any reason but to get the boards I have stored out of there." Brody paused a moment before saying, "I'm telling you one thing, and you damn well better listen and listen carefully, as an officer of the law. If you ever lay a hand on that kid again you'll have me to deal with."

Stanley doubled up one fist while moving the baseball bat back and forth only inches. "And I'll get a whatever it's called to make sure you never step foot on this property again without a warrant." He brought his fist up to a threatening level close to his brother-in-law's face. "Do *you* hear me?"

Brody took two steps forward, invading Stanley's personal space, and in a carefully controlled tone said, "Stanley, don't threaten me, because I can assure you that I'll come out on the winning end. As I recall, my sister bought this café with her inheritance that specifically stated all monies were for her and her only. I believe you were left a hundred dollars. Oh, and, a 1970s Chevy."

In an attempt to defuse the situation before something terrible and irrevocable happened between the brothers-in-law, Avery stepped between them. Both men separated.

"Okay, gentlemen." Avery interceded in what she hoped was an authoritative but not threatening way. "All we need is the boards and we'll be out of your hair, Mr. Mitchell." In her book, first names were reserved for people she liked, and he certainly didn't deserve being called Stanley.

She pulled her uniform jacket back with her elbows, exposing her service weapon and badge as the punctuation to her request. "And I'd suggest you put that baseball bat down, too."

"I didn't know what kind of trouble I was gonna find." He put the bat on the ground near the foundation.

Obviously not accustomed to being called out on his actions, Stanley flashed a cold, sarcastic look at her.

Avery recognized his hateful, smirking behavior was taking its toll on her patience. She wanted to smack a ruler over his hand as the teachers had done when she was in grade school. A hatchet came to mind, but she dismissed it with a cautious internal laugh. The tightening in her chest subsided a bit.

"I don't have the key with me, but I'll get it and will bring the boards over to the sheriff's department after I find them," Stanley said in a sharp, hateful tone. "Will that work for you, Sheriff?" He looked at Avery only, seemingly avoiding Brody's angry stare.

"Yes, sir. That'll be fine. We have people over there 24/7, so I'll let them know to expect you. Please use the front door."

He nodded but didn't move from in front of the storage building until Brody and Avery were on Main Street heading back to the courthouse.

In an attempt to calm Brody and give herself time to digest the events of the day, Avery said, "I don't know about you, but it's been one hell of a day. Why don't we get a bite to eat and call it a night?"

"Got any objections with the Kasota Truck Stop?"

"An omelet with fresh tomatoes and herbal tea sounds good," Avery said. "Oh, we need to go by the department first, because I left my purse in your office."

"I think I can muster up enough cash to buy us dinner, but let's make it clear that we are not on a date but a simple working dinner, so we absolutely aren't doing that nepotism thing."

In not over ten minutes, they drove up in front of the Kasota Truck Stop, which was extremely crowded with big rigs as well as locals and travelers.

"They are really busy," Avery commented.

"If you'd like, we could always go out to my ranch. I have everything for an omelet. I actually do watch what I eat." He smiled at her. "I can fix some breakfast and we can go over the day or even just watch some television. I have cable. Don't know why 'cause I don't watch it, but we could check out the movies."

"You know, I like that idea." As tired as she felt, she still smiled softly over at him. "A movie and breakfast with a good-lookin' Texan sounds like exactly what I need." A rush of *what in the hell did I do, calling him good lookin'?* She hurried on, "Rocky and Jessup can reach us there, and we'll be on call, so I think it's a perfect idea."

"The only person we'll have to deal with is Bruiser, unless he's with Rocky, which he generally is," Brody said as they crossed the railroad tracks and headed for his ranch.

Avery felt sluggish and like she needed to let off a whole smokestack of steam. She laid her head back on the headrest and let only good memories pass through her mind. For some strange reason, Brody VanZant seemed to be in her most current good thoughts.

"I should have gone home and changed clothes. This dern concealment vest is so snug in order for it to fit under a woman's uniform shirt, but after a while it gets hot and really uncomfortable."

"It's not too late. I can turn around—"

"Absolutely not." She sat up straight. "I'm in no mood to answer all of the questions Daddy will have for me. And he knows good and well I cannot answer the majority of them." She sagged back in her seat. "Plus with Mother is not feeling well, she'll want to talk about it. I'm glad they didn't find anything wrong that a fairly simple surgery won't resolve, but I've just got too much on my mind. Plus, Daddy and Mama always have done fine without my advice." She turned toward Brody and met his smile with hers.

"Okay. I understand, but if I'm not being too forward, you're welcome to take off your corset—"

"Concealment vest."

"Okay, you can remove your vest, and if you want big and comfortable I have a T-shirt or two you should like. You can have a newly washed UT shirt or a Dallas Cowboys one." Brody kept his gaze on the road.

"University of Texas, please." She continued to watch the road herself as he turned north off the interstate. "But, of course, the Cowboys will do." She hesitated then added, "I knew you had a ranch and a house in Amarillo, but never knew what ranch you owned." Everything around became vaguely clear, as if a veil of mist was lifting.

"I just figured you knew, but it's the old WBarT."

"But, I remember now, you are the owner of the WBarT. You do know that was my great-great-grandparents' ranch, don't you?" She continued on, "I never imagined it was one of ours, until Mesa mentioned it a while back. So you really didn't know?"

The look on his face said it all. "No."

"My mother was a Sullivan, and that ranch was originally owned by her family; originally by Sloan Sullivan and his wife was Tess Whitgrove. My grandparents lived there until they passed and it was sold. I haven't kept up with it since that time." A happiness Avery hadn't felt in a long time settled around her. "I'm so thrilled that it ended up in such capable hands as yours. Do you run a cattle operation?"

"No. Not at the moment. I never looked at my abstract when I bought the ranch. I stayed mostly in Amarillo while I worked with the special crimes units, so I didn't come out here a lot. I almost never set foot in Kasota Springs during my stint over there. Now I live here exclusively; and ,the old Wolflin family home in Amarillo is sitting there lonely, I guess. I do have a neighbor who looks after it for me."

"That's sad—the lonely house I mean—but I hope the ranch headquarters haven't been changed a lot. I'm sure appliances and stuff like that have been changed out." She smiled, thinking back to some of her schoolgirl memories.

"Not a whole bunch done, except appliances and furniture. Probably the same colors on the wall." Brody laughed. "And the same big ol' Cottonwoods."

"I'm so excited." She laid back her head and let the good memories overshadow one of the worst days in her career, with the exception of the day Lee got shot. *Wow, I can't believe I thought of it as when he got shot instead of when I got him killed because I froze and couldn't get a shot off!*

Brody's voice interrupted her thoughts. "Now that we have dinner planned and what you're going to wear, how about a movie?"

She pulled out her iPhone. "One thing for sure, no cops and robbers, no police stories, no murders, and—"

"Okay, look for Paul Newman or Cary Grant. *Houseboat* is where Sophia Loren slaps him for making the wrong assumptions."

"Cary Grant is out. How about *Hud* with Paul Newman?" Avery asked.

"If it's on, sounds good to me. A lot of it was filmed only a few miles from here in Claude, so maybe we'll find something in the movie we recognize."

She put her phone in her lap, "*Hud* it is. Got the time, and we can find it tonight."

Avery enjoyed every Yucca and Mesquite bush along the path to the main house on the WBarT, and a happiness she hadn't felt in a while consumed her as Brody escorted her from his pickup to the porch.

"It's just like I remember," she said. "Beautiful with so many memories."

After a tour of her family's old ranch house, Avery sat at the kitchen table and watched Brody prepare breakfast for their evening meal. He worked as if he'd been a chef in his former life.

For what seemed like hours, they talked about everything from their families to their Texas Rancher grandfathers, wondering if they knew one another from their days at the WBarT.

"Are you sure I can't help?" Avery asked, but deep inside she enjoyed the herbal tea he just happened to have in the cabinet. His explanation was simple: Clara from Pumpkin's had been doing his cleaning and bought the tea on one of her shopping excursions.

After a hearty dinner of omelets, fresh tomatoes, and hummus, again, that he just happened to have in the refrigerator, she sat at the table enjoying Brody cleaning up and putting the dishes in the dishwasher. She took another sip of tea.

"You could spoil me really easy by doing all the cooking and cleaning up while I drink tea and relax." She put her hands around the delicate cup.

"That's what I wanted. You've had one hell of a day."

"And you haven't?"

"Let's just say we both need a quiet evening." He tossed a dish towel at her. "Okay, dry that fry pan and your work will be done." His broad smile sent a signal of desire to her brain that told her she really wanted to throw the cloth around his neck and pull him down so she could kiss him from tonight until tomorrow. But reality set in. They could not and would not become romantically involved. That was out of the question.

Avery dried the frying pan and hung it on the wall next to two other pans. She pulled at the bottom of her T-shirt and smiled. "This is so comfortable. Thank you."

"Thank you for taking a chance on my cooking," he replied as he laid the towel over the edge of the cabinet. "Let's go see what movies are on."

Dropping down on the couch, Brody patted the cushion next to him. "Here's a nice spot, unless you're scared of getting too close to me."

"I'm not scared in the least. Now find *Hud* or whatever we're going to watch on Netflix. And I didn't tell you thanks for locking up our service weapons. I appreciate it, although I know you know I have a personal one on me, as you do."

They shared a good-hearted laugh.

Once they settled into watching the movie, all of Avery's concerns and worries of the day seemed to dissipate; although with the number of text messages they received from Rocky and Jessup, no doubt the evening could qualify as a working dinner.

"Sorry." Avery reached for her phone. "Hi, Tonya." She stopped to listen while Tonya told her the warrant had been signed and that the two deputies had picked it up. She also updated her on the interview she'd transcribed, without making any comments about being surprised that Danny Scott was being sought for the attempted murder of their sheriff.

Once Avery disconnected and laid her phone on the cushion beside her, she found herself gravitating toward Brody's shoulders, where she rested her head. Although she tried to keep her focus on the movie, she continued to feel the heat coming from Brody. She put her hand on his muscular thigh. Why was she trying to fool herself? She certainly had more than an attraction to him. She was drawn to him by more than his good looks. There was something about the way he lived life, knowing when to live right on the edge and when to stay hidden in the shadows of the woods. He had a reckless charm and passion, plus a protective streak as big as Texas.

Letting her inhibitions go, she put her hands behind his neck, tenderly pulling his face toward her. He pressed his hot mouth against hers. What began as a sweet, slow kiss of temptation became a kiss of hunger. One of need. For only a fraction of a second, she held herself back before giving in to her desires.

He traced her lips, moving his wet, pink tongue across the seam of her mouth, and the last of her control snapped. Every ounce of her body short-circuited. He tore his mouth free long enough to take in a deep breath. Heat exploded within her. He ran his fingers through her hair, pulling the pins out of the top. He let it fall and brushed her blond locks with his fingers.

"No, Brody, we must—"

Brody's cell phone rang with a special tone she didn't recognize. He said very little that made sense to her, except, "Six o'clock at the truck stop." Then he listened. "White cargo van."

Avery sat up straight and pulled her hair back up ran her fingers through it, letting the words *white cargo van* rush through her mind. "White cargo van," she whispered.

Brody stared straight ahead once he hung up, as if searching for the right words.

Avery began, "Brody, look at me."

When he didn't, she simply said, "Tonight didn't happen. We had a nice dinner, watched a movie, and you took me home."

He turned to her. "That's not the problem. Frankly, I enjoyed every second and won't be able to forget no matter what happens." He took in a deep breath. "But, as you've said over and over, if we're to work together, I agree, it can't and won't happen again. But that's not the problem right now."

"What is it?" She felt the pounding of her heart and figured he could also.

"That was Vic. All the months of work on the drug-running ops seems to have gone down the river. Someone, somewhere got wind that the FBI, Texas Highway Patrol, and both of our counties were too close to the *Harbor Crew* cartel out of Mexico, and they've pulled a switch on us. They've found another way to get their drugs up north and down to Dallas." He put his elbows on his knees and rested his head in his hands. "We've been burned, and really badly. Lost tons of money that has been invested, plus our people's protection, but worst of all we've failed and allowed hundreds of pounds of drugs and no telling how many guns out on the street."

Avery placed her hand on his back and rubbed. "Hey, that's the type of work we're in, and not every investigation ends up in a positive fashion. Let's look at the good part of the day." She rubbed a little harder, while his muscles relaxed. "We found out who tried to murder Deuce, and he'll likely be located and brought to justice. Tommy seems a changed man, and with his testimony, Scott will be in a federal prison probably until he dies. And...." She tried to think of something else positive. "Oh yes, and we will have whiteboards to begin our timeline first thing in the morning. White ones just like your brother-in-law's van he didn't want us to see."

Chapter 24

Brody stepped out of the shower with only an oversized towel around his middle. He ran his fingers through his hair and began drying off. He'd spent a restless night alone in his bed. His dreams had drifted between the feeling of Avery in his arms, her kisses, and her soft, beautiful touch on his neck and deep-seated feelings about the Mexican cartel developments or lack thereof. He looked in the mirror and turned his head from side to side. Although he'd had his ponytail cut off weeks ago, he'd kept his dark hair fairly long, in the event he got called back into the special crimes unit to work on the Harbor Crew case. He took a lengthy look at himself, as if he hadn't seen Brody VanZant in the mirror before. A short haircut and shave would do him good, plus he needed to check on the house in Amarillo. Since he hadn't used a local barber, he'd call his old one and see if she could fit him in.

In the background, he heard his iPhone ring, and the only person who had that particular tone was his CI, Vicky.

Pulling the towel tightly around him, he went to the bedroom and grabbed up the phone. "Vic?"

"Yes. Brody, I just wanted to call and let you know how much I've enjoyed working with you for these last couple of years." She hem-hawed a bit, but before he could say anything else, she continued, "I want to make sure everything is okay between us. I hope you don't think I was the one who threw the monkey wrench into all of our months of work."

"There's no way I think that." He sat on the bed. "I trust you too much, and you've proven yourself over and over. Are you coming out from undercover and going back to the APD?"

"I haven't decided what I want to do, but you'll be the first to know. So what are your plans?" Vic asked.

"Don't know. I told Deuce I'd stay here, so I will keep my word. Hope the sheriff will let me partner with Rocky, as she originally planned, and continue as a detective."

"I hope so, but I just wanted you to know that whatever you think is right for you, I'll support you one hundred percent." She hesitated then said, "Oh by the way, I saw the APB out on Danny Scott. I ran across him in Amarillo a day or so ago, and I let the chief know. He's likely in custody as we speak. Scott was drunk as a skunk, so I hope to Hades he put up a fight so they could add more charges to his resume. Got to go. Take care of yourself, and I hope to see you and Sheriff Humphrey again soon."

The phone went dead and he laid it on his table.

Brody sat on his bedside thinking about what would happen to Scott. To betray all of the people who believed in him was unthinkable, and he deserved anything he got, which would likely be life in prison. One thing for sure, Texas didn't mess around with an attempted murder of a police officer. Being such a bastard, likely Scott would spend most of his time in solitary confinement, because the likelihood of him making friends was nil.

Brody picked up the phone and touched Avery's private number.

With a voice as soft as a kitten, she answered, "Brody, are you okay?"

After they exchanged greetings, he gave her all the information Vicky had given him, only to find out she had already received word that Scott was in custody.

Relief rushed through his body, and he recognized a desire to let the feeling sink in.

"Thanks for taking me to get my car last night. Most of all, thanks for following me home to make sure I was safe."

"Anytime...anytime. It's only five-thirty, so what time did you get into the office?"

"I couldn't sleep. Got here about an hour ago. Hey, I've got two new things to add to the whiteboards that Mr. Mitchell brought over."

"Let it rip." He turned on the speaker, stood up, removed the towel, and put on his underwear then tactical pants.

"Well, you'll find this interesting. Thelma and I cleaned out Scott's desk, so Rocky could have it nice and uncluttered when he got in today." She hesitated and he could almost see a smile through the phone with her next words. "When we removed the lower left drawer to get the old torn paper and dirt out, we found an envelope addressed to Deuce, and the elusive search map we've been looking for."

"Did you read the letter?" He held his breath, wondering how she felt about him checking up on Tommy, after he'd been interviewed by Deuce.

"Yes, along with the pictures. Tommy looked sick to me, not high on drugs. I've gone over the missing map and the letter along with it. Sure fills in all of the missing pieces to the puzzle. This should tie up everything for the DA with a great big bow on top."

"I also sent a copy of the letter and pictures to myself, and it's never been opened, so that should add icing on the cake." Brody breathed a sigh of relief.

"Rocky is waving like he wants to talk with you. If it's okay with you, I'll step out and give him my phone."

"Sure."

In only a few seconds, Deputy Robertson's voice boomed across Brody's bedroom. After a brief discussion about what had transpired with Scott, Rocky had another piece of information that set Brody's heart on fire. "Just an FYI, after talking with the sheriff, I went over to your sister's café to introduce myself and have a cup of coffee."

"That's good. She's a very good sister and a likeable person. It's just too bad she's married to such an A-hole," Brody said.

"He wasn't even there. Your sister is very nice. He had to make a run to Amarillo to get some coffee, I think she said. Here is what's interesting. You know I always take Bruiser with me and leave him in the air-conditioned K-9 back of the Tahoe. I knew he needed to take a leak, so I got him out and took him around to the back. You know he's very shy." Rocky laughed.

"Oh, sure. Aren't all guys?" It was Brody's turn to laugh.

"Anyway, he took care of business, but I've never seen him pee so fast. He was almost more than I could handle when he rushed toward their storage building. I let him lead me, and he gave me sign after sign that there's either drugs or a human holed up in there. Bruiser is both a drug dog and tracker. He definitely gave me all the signs."

"That's interesting, because Stanley is the only person who has a key and knows what's inside," Brody said. "Let me think this through, because both Avery and I were there last night to get the whiteboards and Stanley showed up madder that a cat in a room full of rocking chairs. He was pissed out of his mind because we were out there."

"That's what the sheriff said, so I thought you'd want to know since it's your family—"

Brody interrupted him, "Let's get this straight. Winnie is family, and at this point, so is Tommy, but Stanley has a place in Hell with his name on it."

"Understood. Better let you go, so you can get in the office and help the sheriff with the timeline she's so feverishly working on." He hesitated. "As a matter of fact, she just go back, so I'll let you go. See you shortly, bro."

The phone went dead and he stuck it in his pants pocket.

Brody finished dressing and grabbed a fresh cup of coffee. Before he took more than a couple of sips, his phone sounded with Vic's distinctive chime.

"What's up, gal?" He knew better than to answer in any official way.

"How's my sweet thing doing?" his CI asked in a sexy, low tone. He could hear the sounds of big rigs and highway traffic, which pretty much told him where she was calling from.

"Oh honeydew I've been missing you, and since I can't get any action from this darlin' trucker, I thought about you and your *big rig*. How about you meetin' me and bringing along that toy I like so much…. The one we call Bruiser. I'd like to play around with him for a while."

"Meet you at the truck stop." He'd read all the signals. "And bring big ol' Bruiser along?"

"Oh yeah, and I know you have to wear clothes, but I wish you didn't. I'd like you with nothing on, but I'll take a plain shirt and pants I can get you out of as quickly as possible. You know you can satisfy my needs like nobody else." Not waiting for a response, she hung up.

Brody had changed into his Wrangler's almost before he got Rocky on the phone. He grabbed a western-cut shirt from the closet.

"Hey, bro. I just got an cryptic telephone call from my CI that something is coming down at the truck stop. Gotta bring Bruiser for certain, and come in plainclothes." Brody buckled his belt.

"Got some in my locker. Should the sheriff come, too?"

Brody could hear Rocky walking into the locker room.

"Since I don't know exactly what is coming down, I'm not sure. I know she'll want to, but since this really is a major crimes case, if it's what I think it could be, and I don't have time to notify anybody else—"

"Like the FBI, DPS or either city and counties?"

"Exactly. We could create more problems. We don't have the luxury of time being on our side and getting them here, especially since we really don't know what's happening except that she needs us in plainclothes and wants Bruiser. Meet me east of the café but not too far away. Your Tahoe will be fine because it's unmarked and I'm driving my pickup. Undercover man, undercover. See you in twenty." Brody disconnected and headed for his gun safe. He put on a bullet-resistant vest, added his service weapon, handcuff to the back of the belt, and put his shirt on top of it.

"Damn it! It's Thursday, so I'm more positive than ever what's fixin' to happen. Someone fed bad info to my CI. Damn, damn it!" He spoke aloud, almost shouting as he tucked in his shirt and added a Levi's jacket. He grabbed his favorite Stetson from the coat rack by the door and hit his pickup on the run.

He couldn't afford the luxury of sirens and lights to speed his way to the truck stop, but he sure drove as fast with thoughts of other drivers and pedestrians in mind.

In short order, he parked next to Rocky, who was similarly dressed, much like most ranchers in Texas. Brody motioned for Rocky to join him.

"I'm waiting to hear from Vic," Brody offered as Rocky closed the passenger door. "She'll call when she sees we're here, but she has to be careful who's around. You know the drill."

"What changed?"

Brody spent the next few minutes bringing Rocky up to date on his CI's call and the code words she'd added to the conversation.

"That's interesting. It's Thursday, isn't that the day you said the tractor-trailer and van generally show up?"

"It is, so something changed between her first call and the second." Brody kept a vigilant eye on everything around him watching for any signals of trouble. "Did you have any trouble with the sheriff?"

"Not really. I filled her in the best I could, and she said since it was really a special crimes case, she'd step aside, but not to be surprised if she shows up."

"That scares me. If there's trouble, I really don't like the idea that we're going into it by the seat of our pants. She's seasoned, to say the least, but again without a plan for a takedown, if it comes to that, concerns me greatly." Brody ran his hand across his forehead, about the time his iPhone signaled Vicky was calling.

"Hello, sweet thing, I'm almost there." Brody pushed the speakerphone, so Rocky could hear the conversation.

"Honeybuns, I got a room and it'll be ready as soon as possible. Watch out for red lights, police like to stop cowboys who run a red light or have their taillights broke, so be careful. Can't wait to push you against the wall and show you how a woman likes it. See you in a short, short."

Both men kept their eyes on anything that moved around them. Brody pointed out that the semi parked directly next to the west side of the café was the one under suspicion of carrying drugs from the Mexico cartel. As expected, when Rocky drove around the west where the semi was parked, the license and identification number was muddied up.

"Okay, I got part of your CI's message, but parts I didn't understand." Rocky lowered his window and rested his elbow.

"Okay. When she said she had the room ready, she meant she'd made contact with the right people to get all assets on hand. As soon as possible means exactly that. They'll get here ASAP, but the most interesting part is the red light. I've been digesting that, and I'm pretty sure she meant that the tractor-trailer isn't going to get far because it'll be stopped by the DPS for a broken taillight."

Rocky glanced at him. "How does she know it has a broken taillight?"

"I didn't ask, and I don't wanna know."

Before he got the words out, Vicky rounded the corner of the café swinging her purse and a white takeout bag. In a double-sexy walk, she came up to Rocky's open window and held up the bag.

"Hi guys. Are you hungry for anything I have?" She winked at them and lowered her voice, while leaning farther into the window. "I've got a double-cheeseburger and fries. Played a trick on the creep in the semi and grabbed his takeout before he could get back." She raised her voice where anyone around could hear. "Okay, I got your drift. I'm too high for you. You probably only have twenty minutes in you anyway, but it'd still cost you the going rate."

She walked away, flipping them off in the process.

"Woo," Rocky said, then shook his head. "Is she ever hot when she's playing her part. What in the hell did all of that mean?"

"The driver of that semi typically orders a takeout and is out of here within fifteen to twenty minutes, so she bought us some time." Brody couldn't help but smile to himself. "And I'll warn you now if you think Avery is one hundred and fifty percent business, she doesn't hold a light to Vic. She's top-notch and takes her work very serious."

"That's good. When I drove up the white van was parked right next to the semi. I never heard the exact description Mitchell gave you, but the one over there is an early 2000 model Chevy panel truck and is pretty beaten up for its age."

"That matches to a T." Brody looked over to his right and saw a pickup drive around the back. "Damn it to hell and back again, that's one of the Jacks Bluff people. I recognized the markings. They sure don't need to be here when any of this comes down, especially since we don't know what to plan... playing it by the ear." He swore again but used more profanity.

"They'll be in and out of the drive-thru by the time anyone else gets here."

Brody let out a sigh of relief, recognizing the adrenaline in his body beginning to flow faster. He'd done way too many stakeouts not to recognize the changes in his body. "I'm just tied up in knots, not sure what's going on, having to put my trust in a CI who seems to be running the whole thing. Maybe she was the one who wanted me to think the cartel had gotten wind of our progress?" He answered his own question. "No. I trust her too much. There's no way." Brody wasn't sure whether he was trying to convince himself or Rocky.

Brody looked down at a text message. "She pulled it off. Vic gave the DPS time to get in position, so when the semi gets on the highway, they'll stop him, if we haven't gotten him first."

"My blood is rushing so fast, I think I'm gonna have a stroke," Rocky admitted. "I'm used to it. I know you don't have the human trafficking I had to deal with, but you can't imagine opening up the back of a semi and seeing emaciated young women and children who are dirty, scared to death, and haven't eaten in days. I'll never get the look on their faces out of my mind." He squared his shoulders. "Sorry. I didn't mean to make it sound like getting drugs and guns out of the hands of criminals is less important."

"Well, I never thought of it in that way. Both are of the worst of the worst, as far as I'm concerned." Brody leaned forward and gripped the steering wheel as he thought through the possibilities. The desperate need to find the answers and get this part of the mission over. Although he'd only worked with Rocky a couple of times, he had little doubt the newest Bonita County deputy was the top of the heap when it came to stakeouts, and he certainly was giving one hundred percent of his attention and skill to this case.

Rocky broke into his thoughts. "You know, nobody knows me, so how about I drive around where I can get a better view of the trucks and take Bruiser out for a leak?"

"That's a thought." Brody considered the pros and cons. "I like that. The doggie rest area is just on the other side of the drive, so Bruiser can give you a lot of information on whether there's drugs in either of the trucks."

Rocky patted his jacket pocket. "Got plenty of treats, if he finds something. He's pretty sharp. That's one of several reasons I bought him from the department."

"I think he'll be a real asset and sure am glad Deuce had made his agreement with you and Bruiser." Brody couldn't help but let out a easygoing laugh, in conflict with how he felt inside. "I already like that dang Deputy Bruiser, and he seems to like me," he said.

"As long as you don't come between me and him, he'll be fine. But honestly, he likes the ladies more." Rocky grinned.

"Okay, get out of here and let me know what's going on."

Brody continue to clutch the wheel, while he kept a lookout. He watched Rocky get Bruiser out of the Tahoe and take him to the doggie rest area.

To his surprise, Vicky continued to play the part of a Lot Lizard, but as always her favors were turned down. She knew how to pick the right trucker, knowing they had a schedule to keep.

The driver of the semi in question finally came out of the café with a drink in one hand and a carryout sack in the other. He went directly to his truck, but when he saw Bruiser raising all kinds of hell, sniffing and barking at the double doors of the trailer, he dropped everything and ran like a coyote was nipping at his heels.

Brody had barely moved around the café area, when he saw what was going on. He threw on his brakes and bailed out of his pickup. By the time he got to Rocky, Bruiser had been unleashed and was fast on the trail of the driver.

To everyone's surprise, as the trucker got within a few yards of a stand of Cottonwood's and took a leap over the railing, a half a dozen bodies came out of nowhere. But the lawman who brought him down with a knee to his back and wrestling like hell to get his hands in cuffs was none other than Sheriff Avery Danielle Humphrey.

"You didn't tell me you were the police and I didn't do nothing." He threw an elbow toward her face.

"I damn sure did and if you throw another elbow my direction, you'll get the worse Taser shot you can imagine, plus additional charges for assaulting an officer of the law."

Once he was cuffed, she stood up, and Jessup, with the help of some undercover cops, brought the driver to his feet.

Avery wiped her hands on her pants. When the driver, now a perpetrator since he ran from a peace officer, was virtually pulled to the front of the Jacks Bluff pickup, she stepped in front of him and with a voice that softened to a mild roar with hard undertones of serious authority, said, "What in the hell were you running from?"

"I was scared of that damn dog." The man snorted in a dismissive tone while he crossed his legs.

Avery's voice raised two octaves as the other officers closed in on the perp. "I said legs apart, and I meant legs apart. If you don't understand, I can certainly show you what I mean." She stepped toward him. "You are only being detained at the moment, but I can charge you for fleeing from a peace officer. Do you hear me?"

He stared at her and didn't say a word.

"I said, do you hear me?"

"Sure, bossy bitch, I hear you." He snorted.

"Where is our ID and bill of lading?"

The driver stood there with a glazed stare. Brody had seen this many times before—almost every time a person had something to hide.

It took everything in Brody not to step in, but he had no doubt the sheriff could handle herself and there was plenty of support around her, including Jessup, Rocky, and by now a dozen uniformed officers from all branches of law enforcement.

"It's in my briefcase in the passenger's seat," the driver finally said, apparently not wanting to push his luck with a dozen guns pointed at him, as well as two Taser guns. "It's all in order. I'm not hauling anything illegal."

"I'm going to give you your rights, since our K-9 is giving more signals than you'll find at the airport that there's drugs inside." She stared him straight in the eyes. "You have the right...."

An hour later, Brody helped with the search and documentation, while the driver sat restless and vocal in the back of a police cruiser.

The adrenaline rush that had given a feeling of power and strength to Brody began to slow. He could tell by his heightened senses toning down.

Rocky turned to him. "Everything is in order, except for fifty pounds of coffee, which is on the bill of lading but isn't in the trailer. Shows to be a drop-off in Dallas." He shook his head and turned to Avery, who now stood beside Brody supervising. "Bruiser is still going crazy out here, so I'm gonna let him in the trailer, unless you have an objection, Sheriff Humphrey."

"No objection from here. We have more than reasonable cause for a search, so go to it." She looked over at Brody and raised an eyebrow as if to ask if he had any input.

He took it upon himself to answer an unspoken question. "I know of no reason we can't let him up there."

In only seconds, Bruiser sniffed around the whole trailer and gave his handler the signal for drugs. He continued to scratch and whine in front of twelve huge boxes of box springs and mattresses.

Rocky turned back to Avery and Brody. "He's never been wrong. How about we begin by taking them out one at a time and letting Bruiser do his job."

Before the deputy could get the words out of his mouth, Brody was already going up the lift, along with Jessup and a brawny DPS officer.

When they reached the ground, Bruiser went into his spin, lying down and barking, indicating drugs were inside.

"Anybody have a knife on them?" Brody asked about the time Jessup removed one from his gun belt.

Brody made several slashes in the fabric stapled to the bottom of the box spring, revealing tightly wrapped packages of drugs.

"Jackpot!" Deputy Jessup said, as another adrenaline rush hit Brody right between the eyes.

An hour or so later, Avery said, "Deputy Jessup, since you're the only one with a Kasota County vehicle, how about you escort Mr. Romero-Luna of Laredo to his new living facilities, and we'll be in shortly to do an interrogation. He might be the driver, but I'm sure he can give Lieutenant Detective VanZant plenty of information." She pulled out a tightly packaged rectangle of marijuana and handed it to Robertson.

"Want to give them a lesson on where this came from and where it was going?"

"Be glad to," Jessup said.

Rocky began, "See where they burnt in HC and OKC KCK? That means, Harbor Crew to Oklahoma City then Kansas City, Kansas." He reached for a different bundle. "This one is marked HC and AUT HOT. Harbor Crew to Austin, Texas, and Houston." He handed the brick of marijuana back to the officer, who was one of several unloading and counting the bundles.

"Sheriff Humphrey, I need to talk with you," Broday said.

They stepped around the corner, and she asked, "We're out of earshot. What's going on?"

"What happened to the one pound packages of coffee that obviously was in the back of the trailer and is on the bill of lading?"

"I think you know exactly where it is," she stated in a matter-of-fact fashion.

"This time do you want to call your uncle—I mean Judge Humphrey—and get a search warrant? I think we have more than enough cause, especially since Rocky can sign the affidavit as to how Bruiser reacted when he was taking care of business behind the café earlier today?"

"Time is of the essence, because once Mr. Mitchell learns of this arrest and seizure, he'll dispose of any drugs he has." She shook her head. "I don't know how much more you can take. It's been some long, hard weeks hasn't it?"

"That's why I'm in law enforcement, but I praise the Good Lord every day that Deuce will possibly be able to return to the sheriff's department."

Avery looked up at him with an irresistible smile that sent his senses into overdrive. "I've already had Tonya transcribe the events of last night, just in case anything in the future surfaced between Mr. Mitchell and any of us, including Tommy. So, with your affidavit of today's event, we should have no trouble getting that search warrant. What do you think?"

"The truth. As much as I hate to admit it, we'll find more packages of coffee than McDonald's could use in a year."

Chapter 25

Eighteen months later, Avery sat at the kitchen table at Brody's ranch, sipping tea. He had fried bacon, scrambled eggs, and pulled biscuits from the oven.

"Oh, that looks good." Avery grabbed a piece of bacon from the serving plate Brody placed on the table.

"Tastes as good as it smelled cooking." She wiped her lips with her napkin. "Now, you promise not to tell Mama about eating bacon. She'd be so disappointed in me." She couldn't help but laugh at her own comment.

Brody turned away from the stove and gave her a smile to die for. "I promise. I'll keep your secrets as long as you keep me." He placed biscuits on a plate. "Isn't that the rule now?"

She smiled and nodded. "I have to say, I've been through trials during my career and Danny Scott's was the most grueling one I've ever been through. I don't know about you, but I'm still exhausted."

Brody placed the biscuits on the table and took a seat across from her. "I'm like you, it was hard to see Scott up there lying through his teeth, when it would have been better if he'd just fessed up." He buttered two biscuits as he talked. "I couldn't believe that he was the one who snitched on Stanley, making us all believe the Harbor Crew deal had gone down the river, just to throw us off. If he hadn't done that, likely they'd have made another run without anyone catching them. My sister was so devastated that he was involved in the drugs right under her eyes."

"For sure. Not just the drugs for the streets but being the moneyman. Are you sure she'll be okay?" Avery asked.

"She's strong and I'll be there to help her. Talking about Scott, being honest isn't in his personality. It's just a shame that so much money had to be wasted on two trials: the change of venue on one, so many having to testify against him, and not to mention the trials were expedited through the courts."

She took a sip of her tea. "It was sweet-sour to see Deuce up there on the witness stand. With everything he'd gone through and then having to testify. Broke my heart, but so happy he'll be out of his wheelchair, on his feet, and returning to the office soon." She sat her cup down, and continued, "I was really proud of Tommy. He answered each question like a pro. I know one thing, his moving to Huntsville and going to college at Sam Houston to get a degree in law enforcement is the best thing that could have happened to him."

Brody shot her a smile. "I'm proud of the boy. He did what he knew was right and has matured the last year or so more than anybody I've ever seen."

"There's a lot to be proud of. Mother is doing fantastic after her breast surgery. Mesa is rescuing dozens of horses—"

Brody interrupted, "Don't forget Lola Ruth still makes apricot-peach fried pies just for me. And Vic went to work for the police department."

They finished breakfast and sat a while talking about everything from Clara to Rocky and Bruiser.

Laying his napkin beside his plate, Brody said, "Let's let the dishes go for a while. It's our day off, and I want to talk to you." Without any resistance from Avery, he got up, rounded the table, and took her hand.

Once they were comfortable on the sofa, he continued, "I can't let this go." He put his arm across her shoulder and tucked her to his side. "Avery. Look at me, because I'm going to say this one time only, and if you don't respond, I'll have my answer. Avery, as hard as I tried not to create a problem, we have a big one."

Avery placed two fingers on his lips, stopping his words. "I know exactly what you're going to say, but I want to say it first." She moved her fingers and took his face in her hands. Lifting his face to hers, she kissed him, allowing her whole body to fill with wanting. A sense of urgency created an intensity within her that made her kiss him again. Deeply yet allowing the gentle, smoldering flames within her to take fire. "Brody, I love you."

"Sheriff Humphrey, you can't say that because if you kiss me again like you did, to hell with updating the nepotism policy. I'll collect beer cans from the trash and sell them to make a living. I want you so badly that it hurts."

He took her into his arms and kissed her in a way that unlocked her heart.

After pulling back and looking deep into her eyes, he said, "I didn't think you'd ever say those three little words. I've been wanting to tell you, but

I had to keep it deep inside because of everything that was going on with Scott's and Stanley's trials." He pulled her to him and kissed her deeply.

"What are we going to do?" She asked when he finished.

"I've thought and thought about this, and since Deuce will be back in a couple of months, I'm going to give my notice—"

"Oh, no, you aren't about to pull your service weapon and badge out and put them on the table," she said with a light tone.

"My gun is locked up. But, with you here and Jessup maturing into a successful deputy, I think, Avery, I'll get married, if you'll marry me."

"First off, from hereafter would you please call me Dannie, and of course, I'll marry you." She threw her arms around him and kissed him deeply, then pulled away. "But—"

"Yes is all I want to hear. We'll...I mean, Dannie, you and I will work out the rest." He ran his hand up and down her arm. "I figure we can live either at the ranch or in Amarillo. It's a short drive, and I've already checked. I still have a place with the joint task force. The Bonita County Sheriff's Department is the strongest it's ever been, and with Deuce returning and you becoming the new chief deputy, we'll be in a good place."

Avery still was trying to let his words sink in as there was a knock on the door.

"Were you expecting someone?" He stood up, straightened his shirt, and ran his fingers through his hair.

"No." She grabbed her teacup and went to the kitchen to fix another cup.

The booming voice of Rocky Robertson floated through the air. "Hey, I knew you all would want to see this as soon as it came in, so thought I'd drive out and give it to you." He looked around, just as Avery stepped into the living room.

"Oh, good, you're here."

"And the detective in you couldn't recognize the old beat-up county Tahoe sitting out front," she laughed a good-hearted, teasing laugh.

"Ah, so you drive that one." His dimples seemed even deeper than usual as he smiled at her and held out an envelope. "This is what I think you all are waiting for."

She knew exactly what it was but tried not to act too excited. "Want some coffee?"

When Rocky nodded his head, Brody headed for the kitchen.

As quick as was humanly possible, Avery opened the envelope and took out the pages. After a cursory review, she let out a deep, crisp, and clear, "Oh my goodness!" She still wasn't able to believe what she'd just looked over. "Did you look at this, Rocky?"

"No, ma'am. It was marked to you, but I'll readily admit, I was tempted." He and Brody came back into the living room, with Rocky taking a seat in the wingback armchair and Brody leaning against the door facing.

"Oh, my gosh." She exhaled again. "Okay, Brody, come sit with me on the couch so you can hold me up."

Once they were settled in, she began to read aloud. "I'm cutting out the 'yack, yack' part and going to the chance. These are the figures from the Harbor Crew takedown. Of course, it'll be divided up after the trial. I think the most important figure is a little more than six hundred fifteen pounds of marijuana, amounting to $1,144,000. The smaller amounts were eighty-one grams of crack at $7,120; fifty grams of powdered cocaine at $5,000; one hundred twenty-three grams of black heroin at $24,000; and sixty-one grams of methamphetamine for a measly $6,100, making that part of the take $42,000 on top of the marijuana and cash."

Both men let out a hee-law and laughed deep and jovial.

"You're going to love this one. First off, the number of dryer sheets that were in the mattresses trying to mask the smell of drugs could last a washateria a decade. The coffee packs Stanley took had cash in them of over half a million dollars. And that's not all—we knew there were guns. They haven't put a value on them yet, but there were fifty-plus hidden in the mattresses." She turned to Rocky. "And Bruiser is the hero of this, because without him we would have had no reasonable cause to search. I don't know how much our total cash value will be, but it'll be substantial, oh yes, and they confiscated the tractor-trailer and no telling what it'll be sold for. And Bruiser can have all the dog treats he wants from me." She smiled at Rocky and said, "With Thelma's coupons, she'll probably have a big jar of them in the break room just for him."

Avery didn't know what came over her, but suddenly she had a desire to let loose and enjoy the moment. She couldn't help but throw the papers in the air, grab both Brody and Rocky, pulling them from their seats, and make a circle to dance around the room with her.

After some of the adrenaline slowed within Avery, she let loose of Rocky's hand but held tight to Brody's. "Brody, do you want to tell him or should I?"

"I will," he said in a teasing tone. "By the time the tractor and trailer is sold and all of the cash is divided, Bonita County Sheriff's Department can buy me a new Police Pursuit Chevy Tahoe, just like yours." He smiled at Rocky, then turned back to Avery. "Is that that you had in mind? Or is it that we can afford an Impala for you?"

She knitted her brows together and twitched her lips. "That's not exactly what I had in mind."

"Oh, you mean the other thing." He pulled her tight against him. "Rocky, meet the soon-to-be Mrs. Brody VanZant."

For the first time in three years, the thoughts and Lee, along with the shame and guilt, only served to Avery's mind as a positive, loving feeling. The realization that she was not and never had been the cause of his death settled deep inside.

She looked deep into Brody's soul through his eyes and she knew without him saying anything that he knew he was not responsible for any of Stanley's actions.

Together, she had no doubt, they'd have a loving and fun relationship—and she couldn't wait to be his wife.

"I'm not sure if she said yes, or not, but—"

"I said *yes*," she said. Looking at the smile on his face, she added, "Or do I have to sign an affidavit to prove it?"

"Only your signature on our marriage license."

Granny Johnson's Peach-Apricot Fried Pies

Ingredients

Dough
4 cups white flour
2 tsps. salt
1 cup shortening
1 cup milk

Filling
8 oz. dried apricots
6 oz. dried peaches
¾ cup white sugar
2 cups vegetable oil for frying

DIRECTIONS

Crust
In a large bowl, mix together flour and salt. Cut in shortening until crumbly. Stir in milk. Continue stirring until dough forms a soft ball. Divide dough into 18 each 6" balls. Set aside.

Filling
1. In a large saucepan, combine apricots, peaches and sugar. Add enough water to cover. Cook on low heat, covered, until fruit falls apart. Remove lid and continue cooking until all of the water is gone. Note: I prefer to cook my fruit earlier and let it cool.

2. Place oil (or shortening or lard to equal 2 cups) in high-sided skillet. Place over medium heat.

3. Make a ball out of divided dough and roll into a fairly thin 8 inch circle. Spoon an appropriate amount of fruit in the center, fold in half

and either use a fork or a pastry wheel (dipped in cold water or flour) to seal the edges.

4. Fry a few pies at a time in the hot oil, browning on both sides. Drain on paper towels.

5. Cool and enjoy!

I hope you enjoy the pies and memories as much as I did. My readers might be interested to know that my maternal grandmother was Granny Johnson, and this is one of her many recipes. Lola Ruth Hicks was named after my precious mother, Ruth, and my wonderful mother-in-law, Lola. May they rest in peace.

The Troubled Texan

If you enjoyed *Out of a Texas Night,* be sure not to miss Phylliss Miranda's
previous Kasota Springs Romance, *The Troubled Texan.*

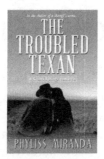

*Small-town Texas isn't big enough for the both of them . . . or
is it just right?*

Sheriff Donovan "Deuce" Cowan has seen his share of trouble, but when
he nearly hauls in Maressa Clarkson for speeding, he's suddenly in over
his head. These days his long-lost high school classmate is calling herself
Rainey Michaels and she sure hasn't come to Kasota Springs by accident.
It seems the Los Angeles Deputy DA has chosen the West Texas town
to hide out from a dangerous convict. It's all Deuce can do not to corral
the sexy spitfire—in the name of keeping her safe, of course. Problem is,
Rainey isn't letting anyone in on her big secret, least of all a hard-bodied,
former pro-footballer sheriff with an overactive protective instinct. So now
she's trying to keep him in line, one slow kiss at a time. . . .

Read on for a special excerpt!

A Lyrical e-book on sale now.

Chapter 1

LIFE WITHOUT PAROLE! the April 12th *Los Angeles Tribune* headline shrieked up at Maressa Clarkson.

The word "failure" might as well have been scrolled in neon. Not being able to get the death penalty for a murderer who made Charles Manson look like a schoolyard bully was totally unacceptable, nothing but a sign of weakness, unworthiness. At least that was the way her father would see the verdict.

District Attorney, Judith Mason, had stood alone with her, the only one to understand the emotional hell Maressa had been going through as lead prosecutor in such a high-profile, gut-wrenching case. Maressa suspected the DA figured that, since she was up for reelection and her conviction record had been challenged by her opponent, she didn't want to get her hands dirty with such a horrific case. She certainly didn't need the stigma of Alonzo Hunter receiving life in prison hanging over her head when he deserved the death penalty.

Besides her own father and her boss, there were probably thousands of citizens of the state of California disappointed in the verdict, but none more than Maressa herself.

Scoping out her desk, she touched a nutmeg-colored folder labeled "People vs. Alonzo F. Hunter" lying open beside volumes of Cal Stats— *Statutes of California* and *West's California Reporter.* An opaque water ring from an empty Diet Dr Pepper can on her other-wise organized desk reminded her that she hadn't eaten a real meal in weeks.

A bonsai plant she had pampered for five years caught her attention. She checked the soil. Still moist. Plucking off a leaf that clung for survival like an umbilical cord, she tossed the dead twig in the wastebasket beside the credenza.

She turned back for a final look and ran her fingers across the brass nameplate: R. Maressa Clarkson, Deputy District Attorney.

The pathetic looking bonsai seemed to plead with her not to be left behind.

Don't look so sad, little guy, With rare spontaneity, she snatched up the front page of the newspaper and wrapped it around the delicate plant, before securing the pot in a corner of her gym bag.

Sliding on her sunglasses, she headed for the door. Cautiously surveying the outer offices, she checked to make sure nobody was around.

Easing the door closed, she exited through the back and headed for a bank of elevators. Luck was on her side; the doors opened immediately and she stepped into the waiting car.

Adjusting her heavy tote bag slung on her arm, she steadied herself, leaning against the mirrored tiles covering three sides of the elevator walls. The coolness of the glass seeped through her olive-drab blouse hanging off her noodle thin shoulders. She had lost more weight. Barely five-foot-two and a slight one hundred and three pounds, she couldn't afford to lose another ounce.

A gaunt, tired image teetering on this side of anorexia screamed back at her. She touched the dark circles under her eyes. Lack of sleep and stress, compounded by the trauma of prosecuting such a horrendously complicated case and her concern for her safety, as well as that of her staff, had taken their toll. Her normally emerald-green eyes now looked more like mucky moss against her pasty complexion. Pinching her cheeks to add a tad of color didn't work. She needed some sun. And rest, lots of it.

The elevator jerked to a stop on the ground floor where she located her new Lexus. She unlocked the doors, and then tossed her car keys on the concrete beneath the automobile. Exiting the parking garage on foot, she walked seven blocks south.

Although the back streets she took were virtually deserted at this time of the morning, she stopped several times to make sure she wasn't being followed.

Halting near a trash bin, she took a deep breath, opened her gym bag and removed the Prada purse that cost more than a month's payment on her condo. Tossing the turquoise-and-gray paisley printed handbag in a shallow growth of weeds behind the receptacle, she walked away. She had a small, cheap purse she had purchased inside her gym bag.

Someone would find her billfold, complete with identification, and figure she was another mugging victim. They'd take the piddling amount of cash she had deliberately left inside and discard the hand-bag. Nothing unusual in a city the size of LA.

Once she crossed back to the main avenue, crowds bustled to work around her like screensavers on speed. Meshing with the smell of designer perfume, tobacco, and leftover lust, she made her way another six blocks west before she flagged down a taxi. She told the driver that she wanted to go to the Los Angeles International Airport, where she paid him and mingled amongst the people before she caught a green-line bus and changed terminals. Weighted down with apprehension, she hailed a second cab.

Maressa removed a note Judith had given her from her pocket, and directed the cabbie to a used car lot in East LA, where she picked up her new identity and an ordinary Chevy Malibu. Not exactly a car she would have chosen, but one serviceable enough for her needs.

"Mrs. Michaels, uh, lady . . . Rainey—"

Jerking her head up, she responded, "What? Yes?"

She needed to get accustomed to her new alias since the last time anyone in her family used her first name was when she was baptized as an infant thirty-two years before. Her father hated the name Maressa, but had agreed to allow it to be put on her birth certificate only to appease her mother. The LA County DA insisted that "Rainey" didn't sound professional and that using Maressa, along with her first initial, would set her apart from the other thousand-plus deputy DAs.

Rainey Michaels did have a secure ring to it.

"Don't act scared. It's a dead giveaway that you're on the run. You paid a lot of money to get lost, so get used to it," chided the slick-talking son-of-slime. "The registration and insurance documents are in here." He handed her an envelope. "Keep 'em with the car 'cause you can't afford to get stopped. Gotcha a New York driver's license . . . everything you wanted, including a burner phone. You okay, Mrs. Michaels?"

"What? Yes, I'm fine. Thanks." She handed over a manila envelope. "All the money is here."

Deal closed, the man slithered back to the hole he called his office.

Slipping behind the wheel, she exited the parking lot . . . off the emotional roller coaster that had taken her for a nasty ride. She needed separation to heal, and plenty of it. Hopefully, given enough time, she could put the daily, sometimes hourly, images of the hideous crimes of Alonzo F. Hunter behind her and begin to live again.

Merging into traffic, she headed toward small-town USA where she could blend in like a single boll of cotton in pale moonlight.

A frightened deputy district attorney didn't resign . . . she vanished.

And in R. Maressa Clarkson's, rather Rainey Michaels's case, she carried way too much baggage with her in the form of horrific memories.

The Tycoon and the Texan

Seven Days to Texas

With a name like Nick Dartmouth, and the fortune it comes with, it's hard not to have a reputation for getting everything you want. So when his former secretary steps onto his foundation's charity auction block, Nick has the perfect opportunity to woo the stunning beauty from Kasota Springs, Texas. But aggressive counterbids force him to make an extreme proposition. Except money itself doesn't guarantee a blissful ride off into the sunset, especially when being won goes against the willful nature of McCall Johnson. Intent on showing Nick they come from two very different—and incompatible—worlds, she's surprised by how well he can handle a horse. For a girl from Texas, that speaks volumes about a man's value. Maybe there's more to this playboy than she expected. . . .

Be My Texas Valentine

In Texas, Valentine's Day is for restless hearts, brave second chances, and passions rekindled. *New York Times* bestselling author Jodi Thomas, Linda Broday, Phyliss Miranda, and DeWanna Pace tempt you with four delicious treats . . .

Out on these rugged plains, love never comes easy. And four daring ladies will do whatever it takes to capture the hearts of four irresistibly sweet-talking Texans. . . . When a quiet foreman comes to the aid of a mystery lady, they'll find that this perfect starlit night is made for courtin'. . . . A determined heiress gambles high to reclaim the rancher she's never stopped wanting. . . . When a spirited lady and a go-getter mayor compete for their town's future, it's two dreams for a lifetime. . . . And to attract a lonely doctor's attention, a shy young woman needs courage—and two unlikely matchmakers. . . .

A Texas Christmas

In the Texas Panhandle, the winters are long, the storms fierce—and the Yuletide nights are sizzling. New York Times bestselling author Jodi Thomas along with DeWanna Pace, Linda Broday, and Phyliss Miranda bring you one tempting holiday delight . . .

On the eve before Christmas a blizzard arrived, transforming a small Texas town into a night to remember. Four ladies desperately in need of saving, four hard-ridin' cowboys who aim to please. . . . When a lone farmer strides to a pretty store owner's rescue, their deepest wishes just might come true. . . . A brave heiress can't believe a rugged angel is riding out of the night to save her and her fellow train passengers—until she gets him under the mistletoe. . . . A quiet loner wants to help a stranded widow have a holiday to remember. . . . And a female saloon owner tired of being scorned by respectable folk gets some *very* naughty help from a handsome greenhorn. . . .

Give Me A Texas Outlaw

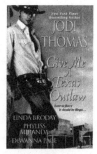

Fearless and irresistible, outlaws are the original bad boys. Now *New York Times* bestselling author Jodi Thomas and Linda Broday, Phyliss Miranda, and DeWanna Pace offer up four sexy and romantic stories for women who love men who know how to pack heat. . . .

If Cozette Camanez's groom doesn't show up for their wedding by dawn, she'll lose her family ranch. Trouble is, the groom doesn't exist—until unsuspecting thief Michael Hughes comes along. Never was an outlaw faced with such a lovely—and willing—target. . . . Larissa Patrick, the beautiful daughter of a wealthy rancher, has been kidnapped. Only one man can save her: gunfighter Johnny Bravo. Rescuing Larissa is the easy part—but getting her home without losing his heart will take the discipline of a saint. And Johnny's no saint. . . . Lawman Ethan Kimble is finally face to face with his quarry: socialite and bank robber Savannah Parker. The only thing between them is a Winchester pointed at his heart—and some undeniable sparks. If Kimble can tame the Texas Flame, they may ignite a passion that breaks every rule. . . . When outlaw Shadow Rivers and desperado Odessa Kilmore escape a hail of bullets and team up on a long journey, both are determined to hide their secrets—and their attraction. No easy task as they discover a love more powerful than their enemies combined. . . .

Give Me A Texas Ranger

Born to protect and serve, these rugged lawmen are the stuff of Texas legend. *New York Times* **bestselling author Jodi Thomas teams up with Linda Broday, Phyliss Miranda and DeWanna Pace to bring you four red-blooded Rangers and the women who tame their hearts. . .**

When Annalane Barkley whispers her dreams to Wynn McCord, the Texas ranger has a new battle on his hands. For the sweet beauty's words awaken his every protective instinct and he knows he's found a woman worth fighting for. . . . When Stoney Burke finds Texanna Wilder in need of rescue, he's caught between his hardened heart and his duty to his best friend's lovely widow. Marriage is merely a solution to keep Texanna safe, but Stoney is suddenly aching for the wedding night. . . . Forced to take feisty Ella Stevenson into custody, Hayden McGraw has his hands full. But when he discovers the spitfire is on his side of the law, they're soon working as a team—up close and very personal. . . . Thomas Longbow only plans to use Laney O'Grady as his cover on his latest assignment. But the passion that explodes between them threatens to expose his plot—and his heart. . . .

Give Me A Cowboy

In the rough-and-ready Texas Panhandle, the rodeo is where to find a real man. *New York Times* bestselling author Jodi Thomas teams up with DeWanna Pace, Linda Broday, and Phyliss Miranda to prove that the right kind of love can tame the wildest heart . . .

Rowdy Darnell was born to be wild and Laurel Hayes knows she shouldn't get involved with him—but oh, how he can kiss. . . . When Augusta Garrison finds out Dally Angelo is hell-bent on riding the bull that killed his father, she's ready to break their engagement—until pure passion takes over. . . . Tempest LeDoux doesn't play by anyone's rules. When a tall gunslinger named McKenna Smith rides into town, Tempest knows he's the one for her—if she can catch him. . . . Alaine LeDoux is pure tomboy—and she likes shooting and riding more than dresses and tea. Good thing Mr. Morgan Payne turns out to be one hell of a cowboy under his citified suit. . . .

Give Me A Texan

Roots that go deep . . . men who stand tall . . . and real women who have what it takes to love and be loved by them. Jodi Thomas and Linda Broday, *NYT* and *USA Today* bestselling authors....teams up with Phyliss Miranda, and DeWanna Pace to bring you four of the best Texas romances ever. . .

Hank Harris wasn't even looking for a woman when he ended up with a wife. Their hasty marriage is for appearances only: a capable, intelligent woman like Aggie is exactly who he needs as a business partner—if only she weren't so damn beautiful, spirited—and in his bed. . . . Payton McCord thought he was one tough cowboy until Amanda Lemmons made him mind his manners. And a woman of her caliber is worth the trouble she causes. . . . Newspaperman Quinten Corbett wasn't expecting his new apprentice to be female. Boston-born Kaira Renaulde is far too refined for a rough-and-tumble frontier town—and far too pretty for his peace of mind. . . . Briar Duncan knows he needs someone to help him raise his headstrong little daughter. But Mina McCoy is more than he bargained for—much more! The woman has the face of an angel and a very definite mind of her own . . .

Meet the Author

New York Times and USA Today bestselling author, **Phyliss Miranda**, a native Texan, lives in the Texas Panhandle with her husband Bob. With plans to write a cookbook, she took her first creative writing class in 2001. One of her favorite parts of being an author is teaching the craft and mentoring beginning writers. She enjoys sharing her love for the new frontier, the Civil War, quilting, and antiques; and still believes in the Code of the Old West.

Phyliss loves to hear from her readers and fellow authors and can be reached at her website, www.phylissmiranda.com. She can also be followed on Facebook, Twitter, or on the Petticoatsandpistols.com blog on Tuesdays.

Printed in the United States
by Baker & Taylor Publisher Services